The Harrowed Runner

Eric S. Kozlowski

Azalea Art Press
Sonoma | California

ISBN: 978-1-943471-33-1

Paintings
by Courtney Kuno Burds

for Charlie

CONTENTS

Part Three

Prologue

It was odd. I could remember much of my youth and yet I could recollect only the sad moments of my adulthood. My memory made me anguish over so many things from long ago. The reminders of my youthful experiences are what caused me such pain.

I can't explain it. I struggled with memories that should have brought me great joy but seemed to only conjure up intense feelings of sadness and debilitating sorrow. It could be the simplest of things in my past or it could be a beautiful image on any given day.

I lived in the Adirondack town limits of Grandby, New York. It was all I knew, and it always seemed cold. The wisps of clean wind, fueled by expanses of evergreens, did not cleanse the difficult life of most of the residents. The rarified air was reserved for families who controlled the food, lumber, and provided the rural inhabitants with seasonal, arduous labor.

The majority dressed in the fur of the animals they trapped, survived by the fish they would catch, and on occasion lived handsomely by the ducks they would shoot. It was isolation, few ventured out of the county. Those who supported the local college were highly educated, they arrived and would disappear by train. They did not stay long and were never considered locals by their transient nature.

I sometimes wonder how my life would have turned out if I had been assigned a different roommate. If only it could have been someone different, it might have changed everything.

I don't remember the exact date I met Simon, although the time is still engraved in my mind. The train arrives at seven o'clock. If I repeat it and say it softly it seems like a prayer, a begging prayer of desperation.

Every so often I say it out loud. I would say it out loud any time I saw a stopping train. I would say it in my heart and soul on cold autumn days.

The fall days are the most difficult. Those are days when I pull cold air into my lungs and it awakens memories of being young. It awakens a feeling of having a chance to start all over, as if I could have another chance.

A different roommate and their arrival might not have been on a train. The time would have been irrelevant and I never would have been considered late. I would never have entered a tavern when my youthful innocence was so delicate and yearning for guidance.

The randomness of our association was created by some elderly part-time worker in the Dean's office utilizing some archaic and unscientific sorting system. She could not have earned much money.

I am sure she took great pride in her duties, but I always imagined her simply dealing information cards from an unsorted stack. I am sure she was diligent and focused, but it was a matter of grabbing cards from a pile.

It was not difficult work and the cards only had to be paired so someone was assigned with someone. It must have been a simple random draw for which I was designated the life-altering association with Simon G. Sheldon II.

It was sad to think what might have happened if she had just taken lunch at a different time. I sometimes think what if she had just left a window open and a summer breeze had been swift enough to displace the cards. It would have changed everything.

Perhaps it was not the card she had intended to have in her hand. If only she had not stopped to drink a cup of tea. If she had not used a damp spoon when adding her customary two cubes of sugar, she might have realized another card was sitting next in line.

I hate to think that she muttered, "Oh well, no worries, this one will do."

I play the scenarios in my head. There are thousands of variables and I will never know. I would learn later about randomness but never fully understand it or its detrimental impact on my life. For some reason, even then I believed I could change randomness, that I could control the outcome of the uncontrollable.

Sometimes in my life it was the measurement of the width of a playing card, the whiskers of a horse's nose, that could induce euphoria or horrific life-altering thoughts of what was next for me. The horse's nose was the hardest, the results of the race, my crippling addiction to winning, decided by a beautiful animal whose brain was minuscule in size.

I don't know the actual date he arrived. I could easily look it up on an old calendar or call the local newspaper who would have all the records from that year. It was one of those days among many quintessential days that evoked happiness and at times, deep and physically crippling sadness.

I do know that it was August, 1917. I was a freshman and petrified about everything. I was scared with uncertainty.

The Western Union telegram simply read:

Harry—major favor—been delayed—inform Dean. My train arrives at seven on Friday —meet me at the hotel next to the station—don't be late. Simon.

Part One

Chapter I

I still have the telegram I had received a few days before he arrived, but I can never muster up the courage to look at it. It sits in my safety deposit box, 13 miles from my home. It's not decaying from age. I am sure it looks as if I had just opened the envelope. It is frozen in time, just a simple yellow sheet of paper.

The telegram has only two companions, my last will and testament and a treasured piece of sterling silver. The shimmering silver piece is relegated to acting as a paperweight where wind and movement are nonexistent.

If I had the courage to look, I know the telegram would have the exact date when it was sent. It would be printed in the first few lines.

I really don't know why I've kept it like a precious relic, in a place where it can't be destroyed, out of view from everyone including me. I guess it may have been because it was the first favor he asked of me.

It was always a major favor he would ask. Simon never requested minor favors. If it was a small favor, it was always a bigger problem. If they were small on the surface they always ended up in some chaotic activity that invariably became a major favor.

It took me a short time to figure that out, but a long time to actually accept it and plan accordingly. It was classic Simon. *Meet me at the hotel.* He could find bars and taverns as if they were leaves falling from a sugar maple tree in the midst of October. Simon locating the Dean's office was a four-year enigma.

He arrived on the Northern "*Creeper,*" the nickname for the New York Central railroad. It chugged along slowly but was always on time. Simon liked that the train moved slowly, the slower the better, as he liked to languish in the opulent bar car.

I guess after all these years it was the name of the train that helped me conjure up the little details of the day he arrived.

Our four-year assigned room was 24 Jenks Hall. Jenks was the customary men's freshman dorm. It was three stories, had 14 rooms on each floor, and a center stairwell as well as a large meeting space as you entered the building.

The building was not constructed as a square. It had been built with reddish stone and the builder had created elegant wings that reached from a center atrium and large meeting room. The school had spared no expense. Large fieldstones were the welcoming mats for the entrances and impeccable brick walkways were accented with newly-planted trees.

Our room was on the right wing and like each end room had an easy access exit down the back stairwells. Our view was the picturesque evergreens and a cattail-lined pond that acted as a buffer to the county road. There was a small parking lot and very easy access to the county road that led to the downtown square.

The room was bleak in nature, plain wooden desks, simple beds, but within a mere few hours upon his arrival on campus Simon would manage to transform the room into a tavern. Twenty-four Jenks became the watering hole, the hangover hospital, hangout, and hostel of Simon's frequent drinking guests.

I was not a drinker when I arrived on campus. I quickly found a taste for strong drink and by my junior year had become an importer of expensive whiskey. My love affair with the Manhattan was instant. That heavenly concoction was enjoyed by the horse racing set that I would soon find so interesting.

I thought of that cocktail often throughout my life. I always laughed that it made me feel so jocular even though one of the main ingredients in the drink was bitters.

It was like yesterday. I remember standing at the highest point of the campus next to six stellar white pillars paying homage to the founding fathers of the college.

They were a unified line of pillars bearing stone labels at the base with their full names. Each founder had put up an astronomical sum of $100,000 in the mid-1800s to buy the land, charter the school, and build the first buildings on the campus.

For some reason, every freshman was required to learn their names. As a freshman, if you were stopped by an upperclassman, you were politely requested to recite the names of Johnson, Gaines, Campbell, Weller, Richardson, and the heroic war hero Gunnison in perfect order.

I was never asked to recite their names. Simon was asked once and laughed and mockingly berated the upperclassman citing that he had no intention of doing something so beneath him even though he knew their names.

Simon was not angered by the condescending request but used it as an inspiration. During our time on campus, Simon would morph their blue blood names into a drinking rhyme. The Dean of Students would eventually catch wind of it and spend the remaining semesters trying to eradicate it from the campus life—to no avail. I had heard that the school stopped the practice after we graduated and incoming students were required to wear colorful caps designating them as new students. It became folklore that they were nicknamed *Simon-Says Beanies*.

Such was the effect of Simon—ignite with rhetoric, build the excitement, watch the turmoil, and rarely if ever be around to clean up the smoldering mess. He seemed to stay only if there was something to gain. New students would come to despise those beanies, caps that were humorous at first sight but made incoming freshmen grimace with embarrassment. Sarcasm was Simon's gift. On the face it was a complex and well-thought-out addition to campus life; underneath, it was a simple joke that was his signature brand of humor.

I had been on campus for a few weeks. I was a football standout and had been recruited to help move the club team to the highest level, as Ivy League games had been scheduled in the coming years.

My father seemed uninterested in my performances on the field. My father believed in hard work and he wanted me to focus on my studies.

My mother, in a moment of emotional weakness, broke my father's trust and shared that he looked forward to visiting the campus and proudly watching the games. My father sternly indicated that I should drive home some weekends to help out at the farm. I had no excuses as my graduation present from the town's high school was a new car.

I was my father's only son. I looked a great deal like him but I seemed more emotional. He rarely showed praise but I always assumed the increasing amounts of responsibility he heaped upon me and the many times we spent on his beloved island retreat were his way of showing his approval.

It was a somber view from the pillars that day. The sweeping vistas were filled with darkening morning clouds, storms on the horizon. I felt compressed by the fog that circled the higher peaks. I should have been uplifted by the fall colors of the Northern Adirondacks—crimson leaves, oranges and light browns could be seen as the sun continuously tried to burn through the morning fog and what I thought were threatening storms.

I was not happy. I felt fear and I internally was tormented, not knowing what to expect.

My life had been narrow, doors were easily opened, friendships encouraged and made, citations given, but not truly earned, all because I was a member of a prominent small town family.

I had been filled with self-doubt, angst, anxiety for the weeks leading up to my first days on campus and the meeting of someone from the city of New York was painfully important.

For some inherent reason I sought outside approval. My small town's adulation was not enough. I needed more from others besides my family and those willing to abdicate their self worth to be my friend.

The clock bells, pulled by some faceless student volunteer, began to ring, the first bells of the day. I did not need to count. There would be seven, chimed in perfect cadence. Simon's train had arrived.

I looked off in the direction of the train station. The circular steam rings of the lead car were fighting with the fog for dominance in the distance skyline. The train, as always, was on time and I was going to be late to meet Simon.

I began my decline to the station. The brick stone path was paved meticulously and the steps were marked sporadically with sayings of college alumni.

The quotes had been engraved on the same reddish stone as Jenks and were placed as the support for the next step. They were easy to read on the way up the stairs, impossible to read on the way down. I am not sure why but I never read these quotations until many years later. This, despite being a path I would travel often. It was odd now to think that I never stopped to read them. It may have been that in 1917 there were only a handful of steps that contained quotations. It may have been that I was usually relatively incoherent when I traveled the steps back to campus.

I reached the last step. I was at the main entrance adorned with an ornate metal arch inscribed with the school's motto in Latin. The words, in coiled bronze scroll work, translated as *Believe in Faith*.

It was believed that Gunnison had yelled the inspirational words while his regiment had charged up an important hill during the final battles of the Civil War. He had been killed during the final battle at the age of 43. The motto was added after his death as a tribute to his bravery.

I turned right onto Park Street. I could see the train was moving forward in a jerking motion as if it might have been positioning to dispatch its passengers. The Franklin Hotel was a mainstay of town and adjacent to the station. I used my running back skills and dashed over the tracks to the front of the hotel. It was regal and had been built to look like the Waldorf Astoria Hotel in New York City.

Its looks were odd for a small town, but it had grown on the community. Despite being a bit out of character, it was country in comfort and had upscale dining on the second floor as well as a tavern that occupied the windowless lower ground floor. It was down the stairs to the left for the bar, up the grand staircase for the dining room.

I assumed, upon my late arrival, that he would be in the dining room, which I quickly scanned. There was nobody resembling a college freshman. I would always remember later that a dining room was never the initial choice of Simon. I never made that mistake again. In search of Simon, I would always check the bar first.

I descended the two flights of stairs and turned right into the corridor that led to the tavern. I looked through the portholes at the doors of the bar where three gentlemen were playing cards, two middle aged. One of the trio was an obvious college freshman.

I am not sure if it was youth or a simple arrogant look that I initially noticed, but I was sure it had to be Simon.

I swung the doors open.

"Harry, you're late." Simon was confident and had an endearing smirk on his face as he shared his observation with the group in an even tone.

The way he spoke made it appear his concentration was elsewhere, but the nuances of his words made you feel like no one else was in the room.

"Do you want a drink?" he seemed to command, rather than ask. Simon instantly gained the attention of the bartender who was at the opposite end of the long bar.

"Simon, learning Latin sober is hard enough," I quipped. I was guessing about the joke as I had grown up in a house where drinking was not only frowned upon but considered a religious sin.

"Believe in Fate," Simon laughed as he mocked and twisted the meaning of the college phrase in his response. Simon, I found, was very cleverly witted.

I had yet to shake his hand, properly introduce myself, and we had started our friendship on what I perceived to be humorous footing. It was funny enough that he was drinking at what most people around town would consider a late breakfast time.

"Meet, *Can't Catch a Jacques* and please say hello to *Pierre the Northerner* who lives in the southern part of Canada," Simon teased. He loved the contradiction he had created about his card partners. He was in control and holding court.

Simon was wearing a dark brown jacket. His face resonated confidence and he seemed rested despite what have must been a long train ride. His black hair was neatly combed. His tie and jacket were neatly pressed and yet his fellow card players looked as if they had been lying in a barn. Pierre and Jacques seemed dirty, downtrodden, and poor.

Simon was taunting them. His smile continued to freeze into a condescending smirk and it was not being appreciated by his rumpled friends.

"It's Legrow." Pierre seemed disoriented and had to focus on his words. He was drunk and hostile as he spoke. He wasn't sure his own pronunciation sounded right.

He felt he had to repeat it, "It's Legrow."

It sounded like gibberish. I was having a hard time understanding his accent but though his demeanor was not pleasant, he was easy to ignore. Pierre had dark brown hair, was gaunt, and he seemed to be sitting favoring the left side of his body as if he had been injured.

Simon playfully asked him, "To peek, Pierre, peek!" Simon was holding the cards tightly in his left hand awaiting a signal from Pierre who was two seats away from Simon at the middle of the bar.

Simon was seated at the end of the bar. There was only room for one seat at the end and the bartender's service opening was to his right. He had a large stack of money which was being stored neatly, utilizing his train ticket as a makeshift envelope.

In a thick Canadian accent Pierre moaned, "Hit moi." A nine of clubs slid in front of the four.

"Incroyable!" Pierre was more animated but had the same disgruntled tone.

"Have a drink!" Simon consoled Pierre as the bartender brought a fresh beer while Simon reached over and retrieved several bills from in front of Pierre. Pierre offered no resistance to Simon taking his money.

"Your poor little stack is not growing. You need to make it LaaaGrowww," Simon howled laughter.

"Quelle domage, I hate to crow my northern friend, Monsieur Legrow!" Simon rhythmically mocked.

Pierre was not amused and seemed more aggressive as if Simon had crossed a line of arrogance. Simon turned his faint mockery onto Jacques. "Need a Jacque, Jacques?" Simon slurred his words as the morning cocktails began to take their toll. Latin might wait another day, I surmised.

Jacques was sitting to the left of Pierre and his stack of money had been dwindling with every hand. Simon quickly stood and moved around his lair to whisper to the bartender while handing him a $5 silver certificate from his right pocket. The bartender quickly left the bar.

Jacques said confidently, "Simon, I not need one this time!"

Simon laughed, "Three Jacques in one sitting, well my measly six is going to need some help." He slowly reconfigured himself back into his seat and made himself comfortable, with his cards held tightly in his hand. He seemed to hesitate while taking a long drink from his glass.

"I need a beverage!" Simon bellowed. "Ah, our overly-tipped Daniel returns. Your job is to make us overly tipsy." Simon laughed at its double meaning.

The bartender quickly returned to his subservient spot and Simon waved his unoccupied hand in a graceful motion for more drinks.

He turned his hidden card over to show a five of spades. Simon instructed me. "Harry, now I need a Jacque!"

Simon continued to goad a bit, saying, "I will take a card."

"ARRETER!" Pierre commanded.

He delivered an ultimatum to Simon. "Cinquante d'argent . . . no dix." Simon motioned the bartender again for a drink.

"Monsieur LeCrow, we have played since the train left New York. You are down. I don't want you to be mad and we're now friends." Simon mocked Pierre's accent, in a low, serious tone. It was a purposely arrogant tone. Simon knew what the the result would be. He was baiting Pierre and his skill at denigrating his name just slightly was enough to antagonize him.

"Activer la carte," demanded Pierre.

"I am not betting you because you will lose," Simon was a bit more assertive.

"You a coward?" Pierre quietly challenged as if was an innocent question.

"It takes courage not to beat someone one when they're losing badly, Mr. Legrow," Simon spoke and looked directly at Pierre.

Simon did not like defending his rejection of not wagering on the next card. His jocular mood was now stern.

"Harry, do you think it is a ten?" Simon asked. He already knew the answer.

I hesitated to answer but Simon had not planned to wait for my response.

Simon turned the card and before it hit the table said, "Dix-vingt-et-un, *Omarkayham*," Simon melodically rang out in a faux French accent.

It was a ten and he had correctly predicted the outcome. I always think his voice would have resonated differently had Pierre not challenged him to the wager on the outcome of the next card.

I had no idea what his chant meant and the ensuing melee would eliminate my interest in finding out.

"Votre CHEAT!" Jacques yelled as he began to rise from his bar stool.

I had been standing to the right of Pierre and quickly put my hand on his shoulder. Neither men were very big but both appeared to have lost a fortune.

"You trick the cards when you move!" Pierre screamed.

Anger and alcohol had fueled their courage for a fight. Simon was five-foot-nine, thinly built, and not going to be any match for either one of them. I glanced down and realized Pierre was protecting a somewhat crippled leg, polio I thought. I immediately felt he was not a threat. I was wrong.

In an instant, Pierre swung his arm around connecting me right above my left eye. I was caught off guard, but standing six-two and having moved hay bales since I could remember, Simon was quickly going to lose the unfriendly company of his new acquaintances.

I turned and decked Pierre with two swift punches. Pierre was no longer a problem. Simon had moved behind the bar while scooping up his winnings from his makeshift security shield. His well-tipped bartender had moved in between Jacques and Simon, trying to play peacemaker. Jacques was not interested in international diplomacy. His target was Simon.

I grabbed Jacques from behind and threw him like a hay bale toward a small group of tables that occupied the area behind us. He rolled like a barrel and his initial signs of discomfort indicated that the barroom brawl was quickly over.

Simon handed Daniel several additional silver certificates. We paid our farm hands well but Simon was now the best employer in town. It was easily a month's wages working for our farm and it was all for pouring liquor.

It was violence and chaos and despite the carnage, Simon hesitated out of decorum before we left.

He stopped showing absolutely no concern for the two people on the floor in pain and thanked Daniel for his kind service. We walked with confident purpose as we exited the downstairs watering hole. We didn't run.

We reached the end of the hallway to the staircase exiting the hotel. I was bleeding fairly badly but acted as if nothing had just happened. The policeman standing there, however, was not as convinced.

"Harry, what is going on?" the officer demanded.

Despite my lack of clarity, my uncle's baritone voice was easily recognizable and our troubles were now certainly magnified.

My father's brother was an identical twin. The only difference was their voices. I sounded nothing like my uncle and despised the fact I somewhat resembled him.

"Uncle Winston, I was just heading to class after picking up my roommate from the train station," I quickly informed, hoping that Simon's presence would help mitigate the problem at hand.

Winston was straight-laced. He had no children of his own and unsuccessfully tried to be close to my sister and me. My father tolerated him. My mother would never say it but she did not care for his condescending and authoritative personality.

"Where is your roommate?" He asked.

I swung around to see Pierre, Jacques, and the bartender held in tow by a second officer that appeared to be a subordinate to my uncle.

"He was settling his bill and heading to campus," I felt comfortable saying. It was not an actual outright lie.

"These gentlemen have a train to catch. They would like to press charges against you for assault and theft," his subordinate reported.

My uncle said nothing further. He curried the Canadians to the end of the corridor, a short animated conversation took place, and the gentlemen who had been the short-term friends of Simon disappeared out the staircase entrance toward the train. The bartender appeared to be pointing at Pierre and Jacques with a tepid finger of accusation. It looked as if his gestures were saying the fight was the Canadians' fault.

My uncle dismissed his subordinate and demanded that Daniel go back to work. He seemed displeased that he could not arrest Simon. He would not dare arrest me, but informed me that I was to bring $50 to pay back a portion of their losses and I was to report to his home Sunday night for supper.

I wish I had not thanked him, but I did. I proceeded upstairs to use the men's room to clean up before I headed to what remained of my classes.

On my way past the regal dining room, there was Simon having breakfast in grand style. A silver tray, with orange juice in a crystal pitcher, coffee, a raised tray of croissants, and a bottle of champagne made for an elegant setting. I should have been angry but the table was set for two.

"Harry, you're late. The eggs are getting cold. What took you so long?" Simon almost indignantly complained.

"Let me guess, they bartered for $30 to leave? Am I right? Tell me I am right, no need I know I am right," he playfully asked. He pulled a neatly concealed wad of money from a hidden pocket in his jacket.

"It was $50. How did you know they would leave for money?" I was stunned that he was so perceptive.

"Well, $50, shame on me," Simon scolded himself.

"I thought Jacques was smarter, well isn't that a hoot! I must have added wrong. Shameful, that is certainly not like me to make an error in gambling arithmetic," he confidently summarized.

"They bartered because time was not kind to them and I had memorized their schedule. They are not Americans, so they were limited in how hard they could press," he continued.

That was Simon. It was the angle, the advantage, always a skilled advanced move to position him for a score, or maybe land him just clear of trouble.

"We need to celebrate," he spoke while he poured two glasses of champagne.

"I am surprised for a small town they had this vintage?" He mocked the menu as if it was poor Pierre.

"I had a fabulous Saratoga. I managed to entertain myself for the long train ride and made a tidy sum off my new friends from Ottawa and we are now roommates," he said with pleasure and increasing enthusiasm. I would have enjoyed him adding my victorious brawl, but we began our first meal together.

It was my first time drinking more than a glass of holiday wine, alcohol that was permitted just once a year. Breakfast lasted until lunch, lunch ended with drinks in the tavern and drinks ended somewhere and at some time.

I will never forget our first arrival to our room. It was the one thing I can recollect from that night and I still laugh every time I think of his instructions.

"Harry for saint's sake, hold the door, use your foot, you're a running back! Boy, our team is in big trouble if you can't keep the door open." He let out a hearty laugh as he realized it was a gem of a put down.

How we found Jenks Hall that night is still a blur. Simon was holding strips of cherry fence, planks of pine and wire. I was holding scarlet leather straps adorned with 'Welcome Class of 1921' and a variety of small pieces of wood that Simon had surgically removed from fences as we returned to our dorm.

I was very drunk. This was new to me but I was having a very fun time trying to maneuver a bunch of lumber at 2:30 in the morning.

"What is this stuff for?" I blurted out. "I have never stolen anything in my life," I protested.

"Simon, I hear the Dean coming up the stairs. Hurry, dump it and turn out the light!" he commanded. Our door closed with a thud. The room was lit only by a small black wall lamp. It was silent except for Simon who seemed to be instantly snoring.

I glanced around the room. His bed had been made. His bags lined the wall to the left end of his bed. His closet was filled with suit jackets, fine shirts, linens, sport shirts, a raccoon coat, hats, pants, and an array of vicuna sweaters.

His textbooks had been positioned on his desk similar to mine. My bed had been remade, several hats added to my closet, and our room had been cleaned from top to bottom. It was something I had not had yet done and never did when I lived at home.

Simon had not been on campus and his room had been readied, belongings unpacked, his study materials prepared, and now he was sound asleep.

"Mr. Charles, please open this door," Dean Hulet spoke in a terse whisper.

I slowly opened the door. The wood, predominantly on my side of the room, lay in a teepee heap. The scarlet welcome straps, torn from somewhere on campus, were fortunately hidden beneath the rubble.

"Have you been drinking? What is the meaning of this mess on your side of the room?" he demanded.

My slurred explanation of building a study area and based on my excessive usage of the words 'study area' earned me a scheduled visit to the dean's office on Monday at ten o'clock.

Dean Hulet had wanted to meet Mr. Sheldon and did not want to wake him as he knew that Simon had made the extra effort to take the early train to get to campus. He had received a nice telegram from Simon's father that his son would be arriving late today because he had helped out his medical practice in an emergency. As the dean left, he instructed me to bring Simon to our meeting for a proper introduction. I was in trouble and now I was escorting the instigator for a meeting with the dean.

"Is he gone?" Simon breathed into his goose feather pillow.

"Thanks for your help, now I am heading to the dean's office," I lamented.

"The dean should be proud of you. You're going to build a study area, I mean a study area, you know what, you should think about building a sttttudddy aaaareeea," Simon laughed as his voice was muffled his pillow.

"Don't worry. I will take care of your study area." His voice actually sounded serious.

I would discover on Saturday evening that Simon had actually sent the telegram himself. The bartender had delivered his bags, set up his side of the room, and his delay arriving at school was only to bet on a horse race in Saratoga Springs.

Simon's time on campus had been less than 24 hours but had netted me what Simon would describe as a classic hangover, a reprimand from the dean, a scheduled lecture from my uncle, a nasty gash above my left eye, and a pile of rubbish on my side of the room.

I awoke on Saturday with my first hangover, I felt sick. My roommate was missing and I had a very fuzzy memory of what had transpired the previous evening. I slowly remembered that I had stolen a bunch of junk, that my criminal activity had been pulling wood from fences and tearing down banners that had been carefully hung by students from the welcoming committee.

I did know that we owed apologies to our neighbors to the right, John Green of Watervilet and Jeffrey Barnes of Chicago. Our room was the last on the hall and directly across was a storage room that Simon would use often as his hiding room. Despite our attempts to be quiet, I was certain our back stairwell entrance the previous night had awoken our next door classmates if not the entire floor.

Barnes was an ardent Chicago sports fan and had ended up in the north country only because his aunt had paid for his schooling, demanding he attend her husband's alma mater. It was a brutal commute to the small town and Barnes detested it. He missed his beloved city.

The college had only about 400 students. News of our drunken rampage, although short in nature, spread quickly and upperclassmen would stop over the next few days to meet the two freshmen who had tussled at the Franklin and arrived well past curfew.

Simon was always well prepared and our visitors were welcomed with Simon's immediate phrase, "Let me get you a drink . . ."

Those who stopped over seemed to all have the same personality and none ever turned down his offer. Many stayed for more than just one drink, most overstayed their welcome and only left when the whiskey had run out.

Simon always said, "More where that came from," as our inebriated guests would stumble into the hallway.

I didn't leave the room until way after sunrise. I was a creature of farm work and the evening had taken its toll on me. I was unable to eat and it felt odd not to be purposeful from the beginning of the day. I found sanctuary in the church reading room, but struggled to study. It was intensely quiet, but even the scratching of my pencil was excruciatingly difficult to bear. I retained a fraction of what I read and finally surrendered and returned to the dorm in the late afternoon.

The Franklin bartender was just leaving our room with a box of tools. Daniel, I would come to learn, was barely 14, but he looked 18. He had been a jack-of-all-trades at a summer camp in the Saranac Lake area. The owner of the Franklin took a liking to his work ethic and asked him to work at the hotel. He was eager to please and had been rewarded for his loyalty to Simon as both customer and friend during the fist fight on our first foray to the Franklin hotel. Simon, I would find, always rewarded loyalty.

Our room now contained a fully-equipped bar with a cherry rail and pine top. Crafted cabinets created the stands that housed crystal, shakers, champagne glasses and several cloths. Simon described it as very posh, a word I had never heard.

"Don't tell me Daniel built this today?" I was still trying to grasp the incredible quality of the craftsmanship. The leather straps we had stolen now adorned both ends of the bar giving our room a festive style.

"When you turn it around, it looks like a desk. It's a studdddy aaarrrreaa," Simon mocked and laughed at me as he spoke.

"Harry, it fits across the hall in the small storage room. I spoke to the moron who cleans up and we can store it there. I made a key without him knowing it," he shared with a calculating tone.

"It stinks in here, I need something with a beer smell. Let's go to the Franklin for dinner. Grab John and Jeff," he commanded with a good laugh.

My stomach turned on the thought. I was sick but thought maybe having more drinks would make me feel better.

We took seats at a table in the tavern as the bar was full. I laughed to myself that just the day before I had rolled Jacques into the very table that was now supporting our drinks. Simon had brought a deck of cards and was rhythmically shuffling them. The people at the bar would turn every so often to see what Simon was doing. He would loudly snap the cards as he dealt them to himself on the table. It was an audible lure and the bar seemed to stop talking when he wanted people to pay attention. I was always amazed that people could be brought to attention just by the the subtle cue that the cards could evoke.

Daniel began his high quality service on Simon and company and in no time the fifteen people in bar were entranced with the *Bone-Ace* game. Simon required only a nickel to play. It only took one curious person from the bar to understand the game and play the first hand. They immediately won and in no time all of the tables had been formed to provide ample playing space for the entire bar.

Simon seemed to lose on purpose and even the most conservative and reluctant of locals joined into the game. Simon became a punching bag, much to the delight of everyone in the bar, who now had a free night of drinking courteous of the charismatic Mr. Sheldon.

Even while he was losing, he was buying drinks for those who played his nickel game. He bought drinks for everybody in the bar. Daniel understood Simon's subtle arm movements and hand gestures as if they had a secret language for ordering drinks. It was comical to watch but the locals never lost sight of the free libations and Daniel was in excellent form, never missing a silent order from 20 feet away.

We eventually sat for dinner in the grand dining room. Simon lost a grand total of $19, a fraction of what he had taken from Jacques the previous day. Simon was still on stage sharing the stories of the money he had won on the summer races at Saratoga Race Course.

John lived near Saratoga Springs and was on the edge of his chair with the tales of the races. Simon's late father had evidently been a noted physician. He spoke about the difficulties of healing people, the advancements of medicine and that his father had dabbled in racing during the summer as his way of relaxing. He didn't speak much of his father after that, he shared that he was a keenly perceptive man.

Simon had made connections with key jockeys and made a significant amount of money on the Saratoga Cup and Travers Stakes. Simon had won money on both races with a horse named *Omarkayham*. John was mesmerized as he had read about the Travers race in the local paper.

His jibe at Jacques made better sense as he was punctuating his card win with the horse's name. He regaled John with his prediction that a well known *Old Rosebud* would be beaten by *Roamer* to win the Saratoga Handicap. Simon had scored against two bookies and continued to win money the remainder of the summer. He complained that one of his bookmakers had disappeared, having taken an errant swim in a local lake.

I knew little of this and simply tried to keep the beer I was drinking from coming back up my gullet. I chatted with Barnes and when I could get any words in edgewise would shake my head with a false understanding, having never heard of these horses or races.

We ended the evening with beers in the tavern. Many of the earlier winners in Simon's nickel giveaway game hung around in hopes that he would return. A small cheer erupted when Simon entered the tavern after dinner. Simon acknowledged them with a nod of his head that he had been beaten badly. The patrons were oblivious to the fact that Simon had lost nothing and had gained a quick reputation that he would exploit for many months to come.

I mentioned the plans for Sunday night at my uncle's home, reminded him he had been kind not to arrest me. I left him to fend for himself. I would be attending church in the morning and the school year would hopefully begin with some structure, at least that is what I hoped.

It was miraculous. Simon arrived before curfew. He mumbled goodnight and clearly had consumed a fair amount of cocktails as his last words were, "That's a bust gentleman, everyone wins."

I tried to share my plans for the next day. I asked Simon to be ready at three o'clock and be prepared for a lengthy lecture from my uncle about our fracas at the Franklin. I was planning to drive to Visger Point before dinner.

I was surprised he acknowledged me, as his last words were, "Your bet, sir." I wasn't sure if his comment was associated with his card game or he actually understood my plans.

We would be heading directly north and since it had been dry the roads would be in relatively smooth condition. My father had worked out a deal with our feed distributor to store and look after my graduation gift. Part celebration, part workhorse, the Model T 1917 Canadian Ford was going to be my summer delivery wagon and during the school year I could use it, on occasion, to celebrate school functions and football wins.

I left Jencks the next day at two o'clock. There was no sign of Simon.

I swiftly spun around the large knobs that were at the top of each staircase. The building was showing the signs of the exuberance of youth looking for the shortest path.

It had become a ritual to spin quickly on the knobs so that your feet would leave the floor. The varnish had worn thin on the innermost floor boards. During the most severe snow storms it became our source of entertainment. The competitive game comprised running from the top stairs and spinning on all three floors. It took no time for Simon to turn the competition into a gambling game.

It was called *Nickel Spin* with the combined best three spins the winner. The numerous competitors spent more time arguing whose feet had left the ground higher on each floor than they did playing the game. No matter who won it would break the boredom of the numerous snow storms that made leaving the dorm difficult.

Invariably, there would be countless arguments about who had won. The losers tended to throw their nickel losses as a sign of protest for what they considered unfair calls by the hall referees. Simon had anointed himself the Chief Steward and he relished announcing the winner after lengthy discussions with the hall referees. On one blizzard-ridden Saturday there were over a hundred students in the meeting room waiting for the results of one of the contentious contests. It was high drama when he announced that after lengthy consideration the contest had been declared a dead heat. He knew a tie would make for extensive discussion and he was right. It made for better arguments as to the winner and the result was one student actually throwing a punch at another competitor.

It was a long walk from the back of campus down the old county road. The stage coach shed setup, although not ideal, provided my father a bit of comfort that I would not joy ride around campus. He wanted me to concentrate on my studies and get a degree he never obtained.

I was relieved to find Simon at Jenks when I returned. We headed to Visger Point, the split between the land owned by my father and that of my uncle. I drove up North Road which ran from the center of town to River Road. Simon begged me to stop at Hamm's Inn that was about halfway to the juncture where you either turned left for my father's property or take the right that took you along my uncle's property.

Hamm's had a large advertisement for beer and a sign for room vacancies. I quickly convinced him that I had a better place to go where beer was more plentiful. Hamm's was a popular local restaurant. The owner was not a friend of my father who had purposely sold a piece of land to another restaurant owner. They had used the prime river land to build the popular River Hotel, which split the two properties.

My uncle's property ran for two miles and curled back with the river's bend arriving at the town's dock and beginning of Maple Street.

I had hoped Simon would be interested in the river's views, but soon realized that the lure of alcohol might shorten our sightseeing. I would need time to coach him on my uncle's attempt to lecture me. More importantly, Simon's unannounced attendance might bring a sterner tone to his condemnation of the fight and gambling.

Visger Point was beautiful and the river peaceful and calm. I regaled Simon with our family history. It was part truth, part lore, but my grandfather had been discovered in a basket on this point in 1839 by the local Indian tribe.

My grandfather was credited with trying the first skiff on the river and began a boating business that he built into a guide boat and tour boat empire. He married my grandmother, Victoria, in 1859. My father and uncle were born quite a bit later in 1875. My father, Henry Walter, had been born a few moments ahead of my Uncle Winston, an indisputable fact that always irritated my uncle.

The family land, 400 acres to the west, was prime farm land with the closest access to Canada. To the east, were 100 acres of coves, pristine river views and unsettled camp land. The land had been transferred to my grandfather when the remaining members of the Indian tribe had moved north into Canada.

Simon was entranced by the closeness of Canada.

"Holy *Omarkayham*, let's hope Woodrow tries to swim across the channel and then sinks," he sarcastically projected.

"What the hell does that mean?" I interjected. I was a great admirer of the candidate for president.

"You don't know what Mr. Wilson will do and I don't agree." He seemed to be lecturing. I continued to share with Simon the government's interest in Visger's Point and Indian Penny Island, also owned by my father, as he seemed generally interested. Meanwhile, his eyes were transfixed on the western narrows. My grandfather had successfully fought the state by allowing a lighthouse to be erected on the point as long as they did not touch Indian Penny Island.

The island lay a quarter mile due east and was the last controlling point to the channel. It's ownership had been a bone of contention since my grandfather's death. My father never spoke of his passing, just saying that it had been a tragic accident in the spring of 1909.

Indian Penny Island had been my father's refuge and he and I had camped on the island ever since I could remember. He planned after my graduation to build a cottage there for our family. He had begun moving local natural red sandstone to serve as the base and was planning a summer residence with sweeping views of the channel. I never asked him why he was waiting for my graduation. I always guessed that he was focused on my obtaining my degree and setting a course in life.

"How did your father get the land with the narrows and island?" Simon questioned.

I knew the story by heart and was happy that my afternoon excursion was winning over the two bar signs we had passed. It would come up at dinner but I figured I would give him the quick version—that my uncle had made the right call when the land was separated and my father always said the parcels had equal value.

He enjoyed the fact that we had to work the land when his brother simply leased the land to wealthy families looking to escape the heat and stench of the cities. Winston built paying customers for us. We delivered farm goods by drift boat and managed a dairy farm with 20 hands. My father was proud that we created things.

Simon seemed interested in how the drift boat worked. I shared that I was an excellent oarsman and could navigate the boats with little effort.

We arrived at the River Hotel, which was empty. One of our farm hands, Lou, was washing some glasses. Lou was happy to see some customers, a bit disenchanted when the second to enter was a Charles. I am not sure if he was concerned that he had a second job or just that I was the son of his boss.

"Hello, Mr. Charles, what can I get you?" Lou asked.

Simon, without force, without jumping in, with not the slightest impression of urgency or control simply said, "Hi, I am Simon, this is Harry, three beers, no misters or sirs."

Simon slid a $5 silver certificate gently on the bar.

"The third beer is for you. We'll have two more in five minutes. If you would like one, take it out of the five. If you can't drink on the job, I am not telling anyone. Please take it as a tip." Simon completed his direction with warmth and charming ease.

Lou glanced at me, I nodded my approval.

"Yes, Sir . . . Simon," he corrected himself.

Simon turned to me. "Time to kill, one hour," he correctly pointed out.

The River Hotel was more tavern than hotel. It only had ten rooms that were rarely occupied. It had a variety of stuffed fish adorning the walls. Muskellunge, bass, perch, northern pike, and a variety of stuffed animals that had been caught or trapped were now frozen on the walls as if they had been just caught or shot.

"Boy, you people like to catch and shoot a lot of innocent animals!" Simon concluded while showing his city side.

"Pretty good eating for the most part," I softly defended.

"There is nothing like fresh river bass cooked right after you caught it." I began to try and be a bit more assertive.

"Harry, drop the "b" on bass. Unless the maître d has a wine list to match the fish, you won't find me cooking a fish I caught!" Simon pompously threw back in my face.

"Oh, I will convert you, you'll see, wait 'til a fish the size of Jacques pulls your arms off for an hour. You won't have old Harry to bail your bass out," I joked.

We drank pretty quickly. Lou appreciated the company and Simon had another bartender in his corner should a fight break out. *Christ,* I thought, *if all the farm hands were bartenders this school year, they could take the growing season off due to Simon's lack of understanding how this much money meant to the people in the north country.*

I tutored Simon on some key stories to get my uncle off the topic of Simon's gambling and fisticuffs entrance to town. He seemed anxious to use my recommendations, but our footing was slightly off kilter when we arrived.

"What do you think of the *Huckster*?" I bragged as I exited the Model T.

Simon, as if on cue, stepped from the car as I completed the sentence in unison with the word 'huckster.' There stood my uncle.

"I am surprised you brought the infamous Sheldon. Mr. Sheldon, gambling is a form of being a huckster. Are you a cheat as well?" my uncle rudely and antagonistically asked.

I realized my gaff and quickly tried to ease the situation.

"I was speaking of the car. It's a 1917 Canadian Huckster, Model T," I informed my uncle. "Should we leave Uncle Winston?" I spoke up, realizing I was being defensive of my friend.

"Nobody is leaving, Mr. Sheldon. Would you like something to drink?" My aunt stepped from the house and took command of the situation by overruling her husband. My uncle was not amused.

Her definition of drink would be clearly different from what Simon had envisioned. As expected, it was lemonade.

"Come inside, we can look at your car later," she finished and cooled the situation.

Aunt Clara was never one to dote over material things. Winston and I made shallow eye contact. He had insulted my friend, and I was already more protective of him than of my own family. Winston had intended to lecture me, but shifting gears was not his strong suit.

"Thank you for letting me join you for dinner. Harry said I was in for a treat," Simon spoke in an ingratiating tone.

"Around here, we call it supper," my aunt shared in a warm and folksy fashion. My aunt had instantly taken a liking to Simon. Her roundish face seemed to light up as if she was under a constant strain. She had black hair like Simon and was fairly large. Her clothes seemed to be too small for her.

My uncle, still reeling from our arrival, sat impatiently ready to unload his speech of temperance on us.

"If it's not too much of an imposition to see the moose antlers?" Simon cautiously asked.

Simon was in for the hour-long version of how my father and uncle tracked the moose from America into Canada across the channel, having parked their car on the ice. They tracked the moose for several hours ending on the border of Canada territory. They shot the moose but the moose was still strong enough to struggle into Canada. Mortified they would be arrested for shooting a moose on Canadian soil, they dragged the moose by their car. The Canadian Mounties had chased them down the narrows on horses.

They were able to get back close to the Charles property and only by the measurement of one half of the moose's antlers were they considered on American soil.

Simon could not fathom that the ice could hold such weight and drag a 1,500-pound moose. Yet, my uncle leaned forward and the saga began. The temperance speech apparently would wait and by the end of the evening we would get off with a fairly benign reprimand.

My uncle seemed relaxed and I shared our sightseeing tour and the topic of the framed Liberty Head 1856 gold coin was our dinner discussion.

I had heard the story countless times and my uncle's take on how the island became Henry Walter's seemed to become hazier with each telling. In the fall of 1908, both Winston and Henry Walter would meet at Visger at the point to flip the coin to divide the land, the winner would choose the west or east. The loser would get the island as consolation. The penny would go to the winner.

My grandfather, always one for an inside joke, secretly named the island after the coin flip and worked with the town to insure that it would always be recognized as such. I always smiled when I looked at nautical maps designating the island as 'IPI.'

My uncle always claimed he never understood the island portion, but it was clearly written in my grandfather's will. It always seemed selfish of my uncle. He had the better river views and no children to leave his property.

As was customary, I would receive the bulk of my father's holdings. My sister was to receive the farmhouse and investment shares in the farm. My father reminded me often that the value of the land was in the future connection to Canada. He always said they must build a bridge. If I needed to sell, I was to sell the farmland first and keep the property adjacent to the narrows.

Simon seemed interested in the land transfer, the coin flip, and my uncle having called 'tails.' The coin was framed in my uncle's study, marked in India ink in handwritten scrolled lettering that read, *1908 Land Transfer Visger Point.* My father had been glad he lost the flip. He said he got a free island out of it and a lifelong getting of my uncle's goat by reminding him of that. My uncle was always proud of his correctly predicting tails at the ripe old age of 33. It was odd he was proud of randomness.

The phone rang. I overheard a simple religious phrase. My aunt whimpered the words, "Dear God."

I now owned an island and 400 acres of farmland. I was now rich. I was now on my own island.

My father had shot himself.

Chapter II

"Why?" my mother uttered softly, just barely audible. Shy to begin with, she simply said 'why,' over and over. In a muffled sob, I could faintly make out that she would have to face sadness for a second time. I immediately thought of her father, Campbell, who had passed away after a long illness before I was born. She had spoken of him often and missed him a great deal. She now was without her husband. I was without a father as well.

I was barely 18, now a wealthy landowner, responsible for my mother, and with a 15-year-old sister who sat motionless in the study. Simon was sitting with her and trying to comfort her but to no avail.

According to Jacob, the barn was gruesome. My father had built a makeshift bunker with hay bales to essentially capture the mess he knew he would create. Jacob had worked for my grandfather, been the most senior worker on the farm, and was privy to all daily operations. My father trusted Jacob and asked him to meet him at the barn at seven o'clock, not a moment early and not to be a moment late. My father planned this to avoid anyone but Jacob finding him.

I consoled Jacob and thanked him for shielding my mother and sister as well as myself from the horrific scene. He was shaken and handed me a set of keys that were on a nearby hay bale in the barn. The note attached said simply, *for Harry*. The ink and handwriting matched the caption underneath of the penny in my uncle's study.

The Reverend arrived, the funeral director, Mayor, neighbors—our farm became a home of condolences and a river of emotions. Dean Hulet arrived, expressed his sympathy, and told me to take my time in getting back to class.

My drunkenness and teepee heap was now in the past and forgotten by virtue of my father's death. The news had spread quickly. Unknowingly, my father had bailed me out of trouble.

Jacob and my uncle had moved swiftly to devise a story to cover his death as a result of a farming accident. The local paper, run by close friends, readily accepted the story. The headline would read, *Prominent Citizen Lost to Tragic Accident*. It would be carried by the Regional Gazette and picked up by several statewide papers.

In the passing years, as the ink in handwritten journals and the newsprint would fade in scrapbooks, my father's death would still be a fabrication created by a second-rate newsman. He had received the account from the owner of the paper and described the tragic agricultural accident verbatim as concocted by my uncle and not the actual self-inflicted gunshot wound that Jacob had described to me.

The story was a lie. It seemed odd, but for some reason the inaccuracy had merit because it was protecting my family, protecting our good name and character.

Simon caught a ride back to campus from Dean Hulet with plans to help coordinate and bring my classmates to the funeral on Tuesday. The house began to return to silence as the remaining dignitaries left for the evening. I settled into my father's study, sitting back in his chair, something I had not done since I was a child sitting on his lap.

I began to open drawers, scavenge through papers, search files, envelopes, bills, and legal documents. The left lower drawer was locked. I reached into my pocket for the keys Jacob had given me, retrieved from the barn. Odd, that I should have his keys, acting as the patriarch of the family. I was now thrust into a role for which I had no understanding or experience. The note *for Harry* flashed in my mind. My father was a planner, he carefully set a course, was this the step he wanted me to take next?

The small copper key opened all the drawers. Several files covered the deep drawer, underneath were two pints of whiskey, one half empty. I was stunned at the sight, my father did not drink, and I could not fathom the meaning and turned sharply to see my mother standing at the entry of the study.

"What is the meaning of this, mother?" I softly demanded.

"Your father would drink, I never knew when, why, and how much. When he left to fish and hunt, it was worse and I never knew when he would return," she sadly finished at the volume of a whisper.

"He was a good provider, a good father," she wept as she finished. She said goodnight and we never spoke about it again.

I began to look at the files along with the whiskey. I retrieved a glass and decided to drink while I cleared his desk. I figured it would help me sleep and ease the pain of his death. The first file made me drink more.

A letter from my uncle dated shortly after Visger's death was a demand for half interest in Indian Penny Island. My father had responded via his attorneys Bond, Quinn, and Baird that the coin flip had determined ownership and the will had made it perfectly clear. Under no circumstances would he transfer ownership of any portion of the property to him. Upon his passing, his son, Harry Walter Charles, would inherit the property to use as he deemed appropriate. I was grieving for my father but felt a great sense of warmth for his faith in my judgment.

The last document was a purchase offer, dated just a month ago, handwritten. Winston had simply said, *Henry Walter, plenty of room for two summer homes, $2,000 for the west end facing narrows, please reconsider. Winston.* I continued to drink the remaining portion of the bottle, took out the India ink pen and wrote what my father would have written in large letters at the top: NO.

My uncle would soon find that I would not be as polite as my father.

I awoke in a morbid haze, not hangover, just morose, joyless, void of sadness, empty, grieving I supposed. Winston arrived shortly before lunch. The plans had been completed for the funeral—a simple route, a simple service, and a complex goodbye.

The talk of the route somehow evoked my thoughts of my grandfather, Captain Visger, sitting in the study when I was just old enough to remember and him sharing the story of traveling to Albany in 1865 to see President Lincoln's body in a specialty-built catafalque.

It was a sadness I did not understand then and did not feel quite right. A beloved president, who had brought together enemies, freed slaves, and was now being mourned by a nation composed both of a vanquished foe, and those who originally stood for what he believed was morally right. He had been shot by an assassin, just one man, just one bullet and now being pulled by six white horses. Now I was ten years older and thinking of my father's white hair, a single bullet shot in his head, being pulled by horses in less than a day.

The idea of a bullet in the brain and why my father secretly drank, unbeknownst to me, did not mar my image of him as an outwardly happy, funny, and caring man. My father was beloved. Tomorrow, there would be no white horses, only townspeople and workers, some who cared little for us, some just looking for a chance to share in a town meal, so poor they would use a man's death as a chance to eat.

Winston cornered me in the study and wanted to discuss family business, closing the door of the home now owned by my sister, as if it was his anointed by age. It was humiliating for him to now stand in front of me as an equal, when just the two days prior he was lecturing me for my antics at the Franklin when he could have easily had me arrested.

"Harry, I had discussed several things with your father, resolutions if you will, of property and a minor dispute regarding the island. I would like you to resolve these in the coming days, focus on your studies, and allow Jacob to manage the farm under my direction until this year is over," Winston confidently instructed.

Now seated at my father's desk, I unlocked the bottom drawer. "Care for a drink?" I casually asked, trying to imitate the bravado of Simon at the Franklin.

"Harry! Shame on you, your father just passed, I don't drink, I am not your father." Winston immediately knew he had revealed a character flaw of the great Charles family. It was a mistake, a lapse in protecting the good name, a lapse in not realizing the impact on me. He was focused on protesting like a lawman and not of a uncle looking to console a young man who had just lost his father to a suicide.

I began pouring a glass of whiskey. I was emboldened by his insulting my father. "I will sell you the west side but $2,000 is too low. Since you have opted to ask at a time when I might be vulnerable, I will ask you for $20,000 and give you until five o'clock this evening," I briskly instructed with sheer bravado.

Winston was red, ashen, and angry. He turned, then stopped.

"Damn you Harry, how dare you speak to me that way. I am a Charles and the eldest male," he informed me of the obvious.

"I made you an offer. From this point forward, not today, not tomorrow, the land I inherited is to be used as I deem appropriate. It is what my father wanted, what Captain Visger worked out when you won the flip. You should have called heads," I sarcastically added.

When it left my lips I knew I should not have said it, but since my uncle had made a calculated effort to try and use the death to his advantage, my father must have known this would happen and made sure I was prepared.

Winston exited in a frenzy. I don't remember if we spoke at the funeral. I had another two glasses of whiskey and decided I needed somebody, anybody to drink with, and my preference was Simon.

I reached campus and parked in front of our residence. Barnes was returning from class.

"Where is Simon?" I desperately asked,

"He's coming back from anatomy class, ask him to play *My Old Kentucky Home* on his rib cage—he removes the collarbones and uses them as drumsticks, it's a hoot!" Barnes laughed as he was talking.

I could see Simon off in the distance with books, a rib cage, and three coeds in tow.

Simon was easily convinced to leave his bad rendition of *My Old Kentucky Home* back at the room and we were off to the Franklin on foot. We grabbed Robinson from Boston, his roommate Chamberlain, Barnes, Harley, Francis, Appleton, Sargent, and Green from our floor as they eagerly wanted to join us on our outing. During the walk, my new friends would casually pass by me and somewhat fumble their words of condolence as we continued our short distance on Park Street.

Simon announced each person as they approached me, Simon relished introducing Walt Robinson in five sequential pronouncements, pausing just briefly after the first Walt, third Walt and after the last two. He would then regal that it was five Walts but sounded like a great deal more. "Walt, Walt, Walt, Walt, Walt, that's five Walts but it sounds like more." Walter would use the slogan to be elected the president of our fraternity.

It felt good that each had made the effort to say something. We were still becoming friends and even the oldest of friends have difficulty extending their condolences. It was getting cold out and it felt like rain. In less than 24 hours, I would be saying goodbye to my father.

The grand dining room was quiet. We headed to the tavern hoping Daniel was working; much to our delight the bar was empty. Daniel's face lit up as Simon, his favorite patron, walked through the door with nine thirsty buddies in tow. Simon smacked his usual certificate on the bar while elongating the name of the Traver's winner to emphasis his need for whiskey.

Simon seemed to have a clever line with his first request for alcohol.

"Beverage please, I am dry, pass me a bev-rye," he tried to create mirth with his opening salvo. They generally rhymed and they were very clever. Many times they made only drunken sense to him.

My yearning for numbness, distance, solitude, isolation with alcohol was quickly replaced with a somber discussion that began with my telling the story of Captain Visger' s visit to Albany to see Lincoln's body. Chamberlain, like many in the group, had lost a family member in the war. His grandfather had fought at Gettysburg. I don't remember how we ended on the topic and the ensuing discussion about Garrett's farm being burned and the assassin being shot, but the consensus was that it was all a plot to overthrow the government.

We were all scholars now, with a mere few days of classes under our belts, wiser than Daniel, loudly opinionated, and within a few hours fairly drunk. We knew everything and where we were short on knowledge, we changed the subject.

We never spoke of the war that was beginning to rage in Europe and if we were planning to go.

Francis, shy at first, transfixed the group in the telling of his great aunt's story of her husband giving up his seat on the lifeboat of the Titanic to a third-class passenger. She wished she had stayed with him, a regret she continues to live with each day.

She spoke often to Francis of waking to see the savior ship, the *Carpathia*, a massive black hull, up against the lifeboat and at that point realizing she had made a mistake. She considered throwing herself into the sea, but realized it took more courage than she possessed. It took courage to commit suicide and she was not courageous enough to kill herself. Her husband had that courage and the honor to do what was right.

The group did not understand how one could give up their seat to a third-class passenger, as if that required some type of thought. I could not understand how they could not remember that my father had just killed himself. I then remembered that the truth of his death was completely different from the version the group knew.

Simon realized that the group had believed the story about a farming accident. He read my face and signaled Daniel for another drink.

We talked for hours about character, tradition, values, wisdom, things we had come to college to learn.

I had suffered the worst of life's experiences in a mere few days—my father's brother seemingly indifferent to family wishes, my gentle caring father leaving his wife and children to question what would drive him to take his own life. Yet, here I was surrounded by new friends, questioning general life mysteries of the world in 1917, why it was what it was and what we would make of it. Simon focused on becoming a doctor, blessed with a terrific bedside manner and a nasty penchant for gambling, drinking, and trouble making.

It wasn't what they said, it was the conviction with which they said it. For some reason I did not share their enthusiasm. I never had, even prior to my father's death.

Simon stood up, a bit wobbly, "A toast, to Harry's father," he continued as our group raised their glasses, "To our next president, please wait until 1921 to pass the dreaded Volstead Act, for I cannot take four years in this penitentiary with just football wagering and nickel *Bone-Ace* to survive!"

John questioned, "Volstead Act?"

Simon enlightened the group, "The prospect of having taverns, alcohol, and the Franklin Hotel rest in the hands of zealots who hate drinkers . . . they think of us as evil, the rural Protestants think of our health, they try and give us wisdom!"

"Evil my ass," Harley blurted out much to the delight of us all.

Daniel, who had put on a green vest, attire he would be seen wearing often, perked up at the conversation. "No booze would doom this town, the nightlife would be gone, and my job would be gone!" Daniel interjected.

Simon quickly added, "Francis, what do you think?"

At the end of the table, Francis had fallen asleep. The table roared in laughter. He would never live it down and his nickname from that point forward was *Faf.* He could thank Harley for his quick moniker of *Fast Asleep Francis*. It did not help that his last name was Fennimore, even Professors unwittingly would call him Faf, not knowing they were contributing to a nickname borne from the first outing at the Franklin where Francis had drank too much.

Francis hated the use of Faf, especially when other students would actually ask what the 'A' stood for in his middle name. He never lived it down but would eventually grow somewhat fond of it.

Simon, part preacher, part politician, and not to be outdone, spoke. "Gentleman, fear not the evils of drink, except you Francis, if you can hear me, prohibition is on the horizon but we will find a source to indulge in the finer things in life, whiskey and beer will flow through the constricted narrows as the Government closes the valves down!"

The group, in unison rang out. "Here, here!"

My need for a diversion had been met. I stuck Simon with the bill, said goodbye, fetched my car and drove to my sister's house to try and sleep before the funeral.

The funeral was at noon. I drove in a light rain to Visger Point at sunrise to think about my father. I collected four stones from the shore of the river, four stones I thought as a nice way to signify what I would achieve by graduating from school. I would place them in his grave and each year after I would bring a stone from Indian Penny Island to share a story of success. I wanted him to be proud of me, I wanted him to know that I loved him, and I hoped he was at peace.

I could not fathom why he had taken his own life—the pain he must have felt, the anguish I now endured, the absolute mystery of it was crushing to me. I walked slowly to the car, turned to the island and vowed to build the cottage he planned after my graduation.

The *Huckster* barely made it back, I had the lanterns on and my father would be mortified that the beautiful car was enduring this torrential rain and mud bath. The dirt roads had given way to muddy avenues and fortunately the processional was only a short horse-drawn carriage ride from the church.

People were overflowing from the main entrance. My mother would have none of that and protocol was put aside, no matter how socially incorrect, due to the weather. She asked everyone to stand. People filled the aisles, hallways, vestibules, and minister's offices. She would have no one outside and people were sitting next to and behind the choir.

The stories of his kindness, his quiet gifts, charity, bequests to those in need, were stories I had never heard or been aware of before. Several individuals had traveled by train from Vermont and Boston. My father had paid for their education, they were now quietly paying for a student on scholarship.

A man rose from the balcony, smiled wide.

"Mr. Charles paid for my dental work, sent me to Syracuse so as not to embarrass me, bought me a steak and corn dinner when I returned, first time since I was ten I could eat corn!"

The mourners laughed their approval for my father. One story after another, it seemed endless. There were tears of joy for his thoughtfulness, his simple acts of kindness, some that made individual differences in people's lives, others that brought unknown silent hope to the entire community.

My uncle completed the service with the eulogy. He spoke glowingly about his brother, their youth, them helping guide river boats with Captain Visger. Despite being identical in looks, he did not remind me of my father. He was stoic, hardened, shallow, resolute. When he spoke, there seemed to be a lack of emotion.

It wasn't a lack of empathy, or kindness, just a sense of shielding his true feelings, maybe fear, and insecurity. *Maybe like an island*, I thought.

The congregation sang a final song, *When the Saints Go Marching In*. We sloshed through a terrible rain, I laid the stones from the river in his grave, we lowered his coffin and I said goodbye to my father.

Simon walked up to me.

"My friend, I can't put into words how difficult this is for you but it will get better with each passing day," he shared in a brotherly tone.

The rain had begun to stop, the mourners began to disperse to our home for a reception and dinner. I felt an urge to hide, and Simon asked if I wanted to go to the River Hotel before heading home. I declined but said I had a copper key and we could spend a few minutes in my father's study.

Simon, seemingly aware that a locked drawer contained ingredients for no good, either a cribbage board, a deck of cards, or strong drink. He knew I was not a card player and felt his odds were pretty good for strong drink.

On such a somber day, it drew Cheshire Cat grins from us both. It was the first time I had even remotely smiled all day and I was thankful Simon was my roommate and friend.

Whatever system the ancient hag had used in assigning rooms, it had worked because I was fortunate to have met Simon, who was now like a brother to me.

Simon and I arrived at the farmhouse. Twelve gridiron men, clad in home jersey brown uniforms, synched in a perfect line, were greeting guests in military fashion. They were unrehearsed but in perfect formation and I was deeply touched.

Death makes people follow symmetry, unable not to conform to protocol. The carriages and Model T's were all in a perfect line despite the wretched conditions.

Coach Kinnon simply said, "I am sorry son, next week we need you back. Your team is also your family." I nodded my head and knew he spoke for my father.

The rain had caused chaos. The storm clouds were moving east toward the channel. The destruction it had caused was minor but the emotional burden it created was quite heavy. I nearly commented that the bottom clapboards of the house were blood splattered but caught myself when I saw my sister, Celia, watching the football players from the upper window.

She was old enough to understand, but the pain she was feeling had triggered an instinct for her to remain a child. I was envious for a moment but now had to act as her father and spend the day consoling and being consoled.

Chapter III

He was a hometown referee born and raised. His bias calls, unnoticed by the 400 spectators who had jammed the stands built for 300, were not lost on the undefeated Connecticut team that had travelled nine hours by train.

The train's breakdown and multiple stops prolonged the trip making the visiting coach less tolerant of the poor calls.

The reporter that covered my father's death would describe his outbursts as those of a petulant child. In reality, the coach's reaction was moderate in relationship to the unfair advantage the ref had given us. It was our final game of the season and the team we were playing was in no condition to play us.

The fans, a mix of students, alumni, town dignitaries, and sports reporters from Connecticut, New York, and Boston were not aware that the referee, dressed all in black and sporting a compressed cap with a white "R" designation, was a distant relative of the running back who had just scored another touchdown.

The stands, confused by the rules of the game, void of a scoreboard, were well aware that the home team was about to complete the transition to big time football by taking down a undefeated Eastern team that had dominated football since the beginning of the sport.

The ref, signaled a "V" as opposed to an "H" for the final touchdown. He enraged the opposing coach by joining in with the announcer using a bullhorn to count down the final seconds.

The fans rejoiced in song, none happier than Simon who had a neatly folded telegram that he had received from his bookmaker in New York. It verified his bet of $50 on our team to win at five-to-one. Simon had just won $250 for simply using the information that the train had been severely delayed.

It had been a season of emotional contrasts. It began with a tragic loss, filled with some very exciting wins and celebrations. I walked past the stands, having completed the day with our new college rushing record. My leather helmet was still on, and despite being a Charles, the cheers were genuine for what I had accomplished.

My uniform was adorned simply with my number. Those willing to fork over the nickel for the program would have known I was Harry Charles, son of the recently deceased Henry Walter Charles. Word would spread quickly. My picture would run in the New York Times three days later with a caption, *Future Star*.

No one knew or would care that I was helped by a third cousin by marriage on my mother's side. I was a bona fide football star.

Simon shared his ill gotten gain and had taken center stage after my day of adulation. He took my family to dinner at the Franklin sparing no expense, even extending an invitation to Aunt Clara and Uncle Winston.

It had been declined immediately and they actually sat at a distant table, much to my mother's chagrin. My mother even drank champagne in honor of the season, my record, and the fact that I signed my first autograph to a guest of the hotel who was from Boston. He said it might be worth something someday. My bravado signature by the end of the evening became barely legible and I was lucky if I could have made an "x" on a piece of paper. Simon kept in close contact with our waiter throughout the evening and his generous tips helped the waiter stay in close contact with Simon despite the overflowing tables and very raucous crowd. Simon would flash a 'V' to me for the sign of victory but would then turn his fingers sideways to tell the waiter to pour doubles—the next round of drinks were to be twice as strong.

I had reached a new level of acceptance, and despite my boorish behavior, the owner was falling all over himself to make sure I was happy. I was a football hero, one of the town's largest employers, a regular guest, and frequent accompaniment of bon vivant, Simon Sheldon.

My uncle's scowls continued to grow larger, if possible, at the number of drinks I had consumed. His table looked farther away, like an island, with each drink.

Simon would later recount how I would repetitively mention that he should join us as opposed to sitting on an island all by himself. Simon had a great deal of fun correcting me when I called him a, "head flapper caller," when I was actually trying to say, "head flipper caller."

The derogatory nature of the comment was not lost on my uncle. My aunt thought it had been meant as a kind invitation but I had punctuated it with drunken sarcasm. Simon said the third slurred request had helped my uncle head to the exit prior to the coffee being served. I would remark later, "What coffee?"

My great evening was interrupted for a horrific vomit session in the lower tavern bathroom. I was sure to tip strongly later as I knew it was one of Daniel's duties to clean the bathroom prior to leaving for the evening.

My sickness, however, gave me the opportunity to consume more alcohol and become proficient at Simon's imported nickel game from Saratoga. The version he played with the bar cronies was different than the one he played against his friends from Ottawa called *Vingt-et-Un*. Knowing Simon, he simply beat Jacques and Pierre at their own game.

Simon held court with the local cronies dealing *Bone-Ace*. I had never played cards. Simon never relinquished control of the deck and the growing crowd simply had to dictate to Simon after getting their initial three cards, if they wanted more cards. The goal was to get to as close to 31 points as one could before going over.

Simon was a magician, or a fabulous manipulator. People would win early, get a free drink, and then eventually lose. Simon was all the while entertaining, interjecting humor, warmth, and buying drinks. Eventually, when they would decide to quit for fear of losing too much money or having consumed too much alcohol, they would push away from the table with a smile on their face.

They would always leave with Simon buying a "better-luck-next-time cocktail." Despite the myriad free drinks, and the smiles on their faces, the herd lost a considerable amount of money as a group.

Simon would laugh on the way back to campus, commenting that the rubes had been a generous and cheerful lot. This night, as best I could recollect, was very lucrative. Simon didn't need the money and I am certain the day after brought a fair amount of remorse from the townspeople who had joyfully given their money to Simon. It was the victory, the thrill of the advantage, the one-ups-man-ship, that was the game. I was ringside, a lucky front row spectator.

He dealt the cards like charmed slices of creativity, mixed with delicate sarcasm, and an uncanny knowledge of facial expressions. He knew if someone should not be playing and whether the loss of a nickel was of paramount human cost.

If that was the case, they would win and he would encourage them to be the auxiliary bartender by asking them to help Daniel serve the overflowing table. The player would graciously exit the game, at Simon's request, and withdraw their monies from the game while maintaining their dignity. They seemed appreciative to be relegated to a servant knowing 50 cents was safely in their pocket.

They felt like they could rejoin at another time when funds were not so scarce, even though they should never play if a nickel would cause financial ruin. He was a master at reading the signs and people somehow knew he had their best interest at heart, no matter how much it cost them.

I never asked him then if he cheated. He may have been just that good, as there was strategy and only a finite number of cards that could be available at any one time. The clarity by which some players won, those who needed to win, was fairly obvious if one looked hard at who on a given night had walked away a winner.

There were a few, not many, who actually won, but repeat winners in consecutive weeks, never. The cloudy haze of free cocktails tended to warp their view and there was none other than the puppeteer master Simon.

He might have cheated, but his charm he could not fake. It was genuine and his heart was always in the right place, a bit misguided, but he loved the win, he loved the control, and he loved being the one who entertained the people with a simple game that only cost a nickel.

I awoke the next day, befuddled as to how I had returned to beloved 24 Jenks. I was curled on the floor, devoid of the blanket given to me by my mother, covered by four of Simon's uglier sweaters.

My bed was occupied by Simon and Simon's bed was occupied by Daniel, who was clad in his customary green vest and work attire. It appeared he had been in a bad fight as his shirt was ripped, there were blood stains on his face, and he had a swollen left eye. We all smelled of strong whiskey while I also had a scent of vomit mixed in.

"For Christ's sake what happened to you?" I mumbled, barely able to put a cogent sentence together.

"Seriously, Harry, you don't remember?" Daniel spoke starkly, indignant to my question.

"No, I don't!" I countered, intrigued by the possible scenarios.

"Near closing time, you started to act a bit big for your britches. I stepped in," Daniel informed.

"Who did you fight, not one of my farm hands, I hope?" I protectively shot back.

"No, you," Daniel sheepishly answered.

"You must be joking," I admonished him in my response.

Simon came to Daniel's defense, "Yup, it was "Southpaw Harry," six-two, drunk as a skunk. You can run for over 300 yards sober but throw back whiskey slower than molasses." Simon tried to add humor to an uncomfortable situation.

"Daniel, I am sorry, you okay?" I apologetically asked.

"Fine, a few scrapes, cut lip, you can buy me a new shirt and pants!" Daniel laughed a bit but grimaced and was serious about his clothes as he spoke.

I reached into my pocket, I had a silver certificate when I started the evening and was delighted to find 17 crumpled dollars in my pocket. I am assuming Simon wanted me to be a future rube.

"Hey, not bad, 17 bucks, did I win this?" I asked him.

He smiled. "You were unbeatable and the night's big winner."

I had no memory of any of it and his attempt to lure me into his seductive *Bone-Ace* game long-term may have gone to waste but at least I had enough to immediately buy my way out of the mess I had caused.

I handed Daniel the seventeen dollars, more than enough to cover the clothes plus a fiscal penalty for the physical harm. I considered him a friend. I didn't apologize but made eye contact to show my remorse. I did not need to say I was sorry twice.

Daniel lived near town and the last I could remember my car was at the Franklin. "Can I drive you home? We will need to fetch the *Huckster*," I helpfully offered, it was the least I could do at having attacked him.

Simon, in the midst of getting dressed, said, "About that, your car is at the farm house."

"What the hell are you talking about, who drove my car?" I was peeved and indignant.

"You did!" Simon added.

"Oh, Christ, how and when did I get back? Did I hit anything?" I was dumbfounded at my lack of understanding.

"After you punched your way out of the Franklin, we drove back with you and Jacob drove us back to Jenks," Daniel explained. "Then you passed out in the back. Jacob didn't want your mother seeing you so drunk."

Simon filled in the blanks. "We carried you to the dorm avoiding the Dean and figured Daniel should stay here. He has to work this morning."

Simon and Daniel both left the room. I was left in a disheveled state. Moments later there was a knock at the door. *Christ, what now?* It was Jacob.

Jacob entered the room with a rehearsed purpose. His reason was to return the car, but his intent was far more important to him. Jacob was 60 but did not look a day over 50. He was hardworking and deliberate, had been dedicated to my grandfather, devoted to my father, and I think fond of me as he had been afforded the opportunity to call me Harry as other help were required to call me Mr. Charles.

"Harry, I had an understanding with your father when he drank that I was always to discuss his directions the next day. Can we agree to do the same?" he began.

"I assume I am not fired," he continued.

I was saddened about my father's drinking and troubled that I had somehow insulted Jacob, the man who had days earlier shielded my family, especially my sister, from the horrific scene that awaited some unsuspecting person in the barn. He had been a trusted friend of our family for over 30-plus years.

"Jacob, I am sorry. I celebrated a bit too much, rushing record and all. Of course not, you will have a place with us always," I sadly offered.

Jacob continued his lesson plan. "I started with Visger in 1887, your father was just 12 and I watched him grow into a fine young man. I have seen you the spitting image, walking, talking, and acting just the same. I would come to call you 'Bright and Cheery Harry' when you were just five. Prior to Henry Walter's passing, he had planned to give me some land to build a house, a place to retire on the river, I thought I would work until you graduate and then turn my duties over to the next in line."

I had a terrible haze over my thought process and was really not thinking straight, but bad judgment or not, I trusted Jacob more than my Uncle Winston, who had a similar conversation about the island just days earlier. My gut told me it was fair.

"Jacob, if that is what my father would have said, I am certain of his trust and commitment to you. Let me meet with Mr. Quinn, while you pick out the land you want, and make it official. I do ask that you stay on until one year after graduation until 1922 as a transition year. We can finalize that later, okay with you?" With smiles and respectful nods, Jacob was now for all intents and purposes my neighbor.

I was discovering that people wanted things from me, simple favors. I had been approached with business ventures, asked for loans from farm hands, I had a stack of correspondence on my father's desk at the farmhouse that I am sure contained a multitude of similar things. They were beginning to bother me.

As the football season was over, the rigors of campus life began to consume me and I was besieged with how it had enveloped me.

I lay in bed. I lost count how many times Simon came and went. The days were growing shorter, the shadows longer. I managed several trips to the farm, spent several nights, met with Mr. Quinn, and rarely left my childhood room or office. I used the copper key to smooth the rough spots.

Jacob received his deed, five acres, and a pretty view of the river with a secluded cove to store a boat. He was handling the farm with great ease and excellence. I could have not cared less.

Jacob was filling new farm hand positions. Lou and two others had enlisted and were headed to Europe to fight in the war. He asked if I would approve an extra month salary for their service to our country, to which I agreed.

It initially struck me that Simon would miss one of his best bartenders at the River Hotel. It was a terrible prospect—Lou would be facing great peril and my primary concern was Simon's ease of getting whiskey during a crowded time at the hotel.

I knew little of the two others leaving and really didn't care.

I found myself in late November standing a lifetime from where I had been just 13 weeks before, in the same spot, same view, and same time that I had been waiting for Simon's train.

Frost now consumed the ground, what leaves remained on the trees were frozen, motionless, dead, everything was dark, hidden by the late rising sun. There was no color, only grey and black. I was isolated, felt empty, desolate, dank, and perplexed by the bleakness of how I was feeling.

It was still. You could hear the steam engine and the rings of steam making soft whispers in the distance. The seven o'clock was approaching. I remembered that on Wednesday, there was an 8:45 am to New York. I knew I was going to be on the train, I did not know why, but I wanted to run away.

I returned to Jenks to the seven majestic chimes. The student volunteer was in perfect sync this morning as I moved quickly up the two flights of stairs to grab a bag and money, only to encounter Simon on his way to class.

"Not headed to Latin, Harry?" he quizzed.

"Not today," I retorted.

"Unlike you. Everything okay? Not using the copper key without me today are we?" he joked.

"At least not in this county," I quipped. Simon stopped.

"Where are you headed? I want in!" he immediately blurted out while catching the ear of Fennimore who was heading to the staircase. Simon had successful predicted my running away and I was now cornered.

"Well if you must pry, I am headed to New York for a business meeting," I lied.

"Rubbish, you will need a Secretary and Sergeant of Arms. Fennimore gather your things, we are headed to 15th East 7th Street, New York business meeting. You're fooling no one. You have been in a morbid mood and you will need assistance on your trip. We leave for the train when our provisions are assembled," he commanded.

We gathered the necessities for our travels, the finest fashions, travel liquor and Simon's gambling jacket, containing an amount equal to a year's tuition. Simon was focusing on making sure his 52 well-shuffled cards, his traveling investment and entertainment club, were added to our provisions.

My initial desire to run from the pillars now had all the makings of watching Simon careen through New York with the velocity of a much faster train than the New York Central. It was Simon on the big stage, Simon in the big league, his league.

I could hardly contain myself. My stride as we left Jenks was more confidant, but came no where near the bravado I had shown weeks before as I exited the field of the last football game. Nevertheless, it was a welcome and vast improvement.

This must have been old hat for Fennimore and Simon, an eight-hour train ride to Grand Central. I had never been more than 30 miles outside of our town. My lone trip to another country was an errant mistake in a homemade raft during a freak storm that landed me on the opposite side of the narrows. I had been only eleven at the time and scared.

My time in Canada had been less than an hour as the storm had passed and my father, adept at rowing, navigated a skiff to retrieve me. I would become an expert, like my father, at navigating the river even in horrible weather.

I was now eighteen, not scared but naive enough to know that the city was bigger than the ego I had obtained as a small town football hero. I had never navigated a big city.

Simon led us to the extreme right of the campus, down Hillside Drive, Fraternity and Sorority row. The homes were majestic and manicured, icons for freshmen as only a small percentage would be asked to join.

I thought nothing of Simon and I joining as Fennimore might not meet the grade. My reputation was secure and Simon had built bravado off the fisticuffs at the Franklin even though he had not thrown a punch. His prowess with a deck of playing cards was becoming legendary. His tomfoolery was making it certain he would be asked to join somewhere, most likely everywhere.

The brick station was practically empty. Simon was more concerned about the lack of people that might have an interest in playing cards. Simon hustled off to the Western Union teller at the end of the station with instructions to get three first-class tickets with sleeping compartments for our trip. I was certain I would not sleep, but his request was accompanied with a clump of folding bills and instructions to get the best sleeping car and accommodations.

Fennimore had made little conversation and didn't seem engaged. I knew little about him, as he was a bit meek. He was bright, wore circular brown glasses and was thin and balding. I assumed he was from a wealthy family as his family had been on the Titanic. I was wrong on all accounts.

"Where are you from?" It was a bit awkward asking given that we had more than likely covered it during our visit to the Franklin.

"Just outside Watertown," he spoke reluctantly, thinking I knew about him already.

"Oh, North Country. for some reason I thought you were from New York." I felt relieved that I might not be alone as a first-time visitor to the City.

"Been to New York before?" I added.

"No, I might be a small fish out of water. It might be better letting the two of you traverse to New York, a bit tight on funds," his volume decreased as he completed his sentence.

"Nonsense, Simon invited you, I have enough to cover us and I will talk to Simon when he gets back. He made money off me in the last game, so don't worry, let's rely on Simon, he seems to always have a plan," I reassured him. I was delighted I would not be the only one gazing like a schoolgirl at a city I had only seen in books.

I had begun to think about what I had said, *Simon has a plan*. Fennimore, a bit mousey, *Fast Asleep Fennimore*. Simon had time to wrangle far more fun companionship —drinkers with wooden legs, jokesters, several upper classmates that had joined him at the Franklin for his robust card games, many who had languished in our room with an inability to quench their thirsts.

The purposeful walk by the fraternities—why not bring a potential sponsor who might speak for him when the time to join came around?

My analysis of Simon was interrupted at the ticket window.

"Next!" A rotund man bellowed through the four brass grates, adorned with intricate scroll work.

"Three first-class sleeping quarters to New York, round trip, thank you," I requested.

"Mr. Charles?" he responded.

"What? Yes." I gazed at him as I spoke but did not recognize the face and name on his badge, *Douglas*.

"I saw your last game. Tremendous effort, 323 yards, no right blocking. You went through holes that evaporated a second after you ran through them," he precisely praised.

I demurely responded, "Thank you, the other team was not up to their game but my offensive line made it easy."

"You're modest! You ran lights out. I put you in the Presidential Car at no extra charge. I can't wait until next season. I am taking the train to the Harvard game in October, it should be a barn burner," he gushed.

"Well you are kind, I will stop down next fall with tickets, I think you know more than Coach Kinnon. Thanks, Doug, for helping with the accommodations," I said with pride.

He was touched that I called him by his first name and I thanked him making sure that he called me Harry.

Simon was pleased with the accommodations, unaware that my running ability and the ticket seller's love of college football had saved him a bundle.

Fennimore kept pacing and I was guessing the $8 ticket was a pretty scary debt he had just incurred. Numbers were Fennimore's game, I was guessing that the expensive start and 48 hours were going to give him a heart attack.

"What's with the Western Union visit?" I quizzed Simon.

"You let old Sheldon handle this. The city is my town. I can tell you I requested a suite at the good old Waldorf Astoria, dinner at seven. We will be meeting and introducing you both to Frank Albans, stock market broker by day, negotiating Investment Consultant by night," he somewhat cryptically completed.

"Let me guess. Your bookmaker?" I barely let him finish.

"Well, Harry, it calls for a visit to the bar car when the *creeper* starts moving. Fennimore, you seem agitated. Out with it, I am beginning to think I need whiskey and it's not nine o'clock yet," Simon morphed into a question.

"Well, this trip might be a bit off the chart for my budget, a bit tight on funds," Fennimore reluctantly shared.

"Okay, I invited you. I can pay your freight and you can pay me back but if you fall asleep before we arrive at the hotel for the night, you pay me double! I have a better idea. I can give you $50 as a loan. At our thirtieth year reunion you pay me back, no interest, serving my yet-to-be-corralled wife and myself two drinks as a thank you," Simon neatly laid out the terms.

Fennimore, like a balloon, burst into laughter, relieved that he could now take part without concern about money. Faf took a piece of paper and envelope from the writing desk that occupied the opulent corner of the suite.

He began to write up a contract of sorts, I was the witness, and despite Simon's protests of the lack of need for this formality, a precise and detailed agreement was executed on November 14, 1917.

Fennimore signaled for the train porter, who took the envelope. It was mailed to himself at the next stop, reiterating that the postal mark would be used as the official stamp that they had executed the binding contract.

In what would become the classic precision of Fennimore, he asked for two twenties and a ten. He indicated that he had $10 in silver coins in his luggage and would pay Simon back for the ticket when we reached New York, unless he wanted to play *Bone-Ace* until lunch.

Simon could not resist the challenge and subsequently ripped the cards up by the time we had rolled into Albany. If my calculations were correct, Fennimore had $12 in neat stacks, and had paid Simon for the train ride. The original fifty was now encased in his wallet.

Simon threw the cards. I wasn't convinced he was that angry.

Simon moaned about the cards he had dealt, asked Fennimore to get the porter to clean up the cards and left the car with the intention of drinking.

He seemed mad that he had lost, but his parting comment of "shouldn't you take a nap?" coupled with my glimpse of his facial movements made me think otherwise.

I gave Fennimore a smirking look of approval as I went to join Simon in the bar car.

I was happy for Fennimore, this was a big trip for him. It was a big trip for us both and I had Fennimore to ease my worry of being in a big city.

"You lost on purpose!" I challenged Simon.

"Nonsense, he beat me fair and square. Bad cards, they run that way," Simon defended himself.

"Mr. Sheldon, what's the plan? Are there many more suitable and humorous drinking companions to join us on this business meeting?" I queried.

"I need a runner this summer for the races and maybe next fall, someone they won't suspect, and Fennimore fits the part," Simon shared.

"You don't need the money, why all the trouble?" I questioned.

"It's a bit of good fun bleeding my blue blood friends from their inherited wealth and I can make Fennimore rich in the process. We can all make some money and I get drinks delivered to my yet-to-be-discovered spouse and yours truly souse at our 30th reunion!" Simon bellowed in laughter at his play on words.

It all seemed odd. I could not fathom these random acts of kindness, letting Faf win, letting a distraught *Bone-Ace* player at the Franklin survive a night at his card table with a tidy profit when in actuality they should not be playing.

The bar car was empty, just Simon and I, elegantly appointed, just what I had sought. I was now privy to Simon's inner workings of a plan. He was hatching something, not a scheme, but a devilish scenario utilizing a runner for the races and for the fall. It mesmerized me with its unknown complexity. A meeting with the book maker, dinner at the Waldorf. Here I was holding cut crystal, sipping top-shelf whiskey and not consumed with mundane things like feed prices, planting schedules, cattle, and harvesting produce.

I was headed to New York, and after two drinks, courage in hand, I again asked Simon, "You lost on purpose?"

Simon, gleeful from the enhanced double said, "Suppose I had, tell me how you knew?"

"You ripped the cards, making it impossible for him to lose any of his winnings and holding him hostage by the loan," I surmised.

"I did not lose on purpose, but there is hope for you. Now for a few more drinks, a light lunch and rest until New York. Our first stop will be McSorley's Old Ale House," Simon regaled with his glass inverted into his mouth.

As if like clockwork, Fennimore was sound asleep when we returned to the car. A ledger had been created on the desk, $72 was written as cash on hand on the top of the page. Loan from Simon, $50, ticket cost $8, and the profits from cards were neatly detailed below.

Simon looked at me whispering "He's a runner alright, the perfect runner. Harry, look, he even accounted for the $10 in coins he has in his suitcase." He shook his head in humorous disgust.

Chapter IV

Fifteen East 7th Street, dark and dank, a world-class tavern filled with dignified gentleman, no women allowed. It reeked of misery and success all at once. Simon exhaled as he walked through the entrance. A gentleman at the door gave him the once over and made no effort to stop him for lack of character.

Simon was with his own kind and his confident walk and manner of ease made him melt quickly into a spot at the bar. Fennimore, stunned by the complexities of the city, appeared as if his fear would make him vomit. I was in the middle of the two, content to take it all in as Simon began to hold court with a patron next to us at the mahogany bar.

"Anybody know the odds on the fight tonight?" Simon projected toward the bartender, waiting for input from the gentry that circled the bar.

An elderly man, clad in a debonair blazer and greenish tie was seated several seats away.

"McCoy, two gets you seven, O'Dowd, five gets you seven," he grumpily proffered.

"Well, looks to be an interesting evening with the underdog at an interesting and tidy two-and-a-half to one.

What do you say Harry, should we take the underdog and make a fast $500?" Simon questioned.

I failed to understand the betting concept but was not afraid of losing a considerable amount of money. Fennimore blended into the bar, unable to speak at the monetary amounts Simon was discussing.

"Champ ain't got a shot, O'Dowd drops him in six," the gentleman added.

Patrons began to banter their opinions about as Simon summoned the bartender for a round of drinks for his new-found friends. He could not have slid the bill more quietly on the bar, but the effect was like a gunshot as the frenzied group of new prognosticators quickly joined the rail.

Simon ordered three whiskeys for us and tipped handsomely as the better whisky was brought off the top shelf of the back of the bar.

The patrons' animated discussion of the fight was tweaked occasionally by Simon fishing for background on the fighters. Simon was looking for the edge.

"Why two-and-a-half-to-one on the dog?" Simon bantered to provoke conversation.

"Seasoning. McCoy should continue his reign. Irishman takes another beating, this time in the ring," a ruffled curmudgeon shouted out.

The bar let out a joyous laugh at the hands of the Irish race. He continued, "The challenger is untested."

Simon glanced at his watch. "Six-thirty. It's time for a chaser," he declared.

Three beers arrived on cue. We were on the clock as Simon ordered another round for his ensemble of fight experts and assorted vultures. The bartender rushed to his beckoning for more drinks.

We left without a care in the world. Fast Asleep Fennimore, not very strong at handling his drinks, was now slow in stride. I was keeping up with Simon.

The Waldorf Astoria was stunning, meticulously appointed. We arrived to greetings from the staff, who were standing around the front desk. Simon plied his trade of gratuities with deft touch, not exposing the silver coins but neatly handing them to every staff member he encountered. We each were called by our last names.

We would not be void of anything for the next two days. We checked into our suites, two adjoining with magnificent views, fresh linens and details of comfort I had never seen.

Despite being modeled after the Astoria, The Franklin was simply not even in the same league. The Franklin was a poor copy. The Astoria was the real deal.

We hastened to the dining room to find Frank Albans reading the sports page and drinks awaiting us at our place settings.

"Simon, you prognosticator, how did your little university pull off such a spectacular win? I laid your bet off and placed a rather nice sum for myself. Five-to-one with Simon on board is too hard to pass up," Albans shared in a very endearing way. It showed the depth of their long-term friendship.

"Dinner's on me!" he added. Frank handed Simon an envelope.

Simon smiled and quickly introduced us. "Albans, this is Fennimore and my roommate, Harry Charles."

Albans stood, hesitated for a moment, "Charles, so this is the reason for the generous odds we won on! Happy to meet you both. Fennimore, are you on the team as well?" Albans inquired.

He glanced at Fennimore and realized his question failed to acknowledge his meek stature.

"No, ardent football supporter and classmate of Simon," Fennimore responded.

"I hear there is a fight tonight., We would like to go. I hear that McCoy is vulnerable?" Simon, again, was looking for information and testing Albans.

"Not sure, money is coming in slowly. I suspect the champ will be one-to-five and two-to-one on the challenger," Albans conned and calculated in one breath.

Fennimore and I made eye contact and seemed in agreement as to the prices of the fighters being offered. Simon was shopping for a betting price and our stop at the tavern was essentially his pre-dinner fight homework.

Dinner was three courses. Fennimore and I had never seen dinner served in this fashion, with wine accompanying each course and whiskey continuing to be drunk as the evening progressed. Country dinners were served all at once. It was stunning. Fennimore allowed his drinks to linger. I seemed ready for more.

Albans seemed vulnerable with the effects of the liquor. Simon began to negotiate.

"Okay Albans, I want to reinvest the $250 on the underdog but I want three-to-one," Simon sternly warned.

"Don't try to short change me!" Simon slurred a bit as he continued. It appeared Simon was putting on an act. The way he stumbled with his words reminded me of the way he acted at the Franklin the morning we met.

"You're not getting three-to-one!" Albans playfully retorted.

"Challenger is untested, that's $250 just for our $17 dinner. I believe McCoy will drop him in six!" Simon jibbed.

"Then take the Champ," Albans laughed.

"Absolutely no fun in one-to-five," Simon continued the comedy of the discussion.

Simon's guard was down and Albans seemed to not realize that he was being baited.

"Harry, he could be parlaying your 324 yards rushing record into a massive sum, or making your effort a simple statistical footnote!" Albans again punctuated with his hearty laugh.

"Okay Simon, I will meet you tomorrow. If you win or lose, I will meet you for breakfast and it will be on me," Albans shared.

Although we had not talked about the game, just Simon's winning, I was struck that he knew of my rushing record. It was odd as he had greeted me as though he had only a minor recognition of me, but was fully aware of my exact rushing yards.

I began to ask Albans how he knew about my record when Simon interrupted with a toast, "To O'Dowd! May the luck of the Irish bring breakfast tomorrow with an envelope as thick as French toast," Simon laughed as he finished.

We were off to the fights as Fennimore whispered to me that he had no idea what French toast was.

"Hell if I know, but it must be thick. If I understand the betting correctly, Simon will have a bundle of silver certificates," I retorted.

Fennimore sought to educate me. "It will be $1,000 including the original $250 from the original football bet."

I found Fennimore's instruction very irritating.

Simon negotiated with a ticket seller outside the boxing hall. The exterior of the old building had long, hand-painted placards hung from the side of the building with magnificent lifelike renditions of the fighters we had come to see. Simon was terse, argumentative, aggressive, and charming. He secured three ringside seats for the princely sum of six dollars. The seats had started at $10, but the overweight, ill-mannered ticket seller was no match for Simon.

"Fennimore, you're betting $25 of your ledger balance on the fight. If we win you will have an additional $73 in the cash-on-hand column," Simon announced.

Fennimore, a bit embarrassed that his ledger sheet had been scrutinized, could only go along. After watching

Simon badger with the oaf in front of the boxing hall, he knew protesting would be meaningless.

Fennimore silently mumbled, "I am not a gambler." He began pulling two tens and a five from his secured wallet.

"Don't I get an even $75 back?" said Fennimore, slightly protesting the arrangement Simon had laid out.

"Well, good for you, you're catching on, however, your fanny is occupying $2 of ringside real estate, no need to put up the dough. We lose you pay me $25, seat is on me. We win you pick up $73," Simon commanded and waved off his attempt to give him the wager.

Simon seemed amused that Fennimore was catching on to the gambling, but a bit perturbed that he was being a bit chintzy with the money he had lost to him on the train. Simon had bequeathed the bankroll using intentionally poor card skills. He felt entitled and that Fennimore should have been more appreciative.

Simon switched his focus. "Harry your wagering $40 to win $120."

I deadpanned, "What is my seat charge?"

"You're a big shot, we'll get Fennimore there shortly, so no charge," he dryly retorted.

The hall was a haze of smoke rings. The combined stench of cigars and alcohol emitted from a majority of the crowd. They had been whipped into a frenzy as the prior fight had ended with what Simon shared was a bum taking a dive.

Many patrons had thrown their nickel programs into the ring. Several had also tried to hit the conniving boxer with whiskey bottles.

It seemed like more fighting might take place in the seats than the ring but Simon, clad in his gambling jacket, stuffed with hidden money, was ready to drink and watch his investment.

He was concerned that the long lines might make it difficult to consume a fair quantity of beer. Fennimore seemed in a daze, was muttering 25 dollars to get me 73 as if it was a prayer of desperation.

I was taking it all in, transfixed on the referee who was splattered with blood from the previous fights.

It brought up the pain of my father's death and a wave of sadness took over me, completely enveloping me. I was unable to focus on the two gladiators that had entered the ring.

Simon turned to me and checked on my understanding. "Harry, they both look like they could win. I like the odds on this fight, I wish I could bet more," he gleefully shared.

Struck by my odd demeanor he quickly and softly asked, "Are you okay? Too much wine at dinner?"

"Just Fennimore's constant irritation," I muttered.

"I am just hoping O'Dowd pummels him. Might be nice to have a wad of cash for the remaining day of the follies of Simon," I retorted.

The comer men were yelling instructions to their fighters. I was now trying to figure out who we had bet on.

"The guy in the white trunks," Simon enlightened us. Fennimore and I must have seemed naïve while trying to soak in the pageantry of our surroundings.

It was choreographed. The announcer was moving around the ring, the fighters preparing in a similar ritual that seemed harmless but might quickly turn violent.

"Looks good, real good, and pretty even in size and build," Simon said, evaluating the humans who were about to beat each other senseless.

The crowd roared as the bell was rung in a quick, repetitive series. I laughed internally. It was certainly not the cadence of an undergraduate chiming the beginning of a day of classes.

The announcer completed reciting the rules, introduced the fighters. The fight had begun with one solid ringing of the bell.

It was magical. They danced and maneuvered, ducked, and swung with violence, but controlled with great athleticism. Neither seemed deterred by each blow, many grazed off their arms, chest, and chins.

A few blows connected on the face of each boxer, punctuated by the gasps and adulation of the crowd. Fennimore was on his feet and yelling encouragement for his investment. Simon was tense, controlled in his concentration and vocal as he began to see his drinking research as one that might pay off.

Round three came quickly. Simon encouraged us with positive refreshments, turned angry when our fighter backed into the comer and became a punching bag. It was drama and a huge financial swing all wrapped up in a man beating another man into unconsciousness.

We were six feet away from the ring, a dollar a foot, and with each landing punch it seemed like a bargain.

My stomach turned on each round as the fighters were beginning to look beaten and bloodied. The $40 I had wagered was a small fortune but I began to want a victory at the personal well being of our opponent. I really didn't care about their health, I now wanted to win.

I had wagered because of Simon. Had my father been alive it would have been fraught with peril, but his death had unleashed reckless behavior in me. I was enjoying every minute of it.

The fight ended. O'Dowd with a relentless pummeling dropped McCoy. It was round six. Simon laughed that the first patron had been dead on and he needed to find him and give him a bit of a reward!

We both laughed as Fennimore, empowered with adrenaline, fell into the seats behind us as he had jumped half his height in excitement. I was now not ready for a drink, I was ready for many drinks.

Simon yelled above the chaos that now ensued, "French toast in the morning."

The champagne, best at the Waldorf, $5 a bottle, was drunk with abandon. Simon cheered each new glass and encouraged Fennimore to add $70 more to the ledger.

"Not until Albans pays me, then it is acknowledged as cash," Fennimore spoke, but barely audibly.

He was drunk but still did not abdicate his need for protocol in his books.

Simon and I laughed at our inside joke. Simon's future runner had the skills to keep track of what was due. Fennimore was passing a secret test. Unbeknownst to him, Simon was paying him with his expertise and betting prowess.

We continued to drink heavily. Fennimore was fast asleep at one o'clock in the morning. I was the last to go to bed just as the sun was coming up. Simon was gone when I awoke at noon the next morning.

I smelled badly, felt sick, and vomited into my mouth a number of times. Fennimore, still drunk and wobbly, was excited as Simon entered the room with a large smile and a very large envelope in his hand.

"Gentleman, hustle up. I have a sure thing at Coney Island today," Simon commanded.

Simon punctuated his statement while handing $70 to Fennimore and $120 to me. Fennimore rudely questioned, "Simon, you are short."

Simon opted not to be perturbed, but with businesslike candor responded, "Don't be chintzy, Fennimore, let's call it an investment advice fee."

Fennimore sobered up very quickly to retrieve his makeshift ledger and proudly added, "Adjusted cash-on-hand, $142, profit from fight, $70, adjusted total reflects overage on seat charge deemed investment advice fee."

We arrived at Simon's church, the racetrack. Wooden grandstands and freshly-painted fences circled the wide expanse of flat, grass-covered land. The track had been ploughed smooth. Delicate undulations made straight lines that curved into the turns and created a beautiful path for the race horses. It was a harrowed track. I could barely get my farm hands to keep a straight line when planting corn and here was a mile of perfectly manicured dirt. The talented work horses and equipment were hidden to the left behind a large barn and several storage sheds.

Horses were parading in a ring directly behind us. Men were fiddling with their bits and saddles while their jockeys were in discussion with the well-dressed owners. It was fascinating.

Simon retrieved long sheets filled with whimsical names. Race One, the name jumped off the page, *Indian Scout*.

Our whirlwind in New York was half over and we were perched with a great view of the track.

"I am looking for today's sure thing," Simon requested.

"Indian Scout, ten to win," I quickly responded.

"Well done Mr. Charles, not the horse but the amount!" Simon proudly spoke.

Fennimore wanted number eight, for his birthdate, and spent several minutes berating Simon with a myriad of questions on how he could bet. It was part hangover and part of his conservative nature to evaluate, but in typical fashion he took the least risk by betting on *Upper Crust* to finish in the top three.

Simon left to haggle with the bookmaker. He returned with even money for Fennimore's charge to show and five-to-one on *Indian Scout*. Simon bet $20 on *Indian Scout* in a show of first time unity. He ignored Fennimore's pick because the payoff was too low.

The bookie did not want to take such large bets but Simon convinced him we would be here for a majority of the afternoon. He relented to Simon, who had sought ten-to-one, when Simon was willing to take half the odds he had first requested.

Simon was a bit angry at the bookie's lack of professionalism and turned his frustration out on Fennimore by calling his bet measly, saying that his wager was the rental cost of a ringside chair.

Unbeknown to Fennimore and I, the race had started. Simon directed our attention to the cloud of dust that was coming at us, 14 horses packed together, the jockeys all steering clear of each other and working their way into a chaotic line. It was magical as their speed continued to increase.

The horses passed the finish line and Fennimore , whose voice was weak from strong drink and yelling at the fight, screamed, "Did I win?"

Simon turned slowly despite the stares and laughter from the surrounding fans, and mocked, "Easy Fennimore, stay awake! There is one more time around. Act like you know what you are doing!"

I smirked with laughter and continued to focus on the horses as they thundered into the last turn.

The jockeys were beating the flanks of their horses with athletic slashes of their whips. I had caught on quickly and watched intently as each jockey thrust their horse toward the lead. My pick, *Indian Scout*, was on the far outside and by what I could tell was closing quickly on the leaders.

I yelled encouragement as six horses hit the line including *Indian Scout* and *Upper Crust*. I had no idea of which horse had won. Fennimore was as clueless as I but Simon knew the exact result.

Fennimore, bewildered by it all, asked again, "Did I win?"

"We did, but you lost," Simon blurted at Fennimore as he bolted from his seat.

"Stay here," he added as he quickly ran toward the bookie that was moving toward the opposite side of the stands.

The dramatic finish was confirmed by the postings on an infield board. *Indian Scout* was first, and number eight had finished fourth.

Fennimore had lost and his over-the-top display of anger showed his concern about money. To my surprise, the stoic Faf knew quite a few swear words.

Simon returned and we happily split $150 of profit.

"I was stiffed last summer. I wanted to make sure before they posted the winner the bookie would not skip," Simon explained.

"Gus wants our action the remainder of the day and knows Albans. He showed he had the means to pay," Simon confidently shared.

Fennimore was on to the next race with intense focus to regain the $2 he had lost.

Our pockets were filled with cash and I discussed with Simon about a gambling jacket.

"I need to send Fennimore on a quick errand later. You and I will go to my tailor and have a jacket made," Simon concluded.

I realized my winnings totaled roughly half the cost of my new car. My dad would not have been amused. My uncle would have been mortified. I didn't care and was still getting my head around how little money meant to me at this time. I was ready to bet again.

The day went by quickly. Gus was eventually broke, as Simon discovered his sure thing that won at six-to-one.

Fennimore was anxious to add $50 to his cash-on-hand column. Simon's gambling jacket was crooked from the bulge the money was making in his secret pocket. I had shoved $100 in my shoe.

Simon made winning look easy. His sure thing was *Some Things Borrowed*. The name was not lost on Gus, who ended up owing Simon $20 as he was short in paying the bet.

Simon gave him $30 back and only wanted the fifty when he saw him again. Gus left with a smile, despite having incurred a financial beating from Simon and company. Simon nicknamed him *Windgust* because all it took was a few good win bets to knock him over.

We spent the remaining time in New York in a fog, traversing several taverns in the Bowery. We stopped at McSorley's Old Ale House and Simon passed a generous silver certificate to the patron who had correctly predicted the outcome of the fight. It was a frenzy of free cocktails and Simon naturally picked up the check for all at the bar.

Nothing would come close to the excitement of our visit to the fisticuffs and racetrack. Simon sent Fennimore to a sports shop and we visited Simon's tailor, who crafted me a natty-looking jacket with a hidden pocket in the same right hand side as Simon's jacket.

We returned to campus. I now knew why Simon demanded sleeping quarters on the train, as the bed was my sanctuary. I was sleep deprived and feeling a bit shaky. Fennimore made no noise for the eight-hour trip back. His pockets were stuffed with over $100 of gambling winnings and an interest-free promissory note, not due until 1951, waiting in his mailbox in Watertown. He appeared to be smiling as he slept.

I awoke to Simon singing, several crumpled papers were on the floor of the stateroom.

"It's about time you awoke. The porter is bringing dinner and coffee. We're an hour away and I was getting bored," Simon whimsically announced.

"Listen to my Class of 1921 anthem! Jiggers for Johnson, gin for Gaines, another cocktail for Campbell, whiskey for Weller, rye for Richardson, makes it a cocktail—cocktail and beverage—it's going to make us pie-eyed, a drinking night that President Gunnison is going to despise!" Simon rhymed with bravado on each ending word of the poetic lyric.

I incorporated the change of beverage into *bev-rye*. Simon would always contend it was he who made the change since he had used the phrase 'beverage dry' many times.

I was still half asleep and wondering what the hell he was doing but it was catchy and his continued tweaking made the rhymes resonate with sarcasm and mockery. I could only imagine that the stodgy founders would not have been amused.

We arrived at the station in the early evening. Simon was unrelenting that we join him for drinks at the Franklin. Simon had prepared the bar by sending a telegram to Barnes to assemble the troops; Daniel had received notice to provide free libations and food and that we would be arriving at eight. The freshman and campus mixer, planned for the gymnasium, had a total attendance of 15 people as Barnes had spread the work quickly.

Simon wanted an audience to hear his new anthem and he had packed the tavern.

It was one of those nights we could never replicate—a perfect combination of classmates, personalities, timing, and overindulgence.

I felt sorry for those who had the poor judgment to ignore the call to the tavern. The bar would be converted into a chorus of drunken revelry. Our classmates were a collection of characters and kindness that could quickly be turned into mayhem and jocularity with overindulgence.

Appleton would begin the night dressed in a natty white sweater with a large "S" sewn on the front. A mere few hours later, a sleeve was missing and the "S" was wavering to the side, held by the narrowest of threads.

The "S" would hang from the rafters the entire time we were on the campus. Appleton would always wonder who had done the ripping of his sweater. None would take credit for their dastardly act.

Simon's poetic rhyme, coupled with the right sarcasm and cadence, made it a fitting tribute to our class as well as a slogan that we would be drinking. It would only take the passing salutation of "cocktail-cocktail-bev-rye" to alert those in earshot that it was time to go to the tavern, it was time to drink.

I would always wonder how many times in my life I would say it, but if I hadn't, Simon would.

It was late spring before we dried out. The year 1918 could not have come any sooner. It was an arduous winter, storm after storm. Snow, wind, and icy rain kept the *Huckster* in dry dock and our self-imposed containment was only broken by idiotic trips to the gymnasium to watch wrestling. The campus was a collection of well-educated but irritable students.

Our repetitive trips to The Franklin became mundane. It was dreary and dreadful.

Simon bought a fancy record player for our room but the lack of sufficient records made the constant playing more wrenching than the silence.

In a state of liquor-induced humor, the records became projectiles down the hall. Many of our hall mates would hide in horror if they heard a song stopped in in mid-play with a despicable sound of the phonograph's needle being scraped across the record. It was their cue to quickly disperse.

The campus began to empty. The farm was doing well. Daniel left for the Adirondacks, Simon headed to New York. The halls began to echo with the sounds of doors closing until the fall. The town became suddenly quiet as the student population bolted for the real world.

My father had driven me to work hard, but I was content to let Jacob handle things. I eased into half days of semi-hard labor and the remainder sitting at the River Hotel sipping beer and muddling through the day. My mother, unaware of my daily ritual, was occupied with the stubbornness of my sister, civic clubs, and her beloved garden club.

In one of my many drunken evenings, I had inadvertently driven the *Huckster* across the town's garden causing considerable damage. My mother called her army of volunteers to replant and care for the damaged bushes and surviving flowers. I made a significant donation and the town's Mayor had a marker and monument built to pay homage to the local citizens who had lost their lives in Europe.

My photo, along with a multitude of volunteers in the background, would run in the local paper with the caption, 'Harry Charles' Generosity Builds War Monument.' The police were in no hurry to figure out who had driven over the flower bed and I, the one who caused the carnage, had become the savior of the garden as well as having my name engraved alongside the heroes who had lost their lives.

It would not be long after that day that we would assemble to commemorate the death of one of our former farm hands. Lou had been killed near a small village in France, evidently pinned down he tried to help a fellow soldier that had been injured. During his attempt he had been surrounded by a small battalion. They ambushed him and unmercifully shot him. He didn't stand a chance and was killed almost instantly. He was called courageous.

Lou had not worked for us long, but I felt obligated to attend the ceremony and service. I was emboldened by a stop at the River Hotel, to honor his job, and returned after to celebrate his life for which I knew little. I had sent Simon a telegram. He sent a generous check to Lou's family.

At the funeral, Lou's father asked who Simon was. I mentioned he was my roommate and had grown fond of Lou while frequenting the River Hotel. Simon felt connected to the town and wanted to help. Lou's father was deeply touched and asked me to bring Simon over for supper in the fall. Simon was hundreds of miles away and getting dinner invitations. I would not hear from him until late July. The telegram simply read, *Saratoga—Adelphi Hotel—August 17th—bring your natty gambling jacket.*

.

Chapter V

It was Victorian opulence. It reeked of money and I was dreadfully underdressed. I had spent six hours by train traversing to Saratoga. There was no fawning Douglas for the upgraded travel compartment. I slummed it in first class. I was exhausted and suddenly held by a behemoth in a tuxedo whose voice bellowed across the front parlor as well as the adjacent bar room.

"Sir, this is a private hotel, guests only," he snobbishly spoke. I could not determine if it was his hotel but his overall demeanor seemed to indicate it was not.

"I have accommodations and take your hand off my shoulder," I pointedly spoke to him.

"Sir, our hotel rooms are spoken for and I know every guest personally," he arrogantly and authoritatively spoke.

The guests in the bar to the left of the parlor slowed their conversations to wait for the outcome of this unwanted disturbance. It was a collection of glitter and glitterati that filled the bar—tuxedo-clad men and women in flowing summer dresses. It was human champagne and the chandeliers flickered on every distressed movement caused by the small town visitor.

"I am meeting Mr. Sheldon the second this evening, we are planning several weeks in Saratoga," I quietly mentioned as I was now not sure if I was in the right place. I was gambling that the moron was not the hotel's owner.

The bar stopped to a whisper and gentlemen rose from their seats and began to approach me with outstretched hands of greeting. I was in the right place. Women smiled, the bartender grinned with excitement. The behemoth's face drained of blood and he looked like he was about to collapse.

He stammered, "Sa, Sir, I must apologize, this is a private hotel, we know our guests and had I been informed you would have been greeted properly. My name is Albert, please allow me to assist you and gather your things."

I began greeting the gentleman who requested I join them. My dress was below grade but it appeared that my humiliation would allow me to calm my nerves with a cocktail, no matter how poorly I was dressed.

I was seated at the end of the bar, conveniently out of view of the parlor and given a drink called a "Manhattan," ordered by James McClennan.

He lifted his glass and with a bravado toasted, "Alcohol should never be external!"

It seemed a bit of a cryptic toast in his delivery but I tipped my head in appreciation and began to sip the concoction of whiskey, bitters, and vermouth, topped off by a twist of orange and a cherry.

The glass, cut crystal, was rough to my fingers, but it sparkled as I tilted it to my mouth.

It was a magical elixir. Despite being nervous, I melted into my glass. My relaxation was short lived as a celebratory roar of excitement began in the bar. I didn't need to look. I knew who it was.

Poor Albert was following Simon, trying to explain his error in detaining me, but Simon was more interested in his entrance.

"Harry!" Simon raised his voice in bravado.

It was a signal to all that I was his friend and the most important person in the room. It seemed just like the first time he had said it at The Franklin.

"You won the Adelphi Handicap! Earl, please, champagne for all." Simon breathed a special spirit into the room with his commanding presence.

"Have you met everyone? I can see Albert must have been in charge upon your arrival. Albert meet Harry," Simon was intuitive enough to make sure that the largest man in the room was his friend.

I rose. "No hard feelings, Albert."

Albert quickly began, "We have met and I want to . . .," Simon cut him off declaring a sacred Simon rule, "None of that."

He was like a boxer as he circled the room. He effortlessly shared names and charming stories with personality and a controlled athleticism of his body. Everyone was anxious to be recognized and he missed no one.

He proudly completed his entrance. "This is Harry Charles, my college roommate and noted football star, a New York newspaper sensation for his efforts!" The group offered a celebratory applause, both for me and Simon's entrance.

"I have brought him here to make money off your fast thoroughbreds and indulge in far too much alcohol and way too much fun." He smirked to the laughter that engulfed the bar. It was classic Simon.

Simon was down to business.

"Who has tomorrow's program and who among us is running a winner so I can pummel the bookmaker on our first day?" Simon jousted with the group.

Jonathan Dunmeyer spoke up, "Be gentle to the bookmakers this summer, you remember that old chap they fished out of Saratoga Lake last year?"

The room began a chorus of the debts he had left many of the gentlemen in the room. Most had been disgusted with the police's investigation that included an unwarranted visit by many to the station due to the bookmaker's journal that documented his losses to the Adelphi elite.

The police simply felt the larger the debt, the more likely the suspect. The police never arrested anyone and chalked his death up to a suicide. The sentiment was there was no reason to continue to looking into his drowning. The police had made a decent investigation even though it was simple theater for the zealots that hated gambling.

"He owed me quite a sum by the end of the meet. I am having trouble finding a bookie that will take my wagers," Dunmeyer complained.

Simon mouthed the words, *What a fibber. He never wins. I should be his bookmaker.*

"It's an eclectic lot in this town. The poor try to take from the rich and the rich use bookmakers to move the gambling money around. A fascinating system," Simon regaled his audience.

"I have a nice filly running tomorrow. The trainer says she should win. Take a chance but get five-to-one to be fair," Gregory Halstaff announced.

Simon muttered, "That's a quick throw out. His trainer hasn't had a winner in two years and yet Greg always seems to have a good one every year."

"From what I understand about statistics, he is due," I quipped.

"Oh, Harry, so much to learn and a mere two weeks to graduate as a gambler and build a tidy sum," Simon said sarcastically.

"I insist that we begin drinking heavily," Simon stated with his customary grin, knowing full well that I needed no encouragement.

The next day was a magical cloud. I awoke a bit hung over, forgetful of the content of the late evening conversations. I was greeted by elegance and a deluge of beautiful smells melded with the cool, calming, Adirondack air.

Puffy clouds highlighted the blue sky as Simon and I awaited the chauffeur, George, who would take us to the race course.

The street was lined with cars that I had never seen. Large and opulent, most seated four in comfort in the back. In the front, was a driver in a constricting black hat who rarely turned his head. I was thankful I had not brought the *Huckster*, it would have been completely outclassed.

I glanced across Union Street and caught a glimpse of a most beautiful girl. I still remember the purple swirls on her dress. Her hat was filled with a bouquet of the finest handmade flowers, it reeked of charm and good taste.

She walked with confidence, smiling as if not having a care in the world. I was in a daze and unbeknownst to me at the time, instantly in love. I tried not to stare but I was mesmerized.

Simon was counting money and paying little attention to my face. The arrival of George and the car disrupted my view and Simon's concentration.

"Damn, was that $1,100, I will try again in the car," Simon said with an air of frustration.

My view was now blocked but I had a snapshot in my head that I would not soon forget.

It was a short ride. The city was filled with beautiful people dressed with class and dignity.

As we drove down Union Avenue, it seemed as if we were watched by all. There were glances of conjecture as those on the street tried to figure who was being driven in opulence to the course.

We arrived at Saratoga Race Course. The shingled Adirondack style of its facade and Victorian turrets made a blend of simplicity, punctuated with detail and creatively scrolled style.

Simon announced, "Welcome to Mr. Traver's vision of perfection. Welcome to Saratoga."

Carved owls stood watch from the rafters, an ode to those who had not been to bed the night before as well as to scare the errant pigeon who might wander among the elite.

We climbed the fairly steep stairs to the veranda for lunch. A blanket of greenery and small trees filled the infield. Simon's well-placed roll of money to the maître d' guaranteed us a perfect view of the finish for the two weeks we would be attending the races.

The infield had an additional track configured with timber and grass mounds. Strategically placed would be our first puzzle, a steeplechase.

I caught a glimpse of the beauty I had seen on the street sitting to our left in the box seats. Her name was Elisabeth Sara Day, daughter of a prominent breeder, owner, and avid gambler. She took my breath away.

"Care for a drink?" Simon laughed as he ordered two Manhattans from our waiter.

"What a glorious place. Where are the bookies?" I inquired. I was now a bona fide gambler.

"We're in a bit of a jam. My great fortune last year has made them all a bit skittish of any serious bets, but don't worry, I will find a horse that will make us a tidy sum," Simon neatly laid out his plan for the day.

The races began. Simon secured small bets on a horse that threw his rider at the fifth fence. He finished last.

Simon laughed his advice. "You never wager much on these races. He jumped fine, but the fence was too high."

"Well, that's not a good start," I grumbled.

I glanced over toward the box seats and saw that she was sitting by herself. I quickly rambled over to the boxes as Simon was concentrating on newspapers containing the horses' past races.

I felt charming by the elixirs I had consumed. "Do you like anything running today?" I asked her."

"Well, you were walking over here, so no. My father has a horse running in the fifth race. He should win." She was charming and very forward.

"My name is Harry Charles and I can run quite fast even when people are trying to tackle me," I bragged.

"My name is Beth. Nice to meet you. How do you like the Adelphi?" she posed.

"It's charming. I like the bar, it's cozy," I quickly responded not realizing that she had noticed me.

I was just starting to speak when Roger Day approached the box seats. He had not noticed me standing next to his daughter.

"Beth, I am trying to secure ten-to-one on him." Roger had been looking down and he immediately stopped talking, realizing that I was listening.

"Hello, enjoying the races?" I asked.

"Always do, I saw you sitting with Simon, friend of yours?" he inquired.

"Why, yes, Simon and I attend college together. He is my roommate," I proudly mentioned.

"Leave my box, now," he sternly said.

I was a bit taken back by his demeanor, but Beth's hazel eyes twinkled encouragement for my quick and uncomfortable departure.

"My apologies for being so forward," I offered.

"Goodbye, sir," Roger admonished in a condescending tone.

I shared with Simon my story of meeting Beth, her quick insertion that her father's horse would win, and my rejection from Roger Day's box.

"Still angry is he, Roger? Had a sure thing last year, jockey tipped me off and I bet so much that he only got a fraction of the odds he had hoped," Simon shared.

After jotting notes in his program, Simon began detailing instructions to me. "Harry take this program and the $400, go to the bar downstairs and wait. Have a drink or two, someone will find you."

"Okay, how will I . . .," I tried to finish, but was truncated by Simon's impatience.

"You will know. Don't acknowledge them, wait until they approach you, leave the program on the bar with the money hidden inside. Don't make any mistakes, the bookies watch me," he flatly stated.

I was off to the bar, $400 stuffed neatly into the ten-cent program, still feeling the sting of my rejection from Mr. Day. I settled in at the bar, which began to fill with the patrons, as the previous race had produced winners looking to celebrate and losers looking to drown their sorrows.

The bar again began to thin as I had my second drink and continued to scan for the person who was to contact me. I was fascinated by the faces of constriction from losing as well as the mirth from the winners when I saw the mousy Fennimore, clad in dapper attire approach the other end of the bar. Neither of us made eye contact even though I wanted to laugh heartily. He was wearing the customary straw hat, but to a bookmaker, he was a serious rube in appearance. Simon was right, he was a perfect runner.

Simon had brought his runner, a runner wearing clothing that was odd for him, making him look foolish, a dope no bookie would expect to have inside knowledge—the quiet and diligent Fennimore!

I thanked the bartender, purposely left the program stuffed with a small fortune and began to leave as Fennimore approached.

"Guess, I might have one more drink, do you mind if I take your seat?" Fennimore inquired in ear shot of the bartender.

I responded with a mild, "No, please do, take my program, I have another upstairs, good day," I said. I walked slowly toward the stairs as I saw Fennimore sit down and covet the program.

Fennimore was left to decipher Simon's notes. The program had the ingredients to make us some money and, unbeknownst to me, make Beth's father very unhappy. He was not going to get ten-to-one on his horse.

The whispers began. *Day's horse is going to win the eighth*. It was fascinating watching people fanatically creating conversation and hearing several nearby tables of people chatting about Beth's father's horse.

I gushed in utter amazement to Simon. "Did you hear that? They are talking about Day's horse. Everyone is saying he is he is going to win."

"It's possible someone made a big bet, those things happen," he smirked and then laughed.

"Simon, did you bet on him?" I quizzed.

"Absolutely not, I do know someone who bet on him, however," Simon laughed out loud.

I glanced at Beth's direction and caught a glare from Mr. Day. It appeared Beth was not very happy at having shared an inside tip that a horse would run well.

Simon mockingly waved.

"Poor Roger the Dodger, not getting ten-to-one today are we?" Simon whispered his taunt. His voice was purposeful, just loud enough for me to hear and try to decipher his plan.

Our first day had been spectacular. Fennimore had placed four bets, three of which had won and been paid handsomely. Roger's horse had won with ease and Fennimore made a terrific runner as he secured six to one. Simon griped a bit, but was proud of how Fennimore had blended into the racing set, straw hat and all.

I would not see Beth until the day before we left to go back to school. It had not been my best night. Simon and I had spent the majority of the afternoon at the Grand Union Hotel where he held court with several jockeys and our friends from the Adelphi.

Beth had sought me out at the Adelphi where I was in no condition to hold a serious conversation. I remembered little of what I had said that evening. She evidently had left looking much like she had after Simon had ruined her father's betting coup.

My first visit had been mesmerizing, a whirlwind. The racing, the pageantry, the wealth, and the banter of each day's racing at the Adelphi was intoxicating. McClennan continued his nightly ritual of toasting us with, "Alcohol should never be external!" It had been lost on most of the gentry in earshot that McClennan had been touting his horse, *External.* The horse was a long shot in the Hopeful Stakes, on the day we were leaving Saratoga.

It was Saratoga's parting gift. *External* won and our train ride back was spent splitting two weeks of winnings in the Presidential Car.

Fennimore had left the train in Watertown. I stashed my winnings using the copper key, and Simon utilized a hidden drawer in the bar Daniel had built.

"I will need this shortly," he proclaimed. We settled back on campus, one minute the vision of success, now just college students.

Chapter VI

Simon spent the Saturdays during the fall of 1918 driving the *Huckster* down Park Street adorned with streamers. I would spend them running through defensive lines and piling up records.

He would excite the crowded street by blaring the car horn which made its signature *Awwwooggaa* sound.

The team would gather at the Franklin for hours of joyous celebration. We were undefeated. Simon would break the burgeoning bar into song with, "Cocktail-cocktail-bev-rye, we just won and will be pie-eyed!"

I would be late to the Franklin to celebrate as I would be interviewed *ad nauseam* by reporters from Boston and New York. They were setting up the Harvard game as an epic battle of a small Northern school versus one that had helped build the collegiate game.

I was the general and the game hinged on my play. They would always ask how it felt to be the favorite. It had been lost on me that it was related to the readers who would be betting on the game and not fueling my ego as the team's best player.

The excitement was building on campus, I made certain to drop tickets off at the train station for Douglas, the team and fans were traveling on Friday, staying over in a rural part of Albany and then taking the train to Cambridge right before the game. Coach Kinnon did not want any distractions.

I was hoping my generosity would provide an upgrade but the train would be packed with students, town dignitaries, and our team. Douglas had shared that the Presidential Car had been reserved for months, even the president of the college would relegated to the back of the train.

"Well, well, the big game, I can't wait. I am bringing the "Boozesters"—Chamberlain, Barnes, Fennimore, Appleton. They all will be in my car conducting appropriate pre-game preparation." Simon made drinking sound like a sport and used his trademark smirk to give it a humorous quality.

"I tried for the upgrade, I should have figured it was you," I laughed.

"Harry, this is the big game, you don't think I would sit in the club car?" he arrogantly bantered.

People were sending me drinks, I wasn't certain Simon liked being overshadowed as Simon usually sent them.

Daniel stopped by our table. "Tavern's quiet, come down and entertain me," he begged.

We finished dinner and the packed dining room applauded as we left. Simon, a bit desperate to be the center of attention, tried to hold court. A few locals were there to drink and not gamble.

Simon drank heavily. I was somewhat well behaved, drinking beer in moderation.

"C'mon, Haaarrrrry, try to outrun old Simon, you're relatively sober!" Simon challenged as we walked back to campus.

"C'mon Mammy, walk a million miles for one of my smiles my Harrrrryyy!" Simon slurred like Al Jolson on one knee. Ironically, it would not be lost on me later that it had been the first record we had thrown down the hallway. It had snapped perfectly in two.

Simon was ahead of me. "Try and get around me Charlie boy," he taunted.

I started to trot and knowing his overindulged state, I simply accelerated and in three steps was laughing my way past him. He lunged to no avail to tackle me. I took my eye off where I was going and caught the first step of the walkway and fell hard. I heard a small pop and my chest hurt.

"Shit, my arm hurts," I moaned.

Simon staggered up.

"Let old Dr. Sheldon take a look. It's a bruise," he said, as he pulled my arms behind me. "I will fix you up."

I still hurt but the adjustment seemed to take the pain away.

Simon ripped the Welcome Class of 1921 banners from the ends of the bar. He configured a figure eight around my shoulders and tightened the straps behind my back.

110

"Just a muscle bruise. Drink this glass of whiskey and don't get up until the afternoon. I will contact the Dean that you will be out of class in the morning. Best not to move much, it will heal quicker," he assured.

"You're going to be the doctor," I smirked and grimaced at the same time. The whiskey seemed to be helping as I contorted and fell somewhat drunkenly into my bed.

I didn't wake until noon. I felt a bit better but was in pain when the straps moved. Simon was gone. Green caught a glimpse of me from the hall and entered our room.

"Jesus, what happened to you?" Green observed. His face told a different story from an inebriated Simon.

"Your arm is black and blue," he informed.

"Dr. Sheldon thinks it's just a bruise."

"He had better change majors," Green bluntly professed. I thought he was laughing but he wasn't.

I stood up and had Jonathan tighten the straps. I felt better.

"Where is your car?" he asked.

"Why?" I asked. I was confused and the oversized whiskey before bed had taken my concentration away. I did not comprehend the seriousness of the injury.

In an urgent manner Green spoke. "I am taking you to see the trainer."

All I remember next was Coach Kinnon yelling at me for being so stupid. He used the word *moron* over and over and I could not help but think of Simon's exact description of the guy that swept the floors and allowed him to store his bar. I had broken my collarbone, playing was out and now our team had no chance of beating Harvard.

I returned to Jenks, grimaced while I packed and waited for Simon. At five o'clock, the time to leave, I began searching the hall.

"Barnes, where is Simon?" I questioned.

"He and Faf left early this morning. He gave me his Presidential Car tickets for the ride to Cambridge," he delightfully shared.

I was sad and confused. There would be no accolades today. I walked with the troops headed to the train. There would be no battle for me and our unbeaten season was now a funeral procession. It was quiet, unlike the raucous crowds that had jammed the stands. There were delicate whispers of concern for victory and complete disregard for my health. They wanted to win and the rumors of my injury were being confirmed as people passed by me.

The word spread quickly on the train that I would not be playing. Here we were, a train full to capacity of players, fans, and dignitaries and we were the only ones who knew that we had little chance to win. My uncle was on the train, too, and he was livid. I replied to his condemnations, saying "I am the one with the cracked collarbone."

We didn't speak the rest of the ride down to Albany. He left the train when we stopped for the night

112

and did not go to Cambridge. He was selfishly angry that I had not told him I would not be playing and simply deserted me without any concern for my well-being.

We arrived quietly outside of Albany Friday night with no reporters to bother the team. Our plan was to stay isolated to avoid any distractions.

We arrived the next day to stands that were packed to capacity two hours before game time.

We left the locker room, walked up a stone corridor, and paraded onto the field. Our opponent had colors similar to ours. Theirs was a school rich in tradition. We were building a future, trying to establish a tradition.

The buzz of excitement became frenzied as I walked onto the field. Coach Kinnon had me dress as if I was playing by taking the field. He didn't want the opponent to know until the very last moment that I was not playing.

It was painful to dress, but the coach's anger fortified my ability to pull my brown jersey over my wounded arm.

The Harvard band had begun to play. When I did not take the field for the first plays, it simply stopped. It was like the band of the Titanic. A hush fell over the entire stadium. The band knew something was horribly wrong.

I returned to the locker room to change, abandoning my team to sit in agony by myself.

I slowly walked back the same steps, closed my eyes, and emerged on the sidelines.

"What the *Omarkayham*? What is Fennimore doing over there?" I whispered.

Fennimore was standing next to the stands wearing a crimson Harvard sweater, positioned near the opposing stands.

I stopped as our team ran off the field after our first attempt to score was unsuccessful. The fans cheered with exuberance, but it was only a hopeful cheer. I caught Simon standing at the left edge of our fans. He was speaking to someone who was blocked by the fans on the sidelines. I kept thinking about Fennimore's odd behavior. *He should be on our side.*

I was trying to make sense of all the chaos. Everything seemed random but I began to think of Simon. He always had a plan.

No, Dear God no! Simon's betting on the game and he knew I could not play, I realized.

Simon could play My Old Kentucky Home using the collarbones from the skeleton rib cage. He must have known it was broken.

"Harry!" It was exuberant and the melodic voice of Beth that I had not heard since Saratoga.

My mood, sullen and sunk by my injury, was suddenly uplifted by her presence. "Beth! What a pleasant surprise!"

Despite the noise of Harvard's offence taking the field, the confusion of Fennimore's behavior, and Simon's desertion, I was focused on Beth.

"I told you I would not miss the big game. Remember when we spoke at the Adelphi?" Beth asked.

I hadn't remembered and had to fabricate my facial expressions and reply. "Sorry you came. I won't be playing today, I injured my shoulder during a scrimmage."

"That's too bad. Sit with me?" she smiled as she spoke.

We spent the afternoon cheering, but I watched each play knowing that it had been designed for me to run through the blocks. She made an unbearable situation bearable.

Many of our plays were just a large pile of bodies. The game turned into a creeper and we stayed fairly close. I saw Simon at halftime talking to someone I recognized. It was Frank Albans. They both looked happy, very happy.

It had been a close game as we only lost by twelve points. Had I played we would have won by three times that. The paper would read *Harvard Beats Upstarts*, with only a passing mention of my not playing. It was the bias journalism held of Harvard continuing its dominance of college football.

The train left the station with a depressed, sadden, and dejected group. Douglas looked as if he had been crying. Many could not make eye contact me as we boarded. Nobody spoke much in the club car. Everyone was ill at ease and I felt a terrible sense of guilt for the loss.

I knew many blamed me for ruining the season and the biggest loss in our short history. It was our transition year and it had been destroyed by an errant step.

What flashed in my mind was Lincoln's train, after the assassination, slowly returning home. I reluctantly joined the Presidential Car, depressed after an hour of uncomfortable glares and broken conversation.

I don't remember hitting Simon or pushing Fennimore. Green broke us up but I could easily have thrown them both off the end of the train. They both had been very lucky that the doors had been locked by a porter who knew that students might become raucous.

Fennimore could not contain himself. "It was brilliant. I bet on Harvard Saturday morning. Albans sent me to a bookmaking shop in Boston!" he boasted.

Simon sheepishly smiled as Fennimore continued to lay out the scheme.

"Albans had been tipped off Friday morning and bet on Harvard in New York as well. It was easy. They figured I knew nothing about football and clad in Harvard attire they took my bet thinking I was some moron wagering on the home team."

"They were happy to take my bet!" he continued.

I had a broken collarbone and a ruined season and Fennimore was treating me like I was a racehorse that had simply fallen at the fifth fence.

"You remember, Harry, Simon sent me to the sports shop to get a Harvard sweater when we were in New York while you were at the tailor," Fennimore filled in the details of the preparation Simon had created.

It was not until several weeks later that things would unravel for Fennimore. A bookmaker had been killed in Boston and the police's investigation centered on the betting that had taken place on the game.

New England reporters began asking questions. Fennimore holed up in Watertown, but was tracked down and was asked if he knew a Douglas A. Campbell, a degenerate gambler that had been killed over losses incurred in the game.

The Boston bookies felt they had been taken with the best player incapacitated. They felt the fix had been made on the game.

Douglas had paid the price of the loss. Fennimore indicated he did not know the bookie, but in actuality he had won money off him twice. Douglas had been the bookie taking our bets at Coney Island. The "A" stood for his middle name, August.

He had been nicknamed *Windgust*. He had been pulled from the depths of the Charles River and pulled into the gambling fix by Albans. Simon would ask me for a favor, meet with the local paper's reporter and squelch the story. I resisted but felt that I needed to protect my integrity and the Charles name. It was not difficult. The reporter who covered my father's fictitious accidental death was easily swayed by Simon's monetary gift. The influence was not that of a Charles but a clump of $5 silver certificates. The reporter was a hack, willing to sell out, and his skill of reporting was based on the number of silver certificates he could shove into his pockets.

Albans, who had only wagered in New York, stayed clear of any trouble.

The president of the University heard the rumors, feared a scandal for the program and allowed the innuendo and gossip to subside without an investigation.

"There was no matter to discuss," was his only comment when pressed by zealot students who wanted a sense of revenge for the loss.

Fennimore, Simon, and Albans made a small fortune at the expense of *Windgust*. In a moment of drunken stupidity, Simon would complain that if Gus had paid him back the 50 he owed him, it would have been waterlogged.

His parting salvo was hoping in the future he could find a bookmaker who could swim.

The season would end with a series of victories. The crowds would thin a bit after our loss to Harvard. I healed sufficiently to set the school's new rushing record. We would lose a fair amount of our team to graduation the following year. We would win many games but the chance to be a Northeast powerhouse was over.

Simon promised not to bet on any more games. His attention had moved to far more pressing matters. The Volstead Act was about to be passed and it had seemed to go unnoticed by many in our small town. Our college days would be dry when we returned in August of 1919 for our junior year.

The brutal winter would lead to a more brutal spring as Simon was on to his next plan.

Part Two

Chapter VII

I remember the spring of 1919 as if it was yesterday, it was hard to forget.

Simon, Barnes, and I, clad in jackets adorned with fraternity pledge pins, spent a lazy afternoon at the River Hotel.

Our barkeeper that day was an older gentleman, angry and bitter. He was not a fan of Simon and cared little for his bravado and wad of money. He was another barkeeper who had cycled after Lou's departure and untimely demise.

He served us slow and was grumpy the entire afternoon. He would simply mutter that it wouldn't be long until the Volstead Act would go into effect and they could fire him whenever they wanted.

Simon would denigrate him every chance he could and it was rather uncomfortable but we drank quietly.

The months of subzero temperatures, little snow, and gusty winds had made the river a frozen brick from shore to shore. The water had frozen in midwave as the wind had created white caps in motion.

The sun was blazing off the river, spots of blue smoothness acted as giant mirrors creating rays of warmth. The hotel was dripping from long icicles that now began to melt. They had been created by the continual fires that roared in the tavern. Thankfully, it would not be long until spring would be upon us.

I stared blankly, quietly reflecting how my eyes had begun to look grayish and hollow. Weeks of studying and utilizing Simon's bar to entertain the troops, who rarely left the dorms, had begun to show itself on my face. The floor in front of our room had begun to have grooves where we had pulled the bar back and forth from the storage room.

The pressure from the season had long been over, the innuendo from the betting scandal and my missing the biggest game had subsided, but I thought about it often. It didn't help that Simon had been spending freely. His gambling jacket clogged with $5 bills had been a result of my mishap at the base of the campus walkway.

Barnes had been taking Simon to school playing *Bone-Ace*. Barnes, mature for his age, was street smart. He rarely led the group in frivolous behavior. He was pointed and used a droll sense of humor to mock and ridicule. He spent the afternoon mumbling to the bartender, "Unpleasant peasant, anymore peanuts, peon." The bartender, Norman, was not amused.

"Simon, I am just a few hands away from a $20 bill," Barnes blankly mentioned.

He had not meant it as funny or sarcastic. It was Barnes simply being Barnes, direct and humorous at the same time.

"Okay, smart scholar. Let's play three hands for ten a piece. All you need is to win one and you will break even with the chance to make a tidy profit," Simon somewhat berated Barnes.

Simon seemed confident that Barnes would take the bet.

"Absolutely not," responded Barnes without any hesitation.

Simon drew a breath and spoke with indignation. "That's not very sporting of you. Well, in that case, it's time to leave." He was terse, as if his honor had been challenged.

"Everyone knows that you don't lose when the serious bets are down," Barnes defended.

"Well, good for you, Barnes you can buy us a departing round. The H-train is leaving the station. Be a big winner and fill my derby flask," Simon requested but it sounded clearly like a demand.

Simon had pulled a sterling silver flask from his jacket. It was embossed with a solid gold horseshoe insignia positioned with the tips of the horseshoe facing upward. It included an elaborate engraved 'S' below the shoe.

"I commissioned this on my first visit to the Kentucky Derby. I bet a fair amount on the horse that finished second. I, of course, had bet to win," Simon told us.

"I would, however, get my money back when the winner, Old Rosebud, ran at Saratoga the following summer. The 'S' reminds me of running second at the Derby," Simon rationalized, confident in his convictions of his wagers.

"I don't know what you paid, but in this neck of the woods the shoe is facing the wrong direction," I bluntly mentioned.

Simon appeared ready to regale us why it was correct when he changed course. "I will pay either of you a $10 bill if you can guess why the horseshoe is actually correct."

Norman, prematurely grey haired and in his late twenties, had found the fountain of youth, suddenly ignoring an afternoon of derogatory comments. His ears perked up with the discussion of winning ten dollars.

"Can I guess?" he politely asked.

Money it seemed, could buy pleasant behavior from Barnes's pleasant peasant.

"You have been a bit of a pill during our visit, but okay, each of you gets a guess," Simon said with a fairly disapproving glare at Norman.

"Had it been the other way the tips of the shoe would have made your arrogant 'S' appear too small," I dispatched with a laugh.

"Harry is out," Simon happily announced.

"It's the way the shoe is placed, for how the horse walks or runs," Barnes confidently spoke.

"Two college men down. Norman, you can claim $20, four shimmering silver certificates!" Simon spoke as he pulled more money from his pocket.

"Barnes, care to bet if he knows the right answer?" Simon broached.

"How much?" Barnes asked.

"Let's make it sporting, twenty and you tip Norman $10 because you have subtly mocked him all afternoon," Simon laid out the bet.

Barnes glanced at Norman who was pensive but dejected as a small fortune for him sat on the bar.

"Okay," Barnes quietly approved.

Simon relegated Norman to the back of the bar. He used a paper napkin and pencil to write the correct answer down and prevent chicanery.

"If he gets it right, give him this as a wonderful souvenir," Simon directed at Barnes.

"Norman, get back here, I am getting thirsty," Simon berated as Norman quickly returned from the back of the tavern.

Norman reinstated himself behind the bar. "I am only guessing, is it so the luck won't run out of the shoe?"

"EXACTLY, you're right, congrats!" Simon blurted out to infuriate Barnes.

Barnes had lost and was not happy. Apologetically he spoke, "Here Norman, a souvenir." as he handed him $10 and the napkin."

Norman took the money. "Keep the souvenir for yourself. I already have one."

Norman pulled out an identical napkin, a twin to the one Simon had written just minutes before, from behind the bar. Barnes had been taken, and taken good!

"I let my guard down, well done Simon," Barnes conceded. The four of us laughed for five solid minutes.

It was brilliant. Norman said the hardest part was playing grumpy the whole afternoon.

I would spend many days in the coming years with Norman as my friend, navigator, and bartender.

"Well done, Norman, it's time for us to leave," Simon proudly announced.

The *Huckster* had metal chains configured around the tires. "Who has been fooling with my car?" I demanded.

Norman put them on. They are for driving on ice, snow, and crossing the channel. We are going to Canada," Simon explained.

I know I would have protested, but my mood had been uplifted by Simon's depleting Barnes winnings with such a well-thought-out plan.

The Model T slid sideways on the ice as we rolled off the embankment near the River Hotel.

Despite the chains, we could not grip on the smooth spots and the car spun semicircles as we picked up speed.

"This is a hoot," Simon blared. "Faster," he encouraged.

The ice was a foot thick in the bay. I accelerated and directed for the point that would lead us to the channel. The thin tires, aided by the chains, crunched through the snow that covered portions of the frozen river.

In a matter of minutes we crossed the channel. Emboldened by an afternoon of libation, I never thought or shared with my crew that below us was the peril of 600 feet of water and lethargic fish, of which we could easily have joined had we hit an errant pocket of weak ice.

We found a fairly smooth beach, climbed a small embankment, and found a road. We were in Canada. Simon pulled a hand-written map from his jacket.

We found a clearing and what appeared to be the only road for miles. "This must be Kings Road," Simon raised his head as he spoke. "Turn right, it's straight for two or three miles."

Barnes, fairly animated for Barnes, spoke up, "Is this legal?"

"As long as we are not hunting, we'll be fine," I informed him.

"We are hunting whiskey. There it is," Simon said and gestured toward the woods.

On the left, sitting back from the road was a large restaurant and bar. It seemed massive. Trucks and horses surrounded the entire building.

As we approached the door, Simon quickly pointed out that above the door was a horseshoe. "Christ, even the Canadians have it wrong," he observed. We all laughed.

We entered through two large walnut doors. *Bienvenue* was carved into an arch at the top of the doors. The word 'welcome' in French separated into two as we opened the doors, as did the name *Vanier's Evergreen* carved in a semicircle in the middle of the door. Whoever had done the carving had used an axe and had been quite precise.

The bar had been consumed with revelry and chatter which halted upon our entrance. Three college men had entered the Evergreen, drinking home of lumbermen, woodsmen, laborers, and dingy, hung-over locals.

Our pledge pins were not badges of loyalty or honor but shimmering lures for trouble.

"Sorry for the disruption, can I buy any Americans a drink?" a controlled Simon asked.

The bar had a nervous laugh.

"Okay, no Americans. How about the whole bar?" Simon raised his voice and a wad of Canadian dollar bills.

The bar roared its approval and it felt like the Ale House in New York. We found spots on the far left of the bar; a stuffed bobcat was perched above our head with a frozen nasty facial expression.

"Let me guess, a lynx?" Simon spoke. His facial disdain indicated his disapproval of his surroundings.

"Bobcat," I corrected.

"Oh Harry, better to keep quiet about your stuffed animal knowledge, it makes you small town," Simon laughed.

Barnes had quickly consumed his first beer. "More," he commanded. "We will need to keep up, Harry," Simon pronounced.

"Barkeep, three more beers and another round for the bar," Simon requested as he pulled more Canadian bills from his pocket. If he was buying our safety, it was working, as the bar cheered with approval.

The drunkards were happy and it appeared not in any mood to bother the foreigners. I never asked him where the Canadian money came from. It was typical Simon, always prepared, even on international soil.

"Barkeep, I want to buy whiskey, who do I talk to?" Simon directed toward Henry, the bearded, portly, and intimidating bartender.

"Shots?" Henry grumbled.

"No, cases of whiskey," Simon requested.

"You must talk to Vanier," he replied.

"Is he here?" Simon asked.

"He will be back," Henry retorted. At the very same time he looked over and added, "There he is at the front door."

"Dear God," I mouthed. It was 'can't catch a jack' Jacques.

"Well, isn't this lucky, my old friend Jacques owns the Evergreen," Simon said with absolutely no concern.

The last time I had seen Jacques was at the end of the hallway at the Franklin. I had rolled him into some tables and was saved by my uncle who paid him off. Simon's plan seemed to lack the understanding that we were pinned down and Barnes was unaware of the potential trouble.

Jacques did a double take. A stunned look engulfed his face. He motioned and called out three French names. On cue, three lumbermen followed him.

"Simon, dare you to come here," Jacques challenged. He missed the how and why but his anger filled in the pieces.

I braced for the worst. Barnes, sensing this was not a good situation, took a large swig of his drink.

"D'argent, I can make you rich," Simon extolled.

"I should have you beaten," Jacques pointed at me with venom. As he spoke his voice raised with increased anger.

"The gendarme, he saves you, you on my land now," Jacques spewed. It flashed in my brain that he was using Simon's logic. He was holding the cards that we had held at the Franklin.

"Where is Pierre?" Simon quietly asked. Jacques was thrown off by the question. "Why you ask this?" Jacques slowed his anger and questioned.

"You can easily beat us up, we have no chance. I will make him rich instead of you," Simon raised each word into a crescendo. The three lumbermen looked on happily with the prospects of a brawl.

It flashed in my mind. The Franklin. Simon sent Daniel out of the bar and he must have called in a disturbance. I never thought of how quickly my uncle had arrived. We had no way to summon such help.

Simon continued, "Rich, more money than you can count." Simon purposefully picked up a silver certificate from the bar, raised it up and allowed it to flutter to the floor. The money was a fishing lure and Jacques was taking the bait.

"How you do this, make me rich?" Jacques questioned.

"Whiskey, Canadian whiskey. America will need alcohol and we can transport it by the river, store it on a private island during prohibition. We sell it for a huge profit," Simon laid out.

Jacques was intrigued. The hook had been set. "How we profit?" he questioned.

"Every case of whiskey will make you $100, we will need hundreds of cases, thousands of dollars over the next two years," Simon explained.

"All you do is move the whiskey to our island every Friday. We will pick it up and sell it, more money than you can count." Simon dramatized his words by lifting the remaining money on the bar.

Jacques was like a large fish running off line.

"How we get paid?" he spoke with animated enthusiasm.

"I have $200 seed money. You buy the first loads of whiskey, we will leave the money on the island each month. It will be easy for you. We will meet at the Franklin on the first Saturday, next September to plan the details." Simon was reeling in Jacques as he spoke.

Simon had a large wad of Canadian money now in his hand, a sign of respect, I thought. He gripped the bills like he had a deck of cards.

Simon had rehearsed. He had planned it to precision. He had minimized the risk by fronting the money and buying trust. He did not consider it a gamble. It was far more than he had won on the train. Jacques motioned the lumbermen away, bought drinks for them and motioned Henry to freshen our glasses.

The fish was in the boat as Jacques began drinking with us. I remember shaking my head in amazement. It had not instantly occurred to me that my father's beloved island would be used for illegal importation of whiskey.

Simon's illegal plan had now made me a bootlegger. Street-smart Barnes smiled his approval.

Simon handed Jacques the $200, we drank for another hour and as improbable as it seemed, we were partners with our combatant upon Simon's arrival our freshman year.

We left in high spirits. Barnes seemed the best of us from a long day of libations to drive the car.

I would have not been a good pilot of the *Huckster*.

Simon laughed at my initial expression upon Jacques' arrival comparing it to the lynx above our heads. I made the mistake again of correcting him that it was a bobcat.

He laughed harder saying he felt a lynx sounded wealthier and craftier. Simon could barely pronounce the words and his enunciation of craft sounded like "rafty." We seemed to laugh the whole way to the beach.

I bounced around the back seat, slid back and forth unable to coordinate a stable sitting position as we glided onto the river and Barnes continued to try and keep the car straight.

Barnes navigated the Canadian Ford across the 1,000 yards and along the bank to the cove where the River Hotel was located.

I remember it in slow motion, but it was a tremendous thud as we were about halfway to the hotel, in the center of the cove. The *Huckster* had hit a pocket created by an upward flow from a spring. It was a great place to catch fish in the summer but the car was now directly vertical. Barnes and Simon in the front were now facing a smashed windshield, positioned parallel, and the doors were encased in the ice. The car was saved by the thick ice. Luckily it had tightly wedged and would be going nowhere for a while.

Barnes simply said, "Reverse is not going to work. We are going to need a very big fish to give us a push."

We wiggled out of the windows. The drive shaft had been snapped, the back wheels were slowly spinning and the tire chains whistled and clanked as they rotated in a circle.

The *Huckster* was now owned by the river.

Simon was laughing hysterically. The car my father had given me would eventually be gone, taken by the warm weather to come. Recovery was unlikely and the damage was extensive, things were leaking from the engine and the front window was a spider web mosaic.

"Holy *Omarkayham*," I shouted as I looked at the mangled mess. The frigid water had pooled around the car and was quickly freezing.

We stumbled to the hotel, emboldened by toasts of goodbye to the *Huckster* from Simon's derby flask.

We were greeted by an entranced group at the hotel.

"We have been watching you guys, you're very lucky," Norman shared in a concerned tone with the group.

"I know, it's damaged beyond repair to boot," I said.

Simon had a plan. "Norman, get me several large boards and white paint. I need a small brush. We will replace the car."

The bar was entranced by what Simon was doing, in less than an hour he created an intriguing sign.

Wager: What Day Will The Car Disappear? One dollar pays Five!

Rules: Pick One Day—Monday through Friday—Weekends are for the house!

It was brilliant, a solid month away from enough warm weather to have the car fall to its watery grave.

Simon created a duplicate second placard that would hang in the Franklin. Norman and Daniel were instructed on taking bets in a ledger, which included name, day of demise, amount bet, and signature of bettor.

Simon was adamant in his instructions to Daniel and Norman, "Nobody can bet more than $2, no exceptions."

Our pawn of a newsman would cover the story, enticed by pictures of a green Benjamin Harrison that he would quickly add to his wallet. Simon liked silver certificates but they were sometimes scarce. The newsman didn't care. He covered the story with the caption of a fundraiser for the town's garden.

Both bars had first-time visitors who wanted to predict when the car would submerge. Even those opposed to drinking would stop and place a wager.

My mother, thinking it was a good cause, played her favorite day of Tuesday. She was upset about the car but recognized it as the follies of college students. I doubt she knew how much my father had spent.

The rules had been simple and there were plenty of people willing to drive by in the morning to see if the *Huckster* had disappeared the previous night. One of the subordinates of my uncle even offered to drive by on his daily rounds. My uncle would have been incensed had he known that one of his staff was spending time sharing the information of a vertically-frozen car. When he was off duty, he never paid for a drink or dinner and never said anything good about my uncle when the free drinks were flowing.

The Franklin installed a spotlight that was ceremoniously turned off at twelve midnight. A patron was selected and given a $2 bet for completing the task of counting down until midnight and shutting the spotlight off.

My car, the cheerleader on football Saturdays, was now a celebrity.

Townspeople had photos taken next to the car, people traveled from all over, many by train, to place a bet and get a view of the '*Titanic of Automobiles*.'

Barnes, as the driver, would sign autographs at the bars. His quick wit and ability to put people at ease with his humor helped the ledger sheets fill quickly. People cherished the chance to shake his hand.

Barnes would say, "My hands, these hands, fended off certain death while the others in the car froze in place." Barnes would hold his hands parallel to his face and simply stare as if they were mythical.

Once the patrons were staring at his hands during the quiet he would simply say, "Amazing aren't they?"

They believed he was being serious and had they known he was the only one remotely sober enough to drive I think they would have been more amused than amazed.

Simon would calculate weekly the payoff on each day, notating that we would clear enough to buy the *Huckster II*. The worst day was Tuesday. It was the day that the Titanic had sank and many patrons had used this as a sign that the car would meet its demise.

The bars were packed each weekend with patrons watching and hoping the car would not disappear into the murky depths.

Students were taking water temperature and ice depth measurements and enlisting the geology and math professors to work on complex predictions to determine when the ice might give way.

Several classes took field trips and studied how the position of the *Huckster* would affect its final demise.

The president of the University, saying it was a learning experience for a good cause, wagered $2 on Friday.

He was quoted several times in the paper, "It's a once in a lifetime event that has turned a potential tragedy into immense fun for the school and town."

I am not certain our inebriated state and drunken return from laying out our bootlegging plan would have made this such an historic event. His photo, the president's huge smile next to the car, made great news.

The owners of both establishments were making tons of money and the three of us never paid for a drink. Several fights broke out as patrons argued about what day it would sink. Norman and Daniel had to calm many patrons who wanted to bet more than two dollars.

Norman and Daniel continued to fill journals with entries and they were being tipped by grateful patrons by helping share their thoughts on the most probable outcome. Simon indicated they would share a percentage depending on what day the car fell. He indicated what days to direct those who could not make up their minds to insure the best profit.

If the car should fall on a Saturday or Sunday we would be buying a car worthy of Union Avenue in Saratoga.

It was early April when the channel began flowing visibly. Simon asked for a minor favor to help Daniel by borrowing the beat-up pickup I had been using from the farm. It was Jacob's work horse and I had commandeered it. He said he needed it on Friday and would have it back to join the patrons on Saturday morning. I thought little of it.

Everyone who packed the bar late Saturday morning knew the end of the *Huckster* was near. Anyone who was anybody in town arrived to the hotel glazed with excitement and anticipation which was embossed on their faces.

People could not venture onto the river anymore for fear of soft spots and the depth of the cold water that had pooled on the surface.

Simon arrived near noon and began hawking, "Weekend Insurance," asking $2 to win four. Several in the crowd, who had made multiple bets using others to skirt the rules, jumped on board. Most, however, were content to try to keep the *Huckster* aloft until Monday by staring periodically and nervously sipping drinks.

Simon was frantically buying drinks this weekend. The phone would ring each hour from the Franklin. "*Huckster* down yet?" It was Daniel's voice on the other end.

It was dinner time, the tavern was swamped and guests were desperate to get a window view during dinner. It was mayhem, but the excitement was incredible. The mayor of the town had never seen anything like it. The president of the college joined immediately after dinner and bought a round for all in the dining room.

Simon had created the most brilliant plan and if the car fell, we would profit immensely.

It was getting late and people were still arriving at the hotel.

I heard a scream. The bar went quiet.

A woman seated against the window spoke in a soft sense of disbelief. "Dear God, it's moving!"

The bar was so quiet it seemed like she had raised her voice. It had been just a whisper, a volume more suitable for a prayer. She was praying it would stay above the ice.

Everyone stopped, not a word was spoken and it was dead quiet. The *Huckster* began to slowly turn sideways and we could see the entire underbelly of the car. It stopped for what seemed like an eternity.

No one wanted to say anything. It was as if the car was mystical, that it had life, and that it was now going to be gone.

The bar was frozen, the car was still and then after what seemed like an hour, in a mere 20 seconds the car tilted directly up, posed majestically, the left wheel slowly spinning as if to say goodbye and then, slowly, it disappeared out of sight.

The time had been exactly 11:40 pm.

The contest was over and the bar seemed sad that it was gone. Despite everyone losing their bet people began toasting the car.

"Goodbye old friend, may you rest in peace," was spoken by an elderly gentleman who had struggled from his chair out of respect.

It was brilliant. Simon had turned a drunken crash into a mythical automobile, compared to an ocean liner that claimed the lives of over 1,500 people.

Simon had limited the bets to $2 per person so as to insure that nobody could complain.

"Disgruntled losers can make trouble," he repeated many times during the contest.

The news was dispatched to the Franklin. The roar inside the bar was different from those who witnessed its end from the hotel. Daniel described it as deafening.

The newsman was fed the story by Simon. The date, April 12, 1919, it was three days short of the fifth anniversary of the sinking of the Titanic but the time had been the exact time the ship had hit the iceberg.

The paper would read, *Charles's Car Sinks—11:40 Saturday Night.* The second line on the front page was, *Identical Time the Titanic Hit the Iceberg.* It would captivate readers. The local paper sold out in less than an hour. The statewide papers experienced the same voracious need for information about the car. It made the front page of the New York Times. A photographer had captured the exact moment it began to sink. The picture would became a highly sought after postcard.

It was a story laced with references about the great ship tilting up and sinking to its grave. The hack of a reporter would win a writing award several years later when he submitted the story to a new magazine. I never saw the story but was told it was the most popular piece in the Reader's Digest during 1923. It had been Simon that created the metaphors, they were perfect. The award should have gone to Simon who had fed him the entire script. It was Simon's creation, after all, and Simon's bravado that made the writer a published sensation.

The spotlight stayed on all night as people reveled like it was New Year's Eve. People actually would make repeated looks at a black hole that now was just a shiny glaze of frozen water.

We left the Franklin after paying off $28 to the seven who had wisely invested in the weekend insurance. It was a loss of $14, but provided an outlet to those who wanted to get their monies back if it was to disappear.

Simon shared, "Those would have been the ones to complain, but even losing or breaking even they now feel like winners."

We drank with Daniel until three o'clock Sunday morning, returning to Jenks with Simon carrying ledgers from both bars. He shared that we would clear $1,800, enough for all to share nicely and get a new car to replace the one that was now in the deep current and sitting in a 600-foot grave.

We entered our room and I tripped over a bunch of bags on the floor. Simon had a pair of wet pants hanging off the bar. "Simon, I almost fell and broke my other collarbone, what are these bags doing here," I questioned.

"An experiment I was working on," he shared.

"I wanted to see the effect of a large amount of salt on ice. Would ice melt faster? And, could I make money off of it?" He didn't smile, almost scientific in his delivery.

As he spoke, he turned out the light.

"You know Harry, it does."

Our room was pitch-black. I could not see if he was smiling but he never laughed.

I didn't know what to think. He risked his life and limb on a frozen river which was ready to give way to the icy depths. He had cheated hundreds of people who had bet on the outcome, but for some reason it did not seem wrong.

It was about winning. I simply shook my head with loyalty and amazement, I went to bed and had no problem falling asleep.

We didn't talk much of the *Huckster*. Simon made a large donation to the Garden Club but turned down any additional notoriety or notation in the paper. We studied dutifully during the week and disappeared into a whiskey haze on the weekends.

I had arranged to take my fraternity brothers on a boat trip through the islands when the weather finally cleared in the spring. We had joined Alpha Zeta, the most prestigious fraternity, and enjoyed our mixers with the sororities. We seemed a bit more studious and spent more time at the house drinking in a refined elegance. I thought Simon would be more interested with the happenings but he seemed content to spend his time at the Franklin.

Fennimore had made the grade, Chamberlain, Barnes, Appleton, Green, and Walt joined as well. Fennimore was aware that he had been helped by his association with Simon and me. The extent was not known but it was later revealed that Simon indicated that he would not join if Fennimore was excluded. Fennimore quickly joined in and was helping the treasurer manage the budgets and party planning. I know that I would not have made the effort on behalf of Faf.

The cruise was on the *Island Wanderer.* Built regally in the 1870s, it now had a carnival quality. It tilted a bit to one side and the large wheel that was its source of power had been trimmed in red. I had made the arrangements with the knowledge that my distant cousin would be at the helm. I had crafted out a tour that would help us map our strategy for the importation planned for the coming fall. Simon, proud of my advanced thinking, was more focused on Fennimore having the right provisions on board. Simon's definition of adequate whiskey conflicted greatly with Faf's thriftiness. It would be a conflict that would rear its ugly head many times in our final two years. Alcohol was plentiful to begin the voyage, scarce when we poured on the shore a few hours later.

I was purposeful in my instructions to the Captain for our trip. I instructed him to run from the town dock, up the channel past the River Hotel cove and return for the education of Simon and Barnes where Jacques and company would move the whiskey. Simon and Barnes were topside for the entire trip. I would point out currents and where we could traverse the bootlegged whiskey in the fall. Simon nodded but never laughed as we cruised by the cove that held my car.

Simon simply looked over at the resting spot and said, "May the *Sunkster* rest in peace."

As we passed the property I owned, Barnes was focused and uninterrupted by my ramblings of where the best spots to land the heavily-laden skiff. He made detailed diagrams and maps which he painstaking recreated for Jacques' eventual use. Barnes was meticulous and understood that the ease by which we moved the whiskey would minimize our exposure. The lighthouse at Visger Point was a perfect marker and would help us avoid detection and provide a key landmark at night.

Barnes noted that Jacob's secluded area was a perfect landing for the skiff, close to the channel but hidden from view. I added that the barn had been positioned with a fair amount of evergreens that shielded prying eyes from the road.

Unbeknown to Jacob, the house and barn he had built had created a perfect fortress to allow us our subterfuge. The home was in full view of the river but the evergreens and small embankment would allow us to land, move the whiskey into the barn and have a place to unload devoid of any view.

We entered the channel and swung close to Indian Penny Island, two acres with a beach access away from the channel. It was Simon's first close-up view of the island. It was an instant reminder that my father was gone.

Barnes continued to drink and draw as we passed my uncle's land and continued the few miles back to the town dock. He said, "Jacob's property is the best for us to move the whiskey, the lighthouse can be our night-time marker and we should have no problem accessing the island and crossing the river to utilize Jacob's barn." It seemed like a good idea. Jacob was a church Elder, a highly-esteemed member of his Methodist congregation. I would request the use of the barn during the school year. I had gifted the land to him and in return he provided his retirement sanctuary as a haven for illicit cargo.

Simon declared the area, "Bootleggers Alley." He would always cryptically refer to our efforts as getting our Bachelors of Arts. It was the perfect moniker and nobody was the wiser.

Simon, completely out of character, asked when we could go fishing at Penny Island. In retrospect, I think he knew that he was helping me heal. He would never say it but gloss it over in times of inebriation and heartfelt discussion.

I had not visited since my father's suicide and had mixed feelings but had reluctantly agreed. Simon didn't want to fish. He was calculating how much weight we could actually fit into the skiff. Unbeknownst to Green and Fennimore they were invited to go as ballast. He called them his "sacks of salt."

It was just a week before the semester was over. We had studied dutifully during the week and would disappear into a blur on the weekends. I knew the river could quickly take prisoners and Simon's experiment was no place for heavy consumption. I knew my voice of reason would not sway the need for libation as our fishing was the cover for our afternoon voyage.

We left early in the morning. The river was calm as a sheet of ice. The water shimmered from the morning sun. It was a perfect day, devoid of wind and a perfect test of currents and ways to traverse the shore line. We were clad in angling gear and outfitted with a collection of the most expensive lures, hooks, and bait. It was the things my father treasured and I was sharing them with my fraternity brothers.

The skiff, 14-feet long, was easy to row and with a bit of resourcefulness it could be piloted with great accuracy. I turned the oars over to Simon and Barnes who worked diligently to get the handle on rowing. In no time they were experts at moving among the small coves and using the current to change directions.

We continued to move up and back with the current and drift fished for a majority of the morning. Simon had been given a pole and was mocking the idea of fishing for our lunch. I was not amused.

The calm nature of the river allowed us to drift from the deep current to secluded coves. Our live bait and lures netted us a few largemouth bass and northern pike. Simon was afforded the opportunity to mock and ask if they would be mounted for the fraternity house. I indicated that they would be our lunch. I had brought provisions and limited the drinking in the skiff as we all were working on empty stomachs.

Simon had not been very attentive to what he was doing when the boat began to move against the current. Simon mentioned that he must have snagged something as the boat was being dragged by his line. He was sitting in the front of the boat and we were slowly moving methodically along the next cove. "Why is this pulling us?" Simon hesitantly asked.

"Simon you have a fish on and by the looks of it, you won't be drinking for another hour," I informed him.

His pole was bent directly over at this point and the skiff continued to move with purpose. The fish was now aware that he was being restricted and Simon was now animated in his conviction to land the mammoth fish. Despite his facial terror, he was intent on having the bragging rights from our camouflaged boat trip.

"I have never seen you so scared," I quipped.

"Not scared, just concentrating at the highest level. This fish is no match for me. It better get ready for a spot on the frat wall," he bragged.

"What the hell is this thing?" Green loudly questioned.

"By the looks of the way it's moving, could be a sturgeon," I said.

"Simon was your bait on the bottom, like money on the floor of the Evergreen?" I asked.

"How the hell do I know? I came to get my BA, not get my arms pulled out of its sockets," he rambled as he strained under the weight of the fish.

The skiff continued to move with sharper pulls and concerted efforts for the fish to free itself. Simon was actually doing a good job as Barnes and Fennimore piloted the skiff in unison with Simon reeling in line.

"Keep your rod tip up, and reel!" I yelled. The line was going slack and I feared the worst but the 10-foot sturgeon showed its dull grey prehistoric nose and jagged fins.

Everyone froze in the boat trying to make sense of a fish they had never seen before. We were the same distance we had been from the boxing ring and it was met with the same gasp and utter amazement.

"That is incredible! What do I do?" Simon nervously pleaded.

"Keep reeling, keep the line tight. He is getting tired and I can get him alongside the boat and net him. I can then club him," I directed. I was now grasping a mahogany club that had been stored under my seat.

Simon continued to pull. It was a game of will and Simon had no intention of losing. The sturgeon turned sideways, his alabaster belly was a sign of waving surrender as he surfaced near the front of the boat.

"That is one ugly Kappa Kappa Gamma—just your speed, Fennimore," Barnes said in a droll tone. Simon continued to pull him toward the side, Fennimore drove the net over its head and I whacked it five quick times, right above the eyes.

"Careful, I want him pretty when he's stuffed," Simon proudly bragged.

We tied the sturgeon to the side of the skiff and rowed back toward Penny Island. "Well, that was fun, can I shoot a lynx on the island?" Simon taunted.

The boat was full of animated friends who had experienced something that they might never accomplish together again. Our test run and river expedition had been a success.

We rowed to the beach, pulled the skiff and the sturgeon on shore. The fish was over 120 pounds and three of the fishing party had to lift it.

"Fennimore, do you want to mount *Sally the Sturgeon?* I mean it for the wall of the frat, you could be the first name on her dance card," Simon prodded.

"I am not having the fraternity pay for it," Faf quickly retorted.

"I am paying for it," I commanded.

Sally would be forever memorialized by our town's taxidermist and barber. He did a magnificent job as well as adding a brass plaque that detailed the weight, length, and of course the emblazoned name of Simon G. Sheldon, II.

The sturgeon would be the welcoming dignitary above the dining hall at the Zeta House. *Sally* would wear hats in the coming years and be decorated in seasonal garb. Simon would regale the next two pledge classes with how he defeated the fish while consuming a well-mixed Manhattan cocktail. His bravado and the innocence of the pledges made the manufactured story become reality.

It would continue to live on as a legendary feat. Twenty years later when I would hear the story told at the River Hotel, I would shake my head and mumble through my drunken stupor, "Classic Simon."

The island was as I remembered. I was happy for the distraction as I began to feel gray and empty now that my father was gone. My gutting of the fish created a bloody mess on the rocks that I was using as a cutting board. It was a saddening process as I relived his suicide and thought of the scene Jacob had encountered.

I made a shore lunch. We had caught enough fish to feed two boats of ballast and everyone was impressed with the delicious fish and plentiful cocktails. We toasted *Sally*, my father, and sang the fraternity song. We roamed the island, Barnes continued to fish and land more bass for us to take back to the fraternity house.

We made drunken plans to meet in Saratoga in the coming August. Fennimore wanted to stay at the Adelphi but Simon would have none of that—he was the runner and had to be separate from the group. Despite Fennimore's protest, he was happy that he was included as well as the one who could startle the bookmakers with heavy wagers. He liked the thought that many in the betting area would want to know more about the crafty plunger known only as Fennimore.

We left the island to a rendition of Simon's class song. We were in drunken unison and our final chorus could have been heard from shore to shore. "Cocktail, cocktail, bev-rye, we will drink until we die," had been added as the last chorus. Drinking had become a religion for us. The water and evergreens acted as our church. The jagged rocks that lined the river were our unoccupied pews. The sound was magnificent and the trees absorbed the memory while acting as our listening parishioners.

That fall, the county and state would go dry. The campus and surrounding towns would have whiskey in plentiful supply courtesy of Simon and the soon-to-be-christened *Drunkster*.

Chapter VIII

"Where is Simon," I mumbled, the words conjuring up fear of being alone, the unknown. The crumpled telegraph in my pocket simply read, *Adelphi, August 11*.

I felt odd, not happy, perplexed that I was not giddy with anticipation. *Do I have the right day?* I questioned myself. I pulled out the telegram and hid in the shadows of the hotel looking to validate my memory. The arches and Victorian scroll work allowed just a few rays of light as the day grew long.

The infrequent, opulent cars driving by would break the symmetry of the perfect lines of the light. The architects could not have known the beauty they would have created when nighttime would fall.

I continued to hide in the shadows. I gradually began to fade, exhausted from my train travels. I had no intention of driving a truck to Saratoga. I imagined the glares I would receive and would be an embarrassment to Beth. Simon had planned to buy a car in New York, something worthy of Union Avenue he had promised on Indian Penny Island.

I needed a drink, but could not summon the courage to enter the enclave of wealth. I turned to enter the hotel when a chauffeured touring car pulled up to the street side entrance.

The driver quickly exited the car, clad completely in black attire. He circled the car to professionally dispense the dignitary seated just out of view.

Best get out of the way, I thought.

"Harry, where are you going?" resonated from the back. It was Simon, his head peering out of the car window.

"Simon, you're late," I deadpanned. "I was just about to quench my thirst, now I won't have to lift the check," I added. I was relieved and tried to conceal it.

The driver assisted Simon from the car.

"What do you think of the new *Drunkster*?" Simon proudly announced.

It was stunning, sleek, with a center tire much like the design of the *Island Wanderer*. The top was beveled and beautiful, chrome adorned at just the right places, polished to perfection. The front of the car had an ornament, a jockey with a whip held in a victorious pose, elegant as if it had just won a big race. It was remarkable. My mouth was wide open, I could barely utter a sound, and amazement had captivated my face.

"Yup, bought her in a cracking good deal. I supplemented our sunken car winnings with a bit of poker profits and could not resist the Pierce Arrow. Stunning, isn't she?" Simon punctuated his bravado by slapping me on the shoulder with his racing newspaper.

The chauffeur, seemingly immune to our private conversation, said, "Harry, she drives like a charm!" The voice didn't match the outfit. I realized it was Albans.

"I must change. I am not a chauffeur, I am a stockbroker!" he bellowed in embarrassment. Albans raised his hands in frustration as the joke had worn thin. I wasn't sure about Albans joining us but Simon was always one step ahead.

The Adelphi was the same, impeccable, only one person at the bar. Surprisingly, Simon did not know him, nor did he want to be known. Albert, the gendarme of the hotel was nowhere to be seen.

"Quiet, not like last year," I somewhat happily shared. It was easy to hide behind Simon in a group; it was easier for me with just friends.

Simon was immediately down to business. His voice lowered as he spoke, "We have much to discuss while Albans is changing."

We began drinking. The elderly gentleman at the bar waved off our offer of champagne and left abruptly, much to the delight of the bartender who seemed to have endured his company and possibly impolite behavior.

"Listen, Harry, Albans wants to book bets this week. Wednesday, *Man o' War* is running in the Sanford. He won't lose. Other than that he should be able to make a nice profit off my array of uninformed racing pals," Simon laid out with purpose.

"No enigmatic Fennimore this summer?" I questioned.

"Barnes, Green, and Fennimore are coming tomorrow. Lucky for the bookmakers I am not betting on Man o' War at one-to-nine," Simon regaled. "Fennimore will lay off the bets that put Albans in a difficult financial bind."

His weathered racing paper was full of ink smudges and precise written notes. It acted as information, but he was intuitive about the human dynamics that would take place on race day. He knew how to profit when the crowd overzealously went one way. Simon would naturally look for the angle to go the opposite direction. It was crafty cards utilizing the small brains of race horses and the large greed of people that could easily overrule their own tendency toward common sense.

Albans entered the bar. "I was ready to buy drinks," he grandly offered as he took the seat I had occupied on my first visit.

"Simon . . . Harry . . .," a subtle controlled voice of confidence rang out.

"McClennan, about time someone who knows how to breed and race a horse showed up," Simon replied. Simon rose to shake his hand.

"Alcohol should never be external! Harry, good for you, I heard you made a tidy profit last year. Let me be the first to reduce your winnings by allowing you to buy a bottle of this establishment's best champagne," McClennan playfully proffered.

"Yes, it would be my honor," I immediately responded.

"Pesky Prohibition, the Saratoga season won't be the same. Shameful," McClennan said regretfully.

Our legal drinking was on borrowed time. The racing days would be playful and as celebratory as my first visit, but tempered when the loss of legal alcohol was mentioned.

"Damn those Protestants, next will be gambling. What will they outlaw after that?" McClennan said with fierce venom.

We were being told to stop drinking and nobody liked it. I was deeply concerned even with the knowledge that I would have a plentiful supply of high-quality whiskey from Canada. I had laughed many times with Simon that I had no idea what was more perilous—bootlegging in a skiff, or the loss of a quality Manhattan made to perfection in the serenity of Saratoga.

The cocktail had a certain cadence in Saratoga, like a beautiful piece of music that danced in my mind and added bravado to my step. It was a melody of taste that somehow was more euphoric on my soul here. I was now without fear after the timid behavior that I faced and mentally battled in front of the Adelphi.

Wednesday morning was like a fraternity party, all of us in joyous good humor to be together. The Adelphi was raucous; Green was startled by its elegance. Barnes fit in perfectly. Clad in a dapper jacket, he would elegantly slide his left hand in his pocket as a signal that a brilliant humorous quip would emanate from his mouth. His life in Chicago made him a natural in Saratoga. Green tended to be the stooge, but as the morning grew long, many would feel the sting of Barnes' witty tongue. He was in rare form, aided by stiff drinks served by our friend Gerard who was at our service behind the altar.

Albans made quiet overtures to the bar's patrons that he would be taking wagers on the races. Simon was not close by, but the gentry knew that he was his sponsor, that Albans could be trusted. Simon had reviewed the program carefully with Albans and left him to his talented negotiating skills. Simon knew the town was filled with charlatans, owners, swindlers, trainers, and jockeys trying to make money and earn prestige by winning at Saratoga. There would be 20,000 people at the races and Albans could easily be snookered by any one of them.

The races looked exciting from the program and the streets were in glorious discussion as loud voices of conviction filled the taverns. *Man o' War* was undefeated and going to win in the fourth race.

Simon said he could not lose, but would never bet on such a heavy favorite. "No fun in that," he advised.

I followed Simon. Barnes and Green were anxious to bet, both hamstrung with a lack of cash, but Simon had secretly bankrolled them with $50 each. It was a fortune for both but they were enveloped by the aura of Saratoga and they felt equal to the wealth around them. They were rich for a moment.

Even I, a wealthy landowner and proprietor of a profitable farm, was struggling to feel equal among the elite.

We left the Adelphi. The day was a bit overcast but it didn't matter. The greyer the day would only enhance the drinking. George, our regular driver, whisked us away to the races. He reminded me of my friend's act at the River Hotel—bitter, sullen, and perturbed, he had to drive wealthy people to the races.

His mood was always worse when he would return to bring us back to the hotel. George spent most of his day with forced pleasantries and trying to put up with drunken chatter from the back of the car. Our whimsical quips and boorish behavior frustrated him but he was rewarded and appeased with a decent gratuity as we would exit the car.

Simon, depending on his consumption, would vary his tips to insure that George was polite and did what he asked. He could be late, but George was to be on time.

The track was abuzz, electric as the races began. Simon had secured a decent table but our later arrival would have required a substantial gratuity and Simon was a bit concerned that the gathering might be a bit raucous for his usual finish line table. Albans had secured several key players who spread the word that a decent bookie was available to take bets. The guarantee was that the bookie would not be fished out of Saratoga Lake at the end of the meet. Albans was in rare form, negotiating and only offering a pittance of odds on *Man o' War*. Everybody wanted to bet on the sure thing.

"What is the purpose?" I grilled Simon. "There is so little return and as much to lose," I questioned.

"Many will just bet for the victory. Losing means nothing, winning means everything," Simon stated.

He was right. I had not thought of it that way. It wasn't losing that was the fear. It was not having the winning ticket. It was taking the risk that has always acted as the victory, no matter what the outcome or cost.

Simon was not going to bet. He liked the horse *Golden Broom* but was not going to try and beat the talk of the town. I wanted to be like Simon so I simply pawned off his advice as I made my way around the track in search of Beth, as Mr. Day's box was occupied by a group of well-dressed owners. Simon had studied the scene as if it was his anatomy class; he knew it all and was mentally tallying the options in his head. It was my collarbone all over again—gain the advantage, and use information to make money.

Green was trying to look elegant but was having difficulty in imitating Barnes' ability to stylishly slide his hand in his pockets. Simon was a bit disturbed by the increasing drunken banter, and indicated that the tailor would have stitched the pockets closed to hold its shape. Barnes jumped on the observation and said it had assisted Green in curling his fingers to hold on to his $50. A squirming Green, as if unleashed from the starting tape, was ready to bet. "I am wagering on *Man o' War*," he gallantly spoke.

"Green, quiet, it's a secret!" Barnes retorted. We all laughed in unison.

"Simon, what do you think of *Upset?*" I queried. "Six-to-one last time, might be ten-to-one today, worth a look." The Racing Form came to life as Simon spoke. I had been reading the form, the numbers and figures were making sense, *Upset* had finished second last out.

Albans was a flurry of activity, notating wagers, providing small slips of papers to a sea of men in straw hats. He seemed a bit nervous, sweating profusely as he approached Simon.

"All well, action on *Man o' War* is very heavy, only giving one-to-ten; so far I have $2,000 to win. I have one odd bet, number four, $500 to win. He wanted fifteen-to-one, I offered ten-to-one and he took it. He has absolutely no chance," Albans finished.

Simon stopped, his head jerked around, "Albans, that's $5,000, you need to lay at least $300 with Faf," he demanded.

"No, it's a ridiculous bet, it's a free $500," Albans laughed as he replied.

"Can you cover it?" Simon casually inquired. His sense of concern had diminished but he seemed perturbed that Albans had deviated from their agreement.

The day was filled with thrilling races but everyone was focused on the fourth. Simon handed me a program, stuffed with money and some notes for Faf. "Tell him to make sure he gets this down." Simon was pointed and made ominous staring eye contact as he spoke.

I returned to the seats after my casual meeting with Faf. The crowd size made the need for Faf minimal, but

Simon had relished the notoriety Faf had gained with the bookmaking crowd.

There was no sign of Beth. I caught a glimpse of Mr. Day. His eyes connected with mine and he quickly looked in the opposite direction. I was a bit sullen that Mr. Day did not acknowledge me, but the Manhattans were plentiful. We laughed and I was hanging with the New York elite. All was right with the world.

Several famous baseball players from Chicago were seen in the Clubhouse. It was shaping up to be an historic day. This day had brought out the rich, the famous, not so rich, and unbeknownst to me, the infamous. All were now equal, having been upstaged and outshined by a single race horse.

People would see us in classy banter and not realize we were just college juniors, absent of genealogy and enormous wealth. I had $600 in my pocket, the cost of the *Huckster*. The Pierce Arrow would make me look wealthy but had people known it had been bought with poker winnings and the rigged sinking of a car, I would have been mocked with facial expressions of disgust.

After race three, the crowd began to come out of their seats. The apron was filled with everybody that could fit, each straining to catch a glimpse of the undefeated darling of the Sanford Stakes.

"Look it's Green's sure thing," Barnes yelled. There was *Man o' War* and he was stunning.

He shimmered as he strolled down the track to be saddled in the paddock.

Albans approached the seats. He had been winning on the early races, and he now felt invincible as he took a chair.

Fennimore had made several small bets for Simon, they all had lost. Simon dispatched Faf again, including the $50 that I had bet on *Upset*. Albans paid little attention to Simon; the horses were arriving at the post.

The day had been unusual as the starter had made many blunders. The first three races had been sent off in disarray. It had been lost on the crowd that the regular starter had been sick, but Simon had mentioned it and he had planned accordingly.

The mirth of the day quickly subsided. *Man o' War* had been left at the start, the horses flew past the stands and the crowd gasped its concern, one-to-ten favorite *Man o' War* was in trouble. If you looked at Albans, you didn't need to look at the horses to know that the favorite was going to have to run a special race to win. Fearful conjecture was murmured. Green shoved his hands so hard into his pockets the stitching gave way.

"If you lose, at least you will look elegant," Barnes mocked with his gifted $50 comfortably in his right pocket. Barnes had not bet and my guess was he had planned not to.

The horses began to turn for home, *Golden Broom* began to retreat, *Upset* took command and *Man o' War* was closing. The crowd, sensing he might get there, roared their approval. Albans was frozen. Simon simply watched and slashed his program gallantly. "C'mon, all you have," he softly encouraged. I was not sure if he was cheering for himself or Albans, it turned out to be both.

Man o' War had been defeated. *Upset* had won the Sanford. Albans abruptly disappeared as the crowd applauded both the winner and the gallant second-place finisher. It dawned on me that Albans had lost a great deal and could not possibly cover the bet he owed on *Upset*.

I caught a glimpse of a deliberate Mr. Day who was quickly approaching our table.

"Where is your bookie?" He pointed his finger as he spoke, but his anger was directed solely at Simon. I was somehow relieved he was now ignoring me.

I was thinking about Beth and less of the $50 I had wagered on the winner of the race.

"Why, Mr. Day, races treating you well?" Simon asked with a condescending tone.

"Cut the false pleasantries, your friend owes me $5,500." Day was angry as he spoke.

"Meet me at the Adelphi, five o'clock, I will see you get paid. Join us for cocktails," Simon's responded politely.

"Five o'clock, no games, Simon," Day turned his back to minimize us as he spoke.

"He had better be there," he threatened. His departing comment was punctuated by his violent exiting stride.

Simon began to scan the crowd; he was looking for Fennimore, not Albans.

Fennimore was now a legend. He had bet $600 to win on *Upset* for Simon at twelve-to-one. His betting days were over as bookies would now avoid him at all cost. It did not matter. We drank at the downstairs bar and people would point and whisper as Fennimore would walk by. Faf had bankrupted a bookmaker from New York and it became the talk of the town.

Bookmakers could be overheard in town to say, "Fear Fennimore."

The mousy Fennimore now had a reputation among 20,000 race goers and he had a sense of accomplishment even though he was merely the puppet. He was getting big for his britches and his failure to pay for the drinks simply grinded my increasing contempt for him.

Albans was nowhere to be found on our return to the Adelphi. We were greeted with a concerned Albert, who had assisted Albans in gathering his things for a chaotic exit.

Simon knew it would happen.

Albert quietly whispered, "Simon it was odd . . . he looked like a chauffeur."

"Nothing to worry about, come have a drink with us." Simon banished hotel rules as an apology.

"Well, that little welch," Simon smiled as he muttered taking the first table to the right.

It was almost five o'clock and Simon had counted $6,000 under the table, securing an envelope from Albert to consolidate the money.

"You know Harry, I know what can happen. I only bet against *Man o' War* because I knew Albans would be in trouble. It happens in horse racing and life," Simon pontificated.

"You're paying Mr. Day?" I asked.

"Yes, if you're sweet on Beth, best to make him somewhat tolerant of me and fond of you," he shared in a brotherly tone.

He quickly became Simon on stage as the bar began to fill with race goers. We had been late to the races, where we had a beautiful but inferior table at the track. Early to the bar, we were on the finish line.

"More drinks, Gerard, champagne for all," Simon commanded.

Mr. Day was punctual, angry in his stride. Simon was quick to congratulate him, interrupting Mr. Day's expected outburst. Mr. Day now knew he was getting paid and the agony of not knowing for the last few hours was over.

Simon handed him the envelope below the table, shielded by my position with my back to the bar. Mr. Day, with decreasing amount of angst, counted the winnings peering under the table and mouthing every time he reached a thousand dollar milestone. Each bill was like a glass of whiskey, his face relaxed, his tempo slowed, and he actually smiled.

As Mr. Day completed counting, he had a bit of a jolt. "Simon this is $6,000, people don't make mistakes in Saratoga with money," he questioned.

"I felt bad that I ruined your winner last summer, thought we might be friends. Harry kicked in his share of his winnings from last year as well," he said. Simon was genuine in his delivery.

Simon smiled with a sense of remorse but carefree that even if he did not win Mr. Day's friendship, he had done the right thing on my behalf.

"Simon, I may have misread you. I like you know horses. Come by my stables tomorrow, I have a horse for you to look at. My Beth planned to come today but will be here Friday," Mr. Day advised. He made a happier glance in my direction. It helped erase his lack of acknowledging me at the races.

We toasted to *Upset* with the finest bubbly available and Mr. Day was simply over the moon.

Albans reentered the hotel. He had been detained by Albert at the entrance, just as I had on my first visit. He looked like a joke wearing the chauffeur outfit. Just two days earlier it had been funny, now he looked pathetic.

Simon waved to Albert. Albans was dispatched upstairs to the room he had violently vacated and quickly returned looking reasonable amongst the gentry. Despite having been refreshed, he was white, perspiring, and in a few minutes, disheveled.

"Simon, I need your help," he begged.

"Mr. Day just left," Simon was blunt.

"I only have $3,000, miserable start," he groused. "The horse broke backwards at the start," he complained, but Simon's body language indicated he really didn't care.

"I told you to lay off $300. I paid Mr. Day, do you owe anyone else?" Simon's voice was stark.

"No," Albans face contorted as he spoke.

"Give me the three. You owe me three more, with $500 extra for covering this. You deviated from what we discussed, don't do it again." Simon was angry but his thin face began to relax to ease the tension.

Albans profusely thanked Simon, unaware that he had helped my relationship with Beth. Simon laid out the plan to be paid back. "Just follow my lead and we can leave in one piece," he instructed.

"No need to be the also ran like the horse *My Swimmer* in the Sanford."

Those in the surrounding tables laughed as Simon had mentioned one of the horses that had run in the Sanford but was really referring to the bookmaker that had been fished out of the lake last year. It wasn't funny to Albans, he was now in deeply in debt to Simon.

Fennimore, Green, and Barnes arrived in fine form. Simon rose and ushered them to their rooms. We all left to avoid a boorish scene as Barnes and Green were in their usual drunken banter.

I secured my winnings, Fennimore took a cut and Simon was loaded. He had bet on *Upset* to protect a friend, made a small fortune, and ingratiated himself to a highly-regarded trainer and all the while Albans had paid for it. It was a stroke of luck, but Simon had minimized his risk.

We were up all night. Revelry and jocularity gained several visits from Arthur after a broken lamp and the infliction of a fat lip on Fennimore. Arthur, trying to keep order, simply elongated his name as he spoke but he knew he held little strength or authority over his friend.

I hadn't broken the lamp, but had tackled Fennimore which resulted in his puffy lip. I could have cared less about the legendary punter of Saratoga. He was grinding on my nerves after refusing to buy drinks at the downstairs bar the previous day. Simon as usual, picked up the check. I was tired of Fennimore being cheap.

The morning was greeted with a terrible hangover for all of us. Barnes, Green, and Fennimore remained at the hotel, their faces just a few inches from their plates and coffee.

Simon and I were curried to the backstretch by George and arrived at Day's barn. The stench did not mix well with the multitude of undigested liquor in my stomach. I gagged and partially vomited as Beth walked into the entrance.

The horses, knowing Beth's voice, began to poke their heads out of the stalls. "There is the special filly," she spoke. The horses whinnied, all speaking in unison to be petted and acknowledged. The stench had taken my breath away; but Beth's beauty had made breathing even a bit more difficult.

The barn was long, 20 horse stalls crowned with cherry and immaculate in detail and construction. They had spared no expense. Gold plates, inscribed with the names of the horses and their lineage were attached to the front of the sliding doors.

"Beth," I muttered, barely audible.

"Harry, my Dad was speaking about you last night." As she spoke and smiled, it lit up the room.

"Your father graciously pummeled a bookmaker that Simon has known over the years, I backed *Upset* as well," I spoke. My voice gained some volume while praising her father and also bragging of my handicapping skills.

"You must sit with us today, the races will be more fun," she happily asked. I gazed at Mr. Day who had entered the same entrance we had come in. I waited for his approval as he had heard the invitation.

"I would like you to join us." He swung a heavy door to its right to expose a beautiful filly. "She is in the fifth. Pretty, isn't she?" Mr. Day did not need an answer as he spoke.

Simon was intrigued and cajoled, "She looks like a runner, bred to run early and win."

"She should run well today. Beth why don't you get us some drinks?" Mr. Day spoke with fatherly care.

Beth happily exited, my eyes watching appreciatively as she bounded down the stable talking to each horse as if they were her long-lost friend. She was wearing tan riding pants, a black jacket, and was dressed to exercise horses. She was absolutely the most beautiful thing, turning into a silhouette as she reached the end of the stables.

Her absence was purposeful. Mr. Day had a plan and it was going to make us a pot of money.

"This filly is burning up the track. She is fast, but I am running her at a mile today. Our jockey has instructions to break toward the lead, drop back, and be well beaten while looking like she is all-out late," he described.

He quickly continued, "Simon, here is a thousand in the envelope. I want you to bet with several bookies and have that crafty Fennimore do the same. Don't be afraid to tout her at a bar or two, either. I am betting a thousand in one spot, the real betting crowd will know I am on her today."

"Why?" I interjected, much to Simon's cringing face.

"When does she run next?" Simon cut me off and did not allow Mr. Day to respond to my irrelevant question. Simon knew the plan.

"Yes, well done, next Tuesday going six furlongs, odds should be fifteen-to-one next time out. We will get eight-to-one when all the bets are spread around. Nobody will question it if we do it quietly next time." Mr. Day smiled, of the logistics of his plan.

"Okay, only Harry and I will know the plan. Albans needs the profit and he tends to share details. You bet $500 with him. I will have him leave on Monday so he won't muck up the race next week. He will be none the wiser. Fennimore will try and get action down. The bookies are avoiding him or offering a pittance of odds. He will take whatever he can get and I won't need to tell him because he will make a ruckus, Let's just say he is overly frugal." Simon was energized despite no sleep. I smiled at his characterization of Faf.

Simon was in sync with Mr. Day. Last year he had toyed with his sure thing. This year we were a consortium, arranging for a betting coup. The right execution would net us a huge amount of money. Mr. Day had positioned us like Jacques.

Beth arrived with a tray of orange juice, a bit weak, not of orange pulp but of alcohol.

She saw my face when I sipped.

"Behave Harry," she shared, knowing that I was thinking it would contain a kick.

She winked at me, knowing that we were in town for a bit of fun.

"Me? You better watch Simon, he is the instigator," I laughed as I raised my crystal glass.

We returned to the hotel, summoned the troops and headed to the track for our command performance. Day's filly was in the late afternoon. We stopped at the United States Hotel for drinks and a bit of acting as if overserved. Simon shared that Day's horse was live and he was going to make a nice profit off his filly. He punctuated it by sloshing his drink, something he would never do. Simon was never one to be overserved in public.

I joined in with a bit of conversation with a gentleman who did not want to talk to me. It was absolutely brilliant as the patrons seemed to take the bait by jotting info in their secret journal, the racing program.

The fun and the furor of the races made each day special. We had seen a great horse get beat the day before and we were going to watch and complain that another good horse had run poorly. We were going to act the same, unbeknownst to Green, Barnes, and Fennimore, who would be our actors, reading lines that they knew by the defeat of *Man o' War*.

It was a contradiction, but held special meaning, knowing an outcome before it happened. It was just salt on ice, waiting for it to melt. There was nothing like it and we all kept the program as our souvenir of the day's results. It was all Simon could do to not bet on the other logical horses in the race. The fear of losing Beth made it easy for me not to profit from the fix.

We joined Mr. Day's table. Green, Barnes, and Fennimore relished being the center of attention. Beth arrived sporting the same dress she had worn the year before. It was more beautiful, more vivid, than the first time I had seen it.

I only placed a few bets. Simon and I were visible to the bettors, and I spent my time chatting with Beth and watching her as everyone watched the races. During the races, once the horses were at the first turn, we would

174

converse as they raced down the backstretch, I would watch her on the first turn, she would watch me as they ran down the stretch when we both thought the other was not looking. We would reconnect once the horses crossed the finish line, picking up where we had left off.

We both hated long races, races over fences were horrid because we had so little time to talk. We would smile in unison when the race was over.

I left under the ruse of getting more champagne, timing my walk among the bookmakers trying to secure a price on Mr. Day's filly. I haggled with several bookmakers and saw Fennimore doing the same thing. I managed six-to-five which would equate to nothing in a half hour.

It was fun to get the stares that had been reserved for Fennimore. I glided back to the seats—the word was out, and Day's horse was a cinch.

Fennimore, Barnes, and Green were unaware that a trap had been set. Albans had taken Mr. Day's bet but avoided any other action, not on Simon's direction but knowing the trainer had placed the bet. Fennimore, Green, and Barnes had bet, Barnes wagering the earth-shattering $2 to win. Fennimore had bet $20 and I was happy the tightwad was going to lose. It was exhilarating to know that he would be in absolute turmoil and angst after the race was over.

I watched in awe as the horses ran to the turn. Just as Day dictated, the filly was on the outside, in third as they went to the backstretch. The jockey had the horse right near the lead and the fans were happy to see the favorite close. They waved their programs in approval. It was a sea of straw hats that would be tilted forward in despair in a mere minute.

Steadily she fell back during the run down the backstretch and dropped toward the rail. He waited to hold her until he was out of sight of the crowd, past the Stewards stands, and only toward the turn, where he met a few tiring horses and had to change lanes. Each move cost her a position and made her run look worse than it had been. His ride had been brilliant, much to the delight of Albans who paid Simon back a portion of the money he owed him, $500 courtesy of Mr. Day.

Barnes, Green, and Fennimore were overserved at the track and their boorish behavior told the entire town how their sure thing was a bust. Simon groused and thumbed his racing papers to continue the part of the victim. We were happy, but if you saw us at the table it would have looked like a funeral. I, somewhat subtle in the background, simply soaked in the spectacular sight of the players' roles. Everyone did what was needed. Our friends were not aware of the plan and they played the best actors of all.

Day played his part, fielding the scathing comments from the tables, of the many disgruntled that she had run poorly.

"I don't think she is fast enough to compete here," he lamented when asked.

The jockey relayed that the horse was breaking his left arm in the stretch as he pulled down on the reins while he slashed his whip, barely hitting the horse. Mr. Day sent the jockey packing with a large envelope, thick as French toast. He made his dismissal a very satisfying end to his Saratoga meet.

I had been invited to dinner with Beth and Mr. Day that evening. Despite his gruff demeanor, he made every effort to take the gentle ribbing from every owner, trainer, and race track patron that made mention of the filly's performance. It was difficult for him, but he knew the dividend was a year's earnings in less than two minutes, just days away. I never mentioned a word of support, but my facial expressions reinforced it had been a tough day.

I wanted dinner to last forever. Eventually as we left Old Bryan Inn, I said goodbye to Mr. Day and turned to give Beth a hug.

It came out of my mouth with little thought. Just three simple words, "Please marry me."

Mr. Day had walked ahead, Beth hugged harder.

"What took you so long? I came all the way to Boston and you had four hours in the stands to ask." she admonished. She stopped and took my hand. "Why of course I will," she said, serious now. "Dad, stop," she shouted up the street.

"Beth, let me talk to him first, I want to do it right," I was serious as I spoke.

"He likes you Harry," she said. I then kissed her with her father watching full view. He had known I had fallen for her, and Simon had already figured it out.

I returned to the Adelphi. Simon was by himself. He had sent Barnes and Green to bed by making them whole on their original stake, a massive $2 to Barnes and $30 to Green. Fennimore drank to calm his large loss on Mr. Day's horse. It was convoluted since he was way ahead, despite losing on the Sanford. Albans had gone to the casino. Unbeknownst to me it was owned by Arnold Rothstein. He was called 'Mr. Big.' Simon despised the casino, he was always the house.

"Harry, you're late," Simon barked. Gerard moved from the bar with a magnum of champagne as Simon continued, "Yes, I will be your best man."

We drank and talked all night. I gushed about Beth, Gerard left.

Even *Man o' War* losing, or the 20,000 people who had witnessed history didn't come close to drinking the magnum of champagne at the Adelphi that night.

We executed Mr. Day's plan. It was quiet, leaving the bookmakers scratching their heads, and we left Saratoga with a pile of money and the knowledge that nobody had figured it out. We had told McClennan about it moments before post time. He plundered his bookmaker and hugged us as we left the hotel later that day. We drove back to campus leaving incredible gratuities to every barkeeper on the way.

The bars we stopped at were sullen and unkempt. Prohibition was weeks away and most had hung a funeral sign their last day of operation. A few that served food professed that they would continue with a, "Yes, we will be open after September 1," but the owners' faces told another story.

Simon's generosity was greater than he could have imagined, as most of the bartenders would be losing their jobs. Simon was planning and it would involve selling whiskey to those he felt showed a sense of true appreciation for his tip. He was making mental notations of those he could trust and be the benefactors of Jacques' risky whiskey.

We arrived late on campus. Fall was already in the air as we stashed our money. Simon's bar had a camouflaged bundle taped to the back. I stashed stacks of bills using the copper key. I never counted how much I had stashed, but it was as thick as proverbial French toast.

Chapter IX

"What an upset," Simon stated with a blank stare. The tavern doors would not open, doors installed the previous year to minimize the noisy disturbances to the dinner guests made by students entering and then drunkenly exiting. Their shenanigans and inebriated revelry had cost the owner business.

We were locked away from the bottles. It was Saturday, the day that Simon had instructed Jacques to show.

I was kicking an old can. Barnes was irritated.

"Stop kicking that," he blurted out. He was tense and not funny for once.

"Will *Can't Catch a Jacques*, show?" I stated.

"No," Barnes followed my comment quickly.

"Sounds like a wager is in order," I retorted.

"Okay, a moose," Barnes shared.

Barnes raised his hands, fingers outstretched and the thumbs were perpendicular to his temples.

"Ten he shows, half moose the train is on time," Barnes continued and dropped his left hand leaving the half antler formed by his right hand.

Simon smiled, "I like that, I bet $200 he would show, so you will need a herd of moose for me to play," Simon laughed.

"Is herd right or is it a pack?" He paused. "This is ridiculous, I am talking about moose when I want a drink." Simon's attitude was now as tense as Barnes as he spoke.

We walked to the front of the Franklin and entered the main door. It was quiet and desolate despite being lunch time. The train was 20 minutes until arrival.

"Where is everyone?" I stammered.

The owner, usually ready to parry quips with Simon, walked from the back and stated, "No alcohol can be served, by the order of the town." We were mortified as he spoke.

"Dry, all we are going to serve is dinner," he said.

"Already, what the *Omarkayham*, miserable this prohibition," Simon stated, his face normally unemotional, was contorted.

"Copper key, Harry," he added quickly.

"Yes, oh dear God, yes," I frantically said. I instantly thought of the woman at the River Hotel. She had said the same phrase about the *Huckster* as it disappeared into the river.

It was the same phrase my aunt had used on the phone after hearing of my father's suicide—a religious phrase now being applied to our need for excitement and fun.

It was a week until our first game. I had pulled a muscle and was sitting out practices and our team looked mediocre at best. I would try, but really was not mentally in the mindset to play football. I wanted to quit, but the cover of the post-game celebrations would help as we drove our cargo around the county.

I was volunteered to spearhead the new tradition of a Friday night town rally and bonfire. Simon choreographed the idea to hide our transportation of whiskey. I had asked Jacob to handle the bonfire and he eagerly agreed. It was unbelievably perfect; most everyone in town would attend the rally. My uncle was informed by the school and would have his entire staff of three policemen handling the safety and crowds of students. Our only games out of town were not until early November, but under my direction they were to be held every Friday.

Instead of preparing for football, I was helping forge our bootlegging operations. We were waiting for our Canadian connection. I left in the Pierce Arrow, leaving Simon and Barnes to wait.

There was no Daniel to overserve us, no cards at the bar, just kicking a rusty can and irritated fraternity brothers.

I returned to see the train pulling into the station. My mother's best crystal glasses had been pilfered for our afternoon with Jacques. It was 11:30 and on time. I was up a half moose.

I didn't watch the exiting passengers. Barnes' face was my barometer. He was staring with concerned effort, then he mouthed a word and his face turned away from the train, Jacques had arrived.

Simon had flashed the money smile.

He was well dressed. I flashed a moose to Barnes and followed it up by a half moose signal. We argued that afternoon about arrival time but eventually Simon mocked Barnes into paying me the whole $15.

"Bienvenue, Monsieur Jacques," Simon pronounced in excellent French Canadian as he welcomed our former combatant.

Jacques smiled like an old friend as he exited the train. Once our foe, Simon had disarmed him. All it took was money and faith. Simon had gambled and had won. And I was happy with my fifteen bucks.

We loaded into the touring car. Barnes drove as we talked on the way to Visger Point.

"Dry, it's dry and the natives are restless," Simon said.

Barnes had given me his meticulously-drawn maps. I already knew the maps in my mind as I pointed to the ease by which we could traverse the river.

"You sure boat get back, current not strong?" Jacques knew the perils even with broken English.

"You go nearest land, cove to cove, easy with two men as you drift. Once you unload, the skiff should be easy to retrace your path. The lighthouse will be your guide," I continued to point to the maps.

"The River Hotel is the next set of lights. We have a spotlight that will be on to help, every Friday," I pointed out.

"How much I bring?" Jacques questioned.

"Safety first. Start with 10 cases. We had a test run and it should be safe. It's 120 bottles at $25 a piece. We split the profit of $20 a bottle—$5 for you, $15 for us," Simon laid out. He had practiced meticulously and had no intention of negotiating.

"Six hundred per load seem small," Jacques shared his discomfort as he was fishing for more.

"Bring more, get more," Simon laughed as he finished.

"Every third delivery, around once a month I will add $100. We may get more, maybe less, but I don't want to squabble on each delivery. We still have to do the selling and take more risk," Simon said.

"We stop at the end of November," he instructed.

When we arrived at Visger Point, we broke out the whiskey and crystal. We drank in style while I pointed to the hidden beach, the River Hotel and the spotlight direction, and our storage garage that we would use on Sundays or in case we ran into problems.

"I want bigger share," Jacques spoke. Like the first time, he was gaining confidence.

"Why? We take all the risk, you simply bring the cases to an island, avoiding any authorities," I interjected.

Much like the conversation with Mr. Day, Simon did not let Jacques answer.

"Mr. Vanier, I will provide an additional $100 every third delivery to avoid having to balance our proceeds and your efforts. Whiskey does not float and selling it is a big offense. I promise if we do better than I expect, I will share the profits with you, alright?" Simon's cadence made it a deal that could not be rejected.

Jacques reached his hand out, Simon acknowledged and the deal was made.

"Merci, I have bought the whiskey with the money gave me last year. When we start?" Jacques thick accent grew stronger as he spoke.

Barnes filled the glasses from our diminishing supply of fun.

Simon paused and continued, "Next Friday, you deliver at dusk, we pick up just as night sets in. You bought 30 cases, your profit equals $600, we split the investment cost, $200. I will leave $500 in a metal box against the rocks in the cove."

"One run every Friday. We sell on Saturday and only sell one day a week to minimize the risk," Simon concluded.

Jacques was confident that he could deliver the whiskey. Simon handed him $500 he had taken from the cherry-stained bar.

"Trust you, my friend." Simon made eye contact and a genuine smile, like the one that I had seen when he paid Mr. Day in Saratoga. I always wondered if it was an act, but he was emotional as he spoke. I am not sure if he was proud of the scheme, himself, or was genuinely honest when he completed these types of interactions.

We drank and toasted the partnership. Once adversaries, we were now friends. Once the whiskey was gone, we returned to the station and Jacques left for the Evergreen.

Simon had bet $700. I picked up a moose-and-a-half from Barnes,

Simon looked at me like a brother. I looked at him.

"Are you sure he will do it?" I spoke softly out of concern.

"Harry, if I am wrong, I will be shocked. He took a train, not just one train to arrive here. Not an easy trip. If he wanted to steal, he could have simply kept the $200. Plus, the time allowed him to decide if he wanted to be rich. It was greed!" Simon confidently spoke.

We left the station to visit Jacob's barn.

It was a perfect scenario, the barn was a great distance from the house he had built. The access road was to the left and it was 200 yards from the prying eyes of Jacob should he be home.

The barn, forest green, blended with the evergreens. Two stories, it had a perfect view of the river from the widow's watch he had built facing the river. There was a double sliding door in the front and a side door to the right. Jacob had dedicated himself to his barn. It was an edifice, with beamed ceilings and a high loft to store hay. It was worthy of a steeple and parishioners. Jacob had seen to his congregation, meticulously welding pieces of scrap metal to create a weathervane that was positioned at the front of the roof. It reached to the heavens, high above the barn—a whimsical Canadian goose just landing, with a copper arrow acting as the directional.

"Well, the Jacques goose is landing," Barnes quipped.

The barn was organized to perfection, with work equipment, gas, oil, and paints and tools neatly organized on shelves.

Simon climbed the ladder to the loft and began throwing bales down. "Six should do," he claimed.

After a few minutes, Simon had organized a vault within the hay. "Just in case we need to store some," he said. "Discard these bales in the river and then let's take a look at the current to see where we should come from in the skiff." I did not need this lesson but obliged his instructions.

It was flawless. The skiff would be at Visger's Point. It would be an easy traverse and the whiskey would help slow the boat in the current. We watched as the bales moved with the current toward the shore and then out to the main channel.

I mentioned about river safety, "Red sky at night, sailors delight; Red sky in morning, sailors take warning." The phrase, unintentionally comical in my delivery, was not taken seriously by Simon or Barnes.

"Wrong, it's red sky in the morning, whiskey drinkers take warning!" Barnes blurted out. I was the only one who didn't laugh.

In a mere seven days, we would be breaking the law of the county. Simon knew it was not a federal crime, yet, as the Volstead Act had not been fully enacted.

"Avoid your uncle at all cost," was all Simon would say in the few days leading up to our first shipment.

Chapter X

Simon had worked with the new fraternity members to organize and implement the start of a bonfire rally on Friday nights before all of our football games. The pledges eagerly seized the opportunity to create a tradition that would act as a focus for the school, town, and most importantly, the fire department and police. They embraced the duty and simply wanted to impress Simon and the upperclassmen of the fraternity. I was the chairman of the committee, but did nothing as I was the figurehead. We were Simon's pawns and the youngsters were oblivious to their role.

Fennimore protested at the cost of the wood. I offered to donate it, but Simon elicited the schools support. He didn't beg but charmingly pointed out the dwindling attendance after the late season loss the previous year. It was a loss that Simon had contributed to and he now had used it twice for his own benefit.

The school thought of it as an excellent way to promote the games and jumped on board with funds to build the fires. The administration worked with the town to provide all the support and logistics.

I somehow received the credit and it inspired a footnote under my picture in our senior yearbook that I had been the 'Pioneer of School Spirit.'

Fennimore took credit for the fraternity savings, an accolade he did not deserve. I was to fill the role of carnival barker, cheering the crowd with a megaphone borrowed from my uncle.

It was utter perfection. The word spread and it seemed like everybody in the neighboring towns as well as the majority of the students and faculty would be in attendance.

Jacob was a volunteer for the recently created fire department and the presence of a blaze would require having his horse-drawn team ready should the fire get out of control as well as directing his volunteers in the cleanup of the drenched, smoldering embers. The emergency equipment was courtesy of the local pharmacist who provided a horse-drawn barrel with a pump hose. The decorative barrel was inscribed with the local pharmacist's advertisement for his soda shop. In bright yellow against the red barrel he had inscribed, *Quench Your Thirst at Latham's Pharmacy*. It was in poor taste but the town readily accepted the money to have a new water dispenser to fight fires.

The last Friday in August, our opening game was to be held ten miles from the campus. I could have languished at this point in my life forever. It was a simple time. I ran with a leather ball and my dearest friends were perpetuating chicanery and sharing a secret only known to us.

It became clockwork. I riled the crowds with chants and cheers while Simon and Barnes were traversing the river, loading whiskey, and hiding it in Jacob's barn. No one paid any attention as they left just as dusk hit and returned while the fire was beginning to burn down and the crowds were dispersing. They even pitched in to help douse the fire, much to the appreciation of my uncle who feared somebody would get injured by the smoke or burned by the sparks. He made sure no one would venture beyond his barriers. He lived for imposing restrictions, for the control. He relished the blockades he had created to keep everyone at a safe distance.

The following day, while I was piling up records and touchdowns, the whiskey was loaded into the *Drunkster*. It was then delivered to an appreciative group of struggling restaurants and the few bars that were trying to stay open by serving food and providing a place for the locals to gossip and gamble nickels on board games. The whiskey kept them in business and they knew that their silence would insure a supply.

I never asked Simon what he said to the buyers, but I always assumed it was the quiet nature of Barnes mixed with Simon's ability to read people's personalities and see if he could trust them. I saw his clairvoyance as we had returned to campus from Saratoga, testing integrity with tips and bravado. It was certainly the whiskey that kept them silent but both of my cohorts knew it was a very difficult balance. One mistake, and a heap of trouble would follow.

It was the drinkers versus the zealots. We all knew that the influx of alcohol would bring scrutiny and Simon loved the contradiction, the victory. The island would be the sanctuary. It was devoid of prying eyes should our scheme get out of hand or we could not sell the whiskey for fear of reprisal.

Our bootlegging continued to be easy despite the unpredictable weather and sometimes bleak Friday evenings. August turned to September and the weather began to turn cold. On the third Friday of September, Simon and Barnes had returned by the end of the game. Simon made a victory sign with his arms, not because we were winning, but because the cases had been retrieved in record time.

Simon nicknamed it his *viculous* pose. It was his scientific word for the need to win while receiving ridiculous profits. And in the meantime, Simon had actually become quite proficient in directing the boat as Barnes would row.

We had stacks of money and paying my cribbage losses to Barnes became a Sunday morning ritual. I was never concerned because the silver certificates were plentiful.

Simon had begun offering discounts for buyers willing to pay with silver certificates. He hated the sound of silver coins, he said it was beneath him. I had begun to hate Sir John Suckling who had invented the addicting game of cribbage. Barnes was beating me badly and I despised it. I loved the competition and hated to lose no matter what the stakes. Conservative Barnes was always aware how much money he was ahead. I never paid much attention.

It was the end of September. Usually cold, it had turned unseasonably warm. Barnes hated rowing in the cold. Swigs of whiskey made it easier but he was happy that Friday had arrived with summer-like temperatures. I don't remember the date but it was one I really did not want to remember.

The trees were beginning to turn autumn colors, but it felt like the heat of July. The school had been aglow with the warm weather. We didn't complain. Coach Kinnon eased up at practice to avoid us being burned out. We all drank heavily that Thursday night, and easily intoxicated by the heat, I was asleep before Fennimore.

I awoke to a scarlet sky. There were thin yellow wisps of color strung between the reddish colors of the morning. It was blazingly hot and I never thought of the significance until many years later. I should have thought then of the simple rhyme that warned sailors, but for some reason it never crossed my mind. I was absent minded, hung over, and dehydrated.

It was a three-quarter moon as the fire was started in the town center. The fire immediately blazed and illuminated the memorial to our fallen town members. It was exciting to see my name embossed as the garden savior as the fire's light began to take center stage from the moon. I was a hero and a football star. My donation had insured my name was featured most prominently.

The list of names, added when word was received of their deaths, looked almost an afterthought. We were a long way from the carnage that continued to be fought in Europe. We lived in a small town and only a few paid a great deal of attention. Most who took the time to stop were families whose loved ones were killed, captured, or simply missing and presumed dead.

The weather had made it the biggest crowd I had seen since the fights in New York. It was exhilarating as I began my rousing speech of support. I yelled about how we would beat our opponent and little did I know our biggest competition was not on the playing field. Everybody was focused on me and not one person realized the moon had disappeared.

The crack of lighting alerted us to a storm that had arrived under the shroud of darkness. The second clap of sound was all I needed to hear. I knew this was a bad storm, a violent summer storm, one that we usually experienced in the middle of a very dry summer.

I surrendered the platform to a subordinate of my uncle who was ready to disperse the crowd as quickly as he could, but it became evident that the driving rain and threatening lighting would require no direction.

I had offered no resistance to his grabbing the bullhorn. I was immediately concerned about Simon and Barnes. The wind began to whip and I knew the river was now the most dangerous place to be. This was far more dangerous than ice giving way. On a frozen river they had a chance to dodge peril. The unpredictable storm made the river's dangers incalculable.

Jacques crossed my mind. Did he make it back against the current or was he engulfed in the chaos of waves, violent lighting, and an unmanageable skiff that by now would be fighting the changing currents?

The stinging rain and deluge was strong enough to extinguish the town fire. It was as heavy a rain as I had ever seen and the wind made walking difficult. If it was more than a squall, it was not going to end well for my cohorts. Our game was just 10 miles away in the morning but the roads would make traveling too difficult. The pep rally was now just a town gathering with turmoil. People were fleeing and fending for themselves.

I would drink later that night. I never thought of it, but I was gambling the game would be cancelled.

I asked Jacob if I could borrow his truck to check on my mother as the lightning continued to periodically strike. Several times the flashes were just outside the town square. Simon and Barnes were in for a difficult journey and it flashed in my mind when I was a young boy stranded on the Canadian shore during a storm. I was now my father, ready to traverse the river in search of my brothers, the brothers of my fraternity.

I had lied to Jacob and drove as fast as I could. The flashes of lighting helped me stay on the road and negotiating the curves which with one error would send me into the trees that lined the road. My headlights were useless as the mud continued to gather around the lights and on top of the truck. It was dangerous but nothing compared to what the bootleggers were facing.

I arrived at Jacob's barn. I could see lanterns flickering inside the barn as I reached the side door.

"Harry you're late," Simon deadpanned. It didn't sound funny like our first meeting at the Franklin.

Barnes was frantic as he spoke, "We saw two men, Harry, their skiff sank. We could not get to them as we were on the island. I never saw them come up."

"Were they in a cove or the channel?" I was anguished and frantically pleaded for information.

"Near a cove, but it looked like they were dragged into the channel. We were loading the first case when the lightning and rain began. It was brutal." Barnes was shaking as he spoke, this was the most animated I had ever seen him.

Simon had hidden one case in his straw vault. "Wretched evening. Two cases of whiskey stranded on the island. I have a bottle back at the dorm, but let's be careful," he said callously as he pulled a bottle from the case. It seemed ironic that the hidden cases on the island were identical to number of men that had most likely drowned.

We began to get into the truck when a flash, a bolt of lightning hit Jacob's barn. The weathervane was electrified and the flash was blinding. It happened just as Barnes closed the door. A few seconds later and we most likely would have been killed. It had been breathtaking as the entire river was lit up for an instant. Through the trees I could see my father's island. Every ripple in the water and every tree seemed frozen. Beautiful. There was another flash of white color. I wanted to wait for another flash.

The fire was instant. The barn was now engulfed in flames and the overhanging evergreen trees, our secretive cover, were now shielding the barn from the bulk of the rain.

"Dear God," I yelled. "We need to get help!" I completed the cry but suddenly realized there was nothing that could be done. The pharmacist's fire barrel, laden with water, would never reach the barn in time.

The nonnegotiable roads, the isolation, the lack of any way to snuff out the intensifying fire would lead to its destruction. All that would be left would be a smoldering ashes and embers. We heard an explosion. The fire had begun to engulf the gas cans and paint that had been so precisely store in his impeccable barn.

"It's a goner," Barnes remarked.

He thought he was being funny, but my friend Jacob would have to rebuild.

"My whiskey, my *bev-rye*," Simon supported the humorless quip of Barnes. He contorted his face like his collarbone had been broken. He continued to mock pain and tears but I did not find it funny.

"We can't say anything about the fire and Jacob can't know we were here," Simon snapped back to seriousness as he detailed what had to take place.

Simon did not ask me if it was acceptable. They had witnessed two people drown, stored whiskey in a burning down barn and now I was the hack of a reporter. I was taking instructions to lie about my whereabouts during the storm. I was not going to win any awards.

We arrived in town. I dispatched Barnes and Simon before we arrived at the square. The rain had subsided, and the few remaining people were my uncle, Jacob, and a crew of his volunteers.

"I could not get to my mother's house, the roads are a mess," I quickly volunteered.

"We have word of a fire," my uncle was resolute as he spoke.

"It's going to be a long night," he spoke again in a braggadocios tone. He inferred that he might be our only savior.

The tone was the same as my father's but his inflections were different. It irritated me and reminded me that I did not like him. When my father spoke he did not have to convince me to believe in what he said. My uncle's voice seemed to plead authoritarian acceptance.

I was anxious to leave and to be back at the dorm. My refuge was the bottle Simon had majestically pulled from the crate in the chaos and I knew we had an additional backup at the dormitory.

I offered to have the fraternity help in the morning.

"It was a short squall. My guess is whatever is burning will be the only fatality," my uncle surmised. He would be wrong and I wanted to correct him but I could say nothing.

"I will call if I need hands." His inflection was thankful, but it rubbed me the wrong way even as he was being nice.

I picked up my cohorts, sharing the discussion I had with my uncle.

"We can't say anything. Let's hope the whiskey crate was destroyed in the fire. Can you ask your aunt if we can come to dinner on Sunday?" Simon asked. The guise of a dinner would help him assess if we could be caught.

He knew my aunt liked him.

We spent the entire night drinking, somewhat afraid of what could come of the deaths and fire. Barnes crippled me with cribbage. I lost because I could not concentrate. Barnes appeared not to have cared about what had happened and seemed intent on repeating, numerous times, how much money I owed him during the night. He was taking advantage of me and I really didn't care. As was customary, we would settle up in the morning. We went to bed just as it was daybreak.

Simon was stoic most of the evening as he contemplated the death of Jacques. Simon only spoke a few times.

He quipped several times after an eventful strong swig, "Jacques and his helper need life *Jacqu-ets*. I am really getting tired of waterlogged money." It was the worst of his drunken insults.

They were drunken slights avoiding the severity of what had happened. Barnes only fueled the volley with singular words.

"Glug," he would add to Simon's swimming jokes.

I awoke to a crashing knock on the door. I assumed Barnes had arrived for his money. I was dead wrong. It was Green.

"Boy, you reek. What the hell were you doing last night, why are you not headed to the game? There is a phone call for you," Green loudly blurted out. He was surprised I was still in bed.

I stumbled to the hall phone. I was still drunk and wondering what the hell Green was talking about. I was sick, incoherently drunk.

"What," I stammered into the phone half asleep, still trying to make sense of Green's question.

"A death." I thought of the men who had disappeared during the squall.

"A drowning? What? Who?" My mind was still trying to make sense of the situation. The sound was getting crisper and clearer as I continued to listen.

I dropped the phone. I now understood. I could barely swallow, barely breathe.

Jacob was dead. I stood silently. I picked up the phone and made plans to be at Jacob's barn. It was beginning to make sense and I realized I had been speaking with my uncle.

I had Fennimore drive me. My head was in pain and I felt dreadfully sick. This was not a happy hangover to be treated in the 24 Jenks hospital.

As we drove, I realized Green had asked me about the game.

"Are we playing today?" I quietly asked Faf.

"Yes, most of the school is not going but the game is still on. I am sorry about Jacob. I am guessing you're not playing." Thankfully, Fennimore bailed me out by feeding me the line I would tell the coach.

I mustered the energy to correct Fennimore. "Jacob was my friend." It was barely a whisper, barely audible to Faf. Fennimore bowed his head and increased the speed of the car.

Coach Kinnon understood my lie and we lost badly to the team we had beaten soundly in our first game of the season. The coach was not happy but understood the ramifications of Jacob's death. I had yet to calculate what it would entail.

There was no one to console and no one to console me. I was summoned, not to help, not to be consoled, but as a witness to listen to my uncle about what had happened.

"Dear God, what happened?" I asked.

"Heart attack, he was overwhelmed with the destruction." The barn was smoldering, one wall was still standing but it was a combination of burned wood, charred cans, an originally red tractor now black and somewhat melted. The hay loft had collapsed and acted like a blockade.

"Chief, come here," I heard from the remains of the barn. There was little left, the fallen loft hindered my view and the fire's carnage was devastating. We could hear, but not see, who was yelling. I then realized it was the subordinate from the hallway at the Franklin.

"Harry, we need to talk about the farm," my uncle was lecturing me as he began to gain momentum walking toward the ruins.

"How about Sunday for dinner?" I had unknowingly completed the task assigned to me by Simon.

"Fine. You know there was a drowning last night," my uncle felt compelled to share with me.

"Who were they?" I lied and questioned at the same time.

"No, it was just one body. I will be working on that today and tomorrow." His voice trailed off as he reached the barn and he turned his back on me.

"Oh, I misunderstood you." I realized the error in my comment and was fortunate my uncle had not noticed it.

I was making better sense now of everything. The loft, the whiskey may have survived. I summoned Fennimore. We left quickly and I could not find Simon and Barnes when I arrived at Jenks.

"Where is Simon?" I yelled down the hall. My hangover had turned angry.

Green exited his room and shared what had been told to him. "Simon and Barnes left on the train, and they won't be back until Thursday or Friday."

I was stunned. Simon left knowing there was trouble. I was Jacob's closest friend, I would be attending to his funeral and I was mortified that the alcohol would be traced to me.

I was angry at Simon and Barnes but was anxious to hear who had drowned and if they would find the other man.

On Sunday, I arrived at my uncle's for dinner, having slept little. I fortified myself before I left the dorm with several glasses of the remaining whiskey from the bottle Simon had taken from the case. There was not much left but enough to inspire courage, to calm despair, to simply help me cope.

I laughed as I thought of a dry county and my very dry-witted uncle. I thought about stopping at the River Hotel but did not want to expose any more illegal alcohol.

The dinner was worse than I could have imagined. Jacob's reputation was ruined. My uncle, straight-laced, exposed Jacob as an illegal importer of alcohol. My aunt and uncle spent the entire dinner consumed with the sadness that Jacob, a church elder, the pinnacle of morals, was in possession of whiskey.

My uncle took it as a personal affront to his authority. His condescending attitude was only enhanced by the silver badge he wore during the week. Numerous times he mentioned Jacob as a scoundrel, as a hypocrite, and loudly pronounced, "The town is to be dry." It made me sick to my stomach.

There was only a mention about the drowning victim, he was a Canadian. His name was Jean Croteau.

I did not ask any other questions. I did not ask my uncle how he found out his name. It was not Vanier and I was somewhat relieved.

I wondered quietly if another body would be found floating, but trapped behind a boat house. The dead bootlegger could easily have been submerged under debris from the storm that had pooled in a crevice created by rocks on the shoreline. The jagged rocks, which I once imagined holding mythical parishioners, an audience to our class song, were now empty. No mythical person of high values would sit and pray for a grave that was harboring a criminal.

The debris would be a mixture of mangled trees and smelly foam created by rotting dead fish. It was possible that the body might never be found. I protected myself by surmising it must have been one of Jacques' thugs from the Evergreen, men who would fight on direction, whose cause was only free food and drink.

I said nothing. I simply talked quietly about Jacob's funeral. My uncle discussed getting someone to run the farm until I graduated. I agreed so as not to cause any problems, giving control to my uncle without a fight.

Jacob's funeral was on Tuesday. I anticipated a large crowd. I was wrong.

The rumors and whispers had devastated Jacob's reputation. The town that once grappled with his single and reclusive nature now realized that it may have been to conceal his immoral behavior. He must have drank secretly. He was a law breaker and a hypocrite.

Everyone was an expert about Jacob's character and they were all wrong. Just a day after his death, the congregation passed judgment on him before, during, and after the Sunday service. The condemning whispers were deafening to me. It was all wrong and I felt powerless to stop or do anything about it.

There were only a handful of people that showed for his funeral. I crafted his eulogy and tried to emphasize his strengths and the kindness that he had shown our family. I thought about the remains of my father's suicide, a secret I could not share to illustrate his compassion and care in protecting the children of his employer. I was trying to make sense of two lies.

I started with the words that he was a good man but the limited audience made resurrecting his reputation impossible. Those who attended simply did not believe the words I was saying and many did not listen very carefully. Many wanted to leave before they arrived. Many seemed to be there without spirit or compassion. To them, he was a criminal and many wanted the pews to be empty.

Several of those attending had said my words were heroic. I didn't feel like a hero. Jacob had witnessed the results of my father's suicide and I was unable to protect his good name in death. His reputation was splattered by cowardly words and his death prevented him from defending himself.

My uncle did not attend and my aunt stayed for only a small portion of the funeral. It was a short service and the burial was held with no former friends as witnesses. He was buried with only the Reverend as his savior and soon enough I was back at the dorm, drinking.

I thought that I should have said the eulogy differently, but I blamed Simon and Barnes. They had deserted me and in turn had deserted Jacob.

I was devastated and angry. Jacob's death was just a few days old and Simon and Barnes were gone.

I went to the storage room and all the bootlegging money was gone. I was headed to the River Hotel to unleash the bottles that had once been inhabitants of my father's island. I needed money and stopped to use the copper key.

My money was gone.

"Mother, was Simon here?" I angrily asked.

"He stopped over with flowers. We had tea, and he is such a kind young man," she exclaimed with a sense of motherly pride.

"Your uncle and Simon seemed to have a nice time together," she added.

The ornate heavy mahogany door was no match for my frustration and bitter anger as I left my mother's home. I shoved the doors open and muttered a dismal response to my mother's glowing tribute to Simon.

On the white porch was a yellow piece of paper, folded as if it was meant to be securely kept. It was a telegram requesting Simon to New York by A. R., instructions to be discussed at Waldorf. Simon was normally the sender. It was odd that the telegram was directing him for once.

I summoned the courage to ask Norman for free alcohol but he had been instructed not to serve during the day. I begged him and told him Simon was out of town and would be back later in the week.

I was angry, drank angrily, and muttered that he had taken all the whiskey, all our money, stole from me utilizing my copper key, and left me begging for strong drink.

Simon and Barnes did not return until October 10th. I remember the date so vividly because they had baseball hats and were talking about the Cincinnati Reds win in the World Series. It was very strange. Barnes was from Chicago, but did not seem unhappy. One of his hometown teams had lost. It actually looked like he was begrudgingly wearing his home team's hat.

Simon handed me $2,000, roughly twice what we had accumulated in our brief bootlegging and I guessed the money he stole from my desk. I never asked where it came from and Simon, sensing my utter disgust with his behavior, never volunteered.

I really didn't care about the money. They asked for my help in catching up on their classwork. I remember shoving Barnes when he asked. I said no on several occasions but Appleton, Green, and others made up their work with the reward of money and a portion of my alcohol.

Unbeknownst to me, Barnes and Simon had retrieved the remaining whiskey from the island. I never saw any of the money that was to be left for the next delivery. Barnes claimed it had been lost, $600, washed away from the boat as they returned to Jacob's barn. The newspaper reported that silver certificates had been found on several of the beaches but I believed it had been the money that the lumberjack Croteau must have lost when he drowned.

They saw a man drown and then stole his money by not leaving it in the box that acted as the safe. It served them right that the river had stolen it from them. I sarcastically thought that a gambling board could not be created to recoup the rain-swept losses.

I didn't talk to either of them for weeks. I ignored their invitations for dinner at the Franklin and was avoiding them at every possible opportunity. I slept at my mother's house for most of October and November and was happy when they left for the Christmas break. I felt betrayed and bewildered. It didn't matter about the money. Two men had died. The death of Jacob was not our fault, but during the storm we could do nothing to save his beloved barn for fear of reprisal.

Simon and Barnes had been cowards not to remain to help with the carnage of the Friday night's storm and the whiskey they had hidden. The rumors had become the town's truth and there was no way to craft an explanation to save Jacob's reputation without them assisting me.

Several townspeople, of dubious character, had tried to make claims on Jacob's remaining property. They had claimed he had owed them money and I simply instructed my attorney to pay them off using the monies I received from Simon. I knew their claims were untrue, but Jacob's reputation would not prevent them prevailing in our town court. I still remember the charlatans to this day. They had attended my father's funeral in an effort to have a free meal.

I also feared that the land, originally my property, could end up owned by others. My attorney had looked out for me by filing a lien after the initial transfer that should Jacob precede me in death, the land would revert back to me. In a matter of a few weeks the land that I had gifted Jacob was now mine again. The Judge used his pulpit to denigrate Jacob as a charlatan and he was happy to return it to the Charles family.

I rented the house he had built to one of our farm workers for a pittance. It was charity, helping someone less fortunate, but it did not make me feel any better about Jacob's death. I had the remaining portion of his barn destroyed and trees planted to fill in the property.

I donated $1,000 to the church. My attorney managed the process and the funds were distributed as if Jacob had bequeathed the gift.

The church could not say enough nice things about Jacob when they received the money, though none of the congregation had showed for his burial. They built a new church hall and a small plaque commemorating the gift was placed in a back hallway, a walkway that would only be used in case of an emergency.

His reputation did not warrant a prominent place. The only person to see the sign on a regular basis was the janitor who found the back door a convenient shortcut to empty the trash. It was odd that it would have to take a fire for the commemorative sign to be acknowledged by fleeing parishioners whose focus would be on simply surviving. I heard many years later that the plaque had ended up in the basement in an old discarded cabinet. The newly-installed fire department chief had requested an emergency sign to be hung in that location. The church janitor did not want to have to hang another sign and simply replaced Jacob's commemorative plaque with the one provided by the fire department.

I actually made a sarcastic remark to the minister one hung over Sunday. My mother overheard the comment and glared at me as if I was a criminal. She apologized for my behavior, branding me a moral criminal, when in actuality it was the church that was the criminal, acting hypocritically in condemning him while taking money that had been given to them.

I was angry at my mother for weeks. I couldn't understand why she would apologize for my behavior when the congregation had simply disowned one of their fellow family members. It was a Methodist Church. It preached kindness and love, but it was filled with hypocrisy and downtrodden people who had disparaged a man who exemplified their supposedly core religious values.

Chapter XI

We managed to survive the remainder of our junior year. It was not the follies we had enjoyed, the county had seen to that. We drank in secret. We had to ration our drinking as our pipeline was a regular delivery from a connection Simon had in Long Island. The box would come from New York and it was marked as auto parts on the side of the box. Douglas, who had been promoted to station manager, was swayed by the promise of free football tickets in the fall to store the boxes for us upon their arrival. He was taking a risk but he felt that he was my friend.

Alcohol was expensive and not everybody could drink because of the cost. Fennimore was cheap and my attempts to have the fraternity pay for a supply for the final parties of the year was denied by his recommendation to the fraternity president.

The semester ended and the town quieted to a hush. The Franklin closed. In a matter of a few weeks it began to look run down and the owner tried to sell it with a feeble sign he hung on the door. The betting cards Simon had created for the *Huckster* had been more diligently prepared. It did not take long for him to realize that he had no chance to unload it without the opportunity to sell alcohol.

It was our final summer as college students. I did not feel solitude in my work. My mother was consumed with the marriage of my sister, who had been courted by the son of my attorney. Her fiancé, William, Jr., was a decent young man, straight-laced, and a year behind me in school. He was well liked and my aunt and uncle seemed to fawn over him at every family dinner and gathering.

The saving grace was that Simon had been invited to the wedding. I was going to introduce Beth to my family and Simon was bringing his fiancée, Rebecca Groton.

I continued to spar with my uncle after I fired the farm manager he had hired. The manager, who had questioned my work ethic, seemed to only spend time sharing his exploits with my uncle. The last straw was when he had characterized me as, "having shortfalls in effort."

It was the middle of August. It seemed to rain every day, but I was buoyed by the arrival of the train bringing Rebecca, Simon, and Beth. The three were meeting in Albany and taking the Presidential Car to town.

They arrived on the most spectacular day, it was warm and sunny and Simon's exit from the train was converted from graceful elegance to the *viculous* pose when in saw me. He had refreshments in tow. Rebecca was attractive, with brownish hair, and a soft narrow face.

She was a bit taller than Simon and was impeccably attired and seemed perturbed by the long trip to a small town.

When Beth emerged from the train, my breath was short. She was beautiful and wearing the purple dress I had seen her wear the first time I saw her from a distance. Her hair was free, Rebecca's hair was taut and short. Beth seemed poor compared to Rebecca and Simon. I was surprised I made the observation. Beth seemed overtly happy. Rebecca seemed shy and a bit confused by her surroundings.

Simon seemed different with Rebecca, less in control, more distant than he was in a small group. We were different couples but we quickly became inseparable. Simon's derby flask accompanied us on every dinner, river tour and my family's gatherings before the wedding.

Simon and Rebecca were on stage. I was comfortable quietly introducing Beth and was pleased that my mother seemed to approve of her. I didn't say much about the horses but talked about the farm that she worked at with her father. Beth's mother had passed away when she was young and it seemed like my mother knew there was a maturity in her beyond her years. My mother seemed happy when I told her we planned to marry after I graduated. My uncle seemed neutral. I don't think he disliked her, he simply disliked me. The wedding was a distraction from my talk of marriage to Beth and I don't think my uncle ever congratulated me.

The wedding was traditional, my sister was beautiful and the Methodist church was festive for once.

Jacob's and my father's funerals were the only occasions I had been sitting in the front row. My mother's garden club had outdone themselves, as the church was filled with freshly-cut flowers. Simon's donation had helped build a small greenhouse and I am not sure my Mother would have been so appreciative if she knew Simon had rigged the outcome of the demise of my car.

Simon called my mother's flower brigade, the *Plucksters.*

I had planned the reception party on the land in the narrows. The river background and the large trees were a perfect spot for the makeshift dance floor and people could walk to my mother's house for time to rest. My farm hands had built a large fire to cook fish and chicken and it was a simple country gathering in honor of my sister and William, Jr. It was not lost on me that the last fire I had seen destroyed Jacob's barn.

Simon and I disappeared often during the party. I walked away from the wedding. I could see the path, and the narrows afforded us a view of the place we had climbed the icy bank. It seemed peaceful, tranquil, not the robust joy of college kids on a carefree laughing journey. The river, the current swift but silent, seemed so odd in relation to our drunken voyage into Canada. Simon laughed as we arrived at the clearing, a view directly across from where the car seemed to rise with no problem. I remember my accelerating the car, all of us hoping we would make the climb and praying that we would make it.

Drinking seemed to remind me that it nullified my concern at the time.

"I wonder if Jacques died," Simon said, bluntly and our mood seemed quietly tempered. There was care in his voice but clearly no remorse.

"Derby flask?" I asked.

"What a grand idea, I wish I thought of it myself," Simon mused as the flask was already out of his coat. The silver flask caught the sun as it emerged from his pocket. It was like a silver fishing lure, enticing both of us for strong drink.

"What's next, Harry?"

"River Hotel. I assume Norman will secretly keep Rebecca and Beth in the dark," I replied, while preparing for a swig of whiskey.

"No, Harry, it's 1920, in just a few semesters it's over, and on to next steps, new hurdles. It went fast." His tone diminished in an expression of introspection. I don't know why but it seemed to jolt me, I really had not thought of a plan as plans seemed to fall in place for me, thrust by circumstances over which I had no control. They seemed random even though I thought I had control of my future.

I seemed defensive as I spoke, "Still time."

"You're late," Simon laughed but it resonated with me. I made sure the flask was empty before handing it to Simon, the horseshoe was pointing the wrong direction.

"Shame on you," Simon mocked as he grabbed the flask, turning it in the correct position. I assumed that he had been pointing out the error of the horseshoe's direction. I could not have been more wrong. I sensed he was perturbed that he had to refill the flask.

The wedding was increasingly festive. Simon readied the flask from a whiskey bottle he had hidden near the river, directly across from the point we had entered Canada during our winter exploits.

The afternoon was filled with laughter. There were some tears that my father was not there but my uncle played the role of the patriarch, giving my sister away and usurping my role as host.

My mother seemed happy as her flowers were her emotional support and she was surrounded by friends and family who knew that the pain of losing her husband would never subside, but for one day she could alleviate the empty space in her heart.

The river began to shimmer as the party ended. My sister had left an hour earlier, headed by train to Niagara Falls for her honeymoon. She would be surprised and telegraphed from the train that with the help of Douglas and Simon she was in the Presidential Car for the entire trip. Simon and Rebecca had made the honeymoon begin on a grand note and my mother was appreciative. Simon was family at that very moment.

My mother, exhausted by the day, was playing chaperone to Beth and Rebecca, a requirement of Mr. Day that would was to be respected. It was a favorable arrangement as Simon and I were at the River Hotel. The train was leaving at its punctual 8:45 am, the plan was to meet at the station. Rebecca seemed relieved to be out of the spotlight, but Beth seemed nervous for some reason.

It seemed I was being rushed to leave the field as my farm hands were removing the dance floor, flowers, and uneaten food. Beth seemed increasingly upset and my continual prodding, asking her what was bothering her, seemed to anger her more.

Rebecca and Simon seemed distant and I was a bit disappointed that we were not eating with my mother. Simon truncated that plan by indicating we were going to the hotel.

My uncle stopped me as we were leaving and motioned Simon to escort the ladies back to the house.

I tried to object, but he cut me off.

"You need to conduct yourself as a Charles," he dictated while grabbing my collar. I immediately thought of Pierre at the Franklin. I was not happy.

"Uncle, take your hands off me!" I was tired and I was having trouble pronouncing the words as I spoke with anger. I pushed him away.

"Harry, you are an embarrassment to our family," he yelled. I was concerned Beth could hear him as they were still visible but a fair way down the path.

My uncle grabbed me again. I pushed him back with uncontrolled force. He fell hard and was lying on his side. He stumbled getting up.

"Harry, how dare you," he spoke, knowing that he was no match for me. I stared at him and he knew immediately that I was not going to take any more badgering from him.

I helped him up, then turned and walked away. My uncle had been defeated. I would see him later that night, but for the moment I felt that I had stood up for myself.

Despite the confrontation, I arrived at my mother's house in high spirits to find Rebecca and Beth enjoying tea. Simon ushered me out and Beth's eyes seemed to plead for me to behave. In the mood I was in, I was to have none of that. I avoided her gaze.

When we arrived at the hotel, Simon mentioned several times that, "Pace makes the race." He laughed as he compared me to a horse that ran fast but did not win the race because he was tired. I *was* tired and simply wanted quiet. It had been a long day punctuated by my uncle's lack of control about me. I realized then how much he hated me and I despised him deeply for it. He was not my father. I never would have pushed my father away, never.

The hotel was quiet. *Perfect*, I thought. Norman procured our libations and for the three others at the bar, who sat stoically drinking sarsaparilla. It was dark and the spotlight illuminated the very spot that the *Huckster* had gone down. The owner had liked the way it looked and reminded people, despite no alcohol, that they had food and were open for conversation.

The hotel survived because of the rooms. Without those, he claimed, he would have shut down. That is what he said, but he served alcohol to those he could trust, including the town Justice and several who worked for my uncle. The mere fact that several prominent people drank, much to my delight, reinforced that my uncle was not well respected.

The Volstead Act was a death blow, a paper siren that taverns were to meet their demise. The Puritans were winning, the drinkers who enjoyed entertainment and amusement were being forced to change.

I was oblivious, but Simon seemed focused and pensive. He was anxious to get to Saratoga. Things would change quickly as the farm manager I had fired entered the bar.

"Harry, surprised you're not working?" he sarcastically muttered.

"It's Mr. Charles to you. Owning land has it's privileges. Find a job after I fired you?" I questioned, equally sarcastic. I held the highest card and he knew it.

"How dare you!" he bellowed.

I know why I hit him, I just did not know exactly what happened next.

He was evidently on the floor, bleeding, Simon ushered me out of the bar. He wasn't amused, but pulled me into the parking lot. I fought my leaving and his urgency was not my concern.

Our exit, delayed by my stubbornness, was not quick enough as we attempted to leave the parking lot. Officer Warner was intent on stopping us. It was the first time I heard his name as Simon showed initial respect pronouncing his name, including his title of deputy. He was meek, thin, and posed no threat to my uncle's dictatorial authority.

"Fights and drunkenness seem to follow you both around," he said, trying to resemble my uncle's delivery. It was a poor imitation.

"Drunkenness, yes, fighting no. Harry was defending himself," Simon retaliated in a serious tone.

My uncle arrived. He slammed the door and said we were under arrest as he approached the car.

"How about a head start? Penal laws are in our favor, Officer Dick," Simon shot back. He pulled no punches, using the slang for an officer of the law.

"Lucky Clara likes you Simon, because I don't." My uncle's matter-of-fact reply seemed to be begging a response from Simon. He ignored Simon's derogatory remark.

"Sir, from what I surmised, your selection for a farm manager failed to acknowledge that he is a rude, classless man, certainly not worthy of working for Harry," Simon defended me in a strong voice, which seemed to shove my uncle down a few cribbage pegs.

My uncle had the deputy detain us while he went inside to speak to Norman.

Minutes later, my exasperated uncle approached the car delivering his verdict.

"I can't arrest you for fighting, Norman has indicated that you were provoked. I can however, arrest you both for public drunkenness." He seemed happy as he spoke, but saddened that he could not arrest me on more serious charges.

"I am not drunk, and look Harry is now sleeping. He needs his rest for next season," Simon pointed out to distract my uncle as the car rolled backwards. He started the car and drove quickly around my uncle and the startled deputy.

"Bye!" Simon mocked, while producing the *Awwwooggaa* sound from the horn to send one more signal that he was beneath him and had no authority despite his shiny badge.

As usual, Simon had a plan. I broke into Jenks Hall as Simon stashed the car in the storage spot arranged by my father. We were fugitives, not criminals, but fugitives from the justice of my uncle. Simon produced a bottle from the storage closet that he had hidden prior to our leaving for the summer. Incredible, I thought, even as fugitives, he had prepared for an escape of fun.

We had candles, and kept in the room with the shades drawn, Simon walked outside to make sure the glow was not noticeable, and I drank heavily for the few minutes he was gone. We rambled in conversation, most gibberish. There was no content but it all sounded profound.

The only valuable part was our plan to leave. It was simple. We would drive to Watertown, stash the car at Fennimore's house, then meet Rebecca and Beth on the train. Sobriety was not necessary and we never went to sleep, as the excitement of the plan was our energy and our camaraderie that kept us awake. We left Jenks under the cover of darkness in the early morning, arrived at Fennimore's house and had him drive us to the station to join the train. Faf would pick us up on our return and we would be at campus in time for my first practice and the beginning of our senior year.

We joined the train, but there was no Rebecca, no Beth, no Presidential Car. We were a no show and our car was sold to another passenger. We were relegated to the worst car and it was a long trip as we both began to feel the effects of overindulgence. We sat most of the trip in the bar car, which only served food and no drinks.

When we arrived in Saratoga, Simon was anxious, somewhat nervous. This was a first for him. We arrived at the Adelphi, quickly relegated Albert to purchase clothes while we hid in the room. Simon was calling New York, while I called Beth at her home. No answer. My mother shared that they had left later that day and that my uncle was looking for Simon and I.

"No reason to worry, we're fine," was my casual response.

The bar, still opulent, had been turned into a makeshift room for breakfast and teas.

Simon connected with a cohort for a bottle of whiskey and after several drinks in the room shared that he had to meet a friend of his father's at the the race track the next day. He wanted me to come along, but he wanted me to appear that I was not with him.

"Why, I am not a runner?" I questioned.

"Well, we have a problem." He pulled a newspaper that he had grabbed on our way into the hotel. I assumed it was racing news, but I was wrong. In bold print, it read: *Black Sox Scandal Widens.*

"I have a considerable amount of money to give to a noted gambler and he is a man of questionable character, unsavory is the best word to describe him. I was a runner for the World Series last year, placing large bets on the outcome of the games," Simon told me. I could tell it had been rehearsed.

"Harry, it was fixed." He seemed hesitant as he spoke. Admitting trouble was not easy for Simon.

"I am trying not to be implicated and I simply need to pay Arnold the monies owed and then we need to leave town," he without bravado, just fear in his voice.

"Albert the hotel dick?" I thought it was funny, it was not.

"No, not Albert. If only it was Albert—that lummox I could handle. The guy I need to pay could easily turn me in and implicate me as a part of the plan. His name is Arnold Rothstein," Simon elaborated.

"Would you do me a favor?" he asked.

"Sure, what is it?" There was no question that I would help.

"I need to buy time. I will tell Arnold that you will fix the game we play in October against Yale. I indicated that we will work out the details later and it will make him keep me out of the scandal. You won't play, feign an injury a few weeks before, and then I will tell Arnold. I am giving him $5,000 more than I owe him. He will get to keep that and it should make him content enough not to include me. The money is a gesture of gratitude," he spoke as if it was a done deal.

Simon was my brother and I quickly agreed. He clearly needed my help. I was simply to sit at a far-away table and motion that I was going to help. If Arnold wanted to speak with me, I would simply recite what we had discussed.

We arrived at Saratoga Race Course with no fanfare. The place was packed, but Simon secured a table for me and was waiting for Arnold.

The fans were there once again to see *Man o' War*. We were there to pay a debt and had not really thought about or discussed the races. I was hoping Beth would be there. My attempts to reach her had been unsuccessful. There was no sign of Mr. Day and I simply blended in.

The races were fun to watch but there were no wagering schemes, no sure things except *Man o' War*, and no Simon to help with my big bets. I lost a considerable amount of money left to my own deciphering of the program and racing information. I tallied up my losses to a lack of strong whiskey.

Simon finally surfaced with a short, thin man dressed in a meticulous summer suit, floral tie. He was immaculate, and collected even in the summer warmth.

It immediately struck me: the 'A. R.' on the telegram, the baseball players in the clubhouse last year.

Simon was a part of this plan, which had taken months of preparation and execution, and I had better play my part.

Simon immediately introduced me, "Mr. Rothstein, this is Harry Charles, noted football player." I rose.

"It is an honor to meet you," I said, knowing that my job was to convince him. Arnold was shorter than Simon, but he was ominous in his mannerisms. I was immediately uncomfortable but played my role.

He was direct as he spoke, "Simon indicates you will help in October."

"Yes sir, Simon has my full cooperation and I will do what he asks, he is a brother to me," I recited.

"Good," he confirmed. Simon was off the hook. Both men smiled with somewhat devious looks, but I could tell that Simon's was of simple relief.

We left before *Man o' War* raced. My previous winning horse, *Upset,* was in the race, but we grabbed the first train and we headed back to campus to start our senior year. One problem was safely behind us now. Now, there was only my uncle to deal with.

Man o' War won easily and I would have lost more had we stayed to bet on *Upset.* I did lose a full moose as a side bet with Simon, he graciously let me off the hook for my assistance with Arnold.

We opted to not have Fennimore drive us, we took our chances and stayed on the train. We arrived in a driving rainstorm, it was cold and dreary. It was going to be a long walk back to Jenks.

As we exited the station, having just walked out onto Park Street, my uncle drove up to us.

"Seems like drunkards always end up wet," he scowled. He had no idea that it was the most profound thing he had ever said to me.

Simon mumbled, "No, bookmakers." We both laughed at the inside joke. My uncle was not amused.

Simon and I both seemed content to be arrested, if only to avoid the walk.

"Not a another word out of both of you," he directed. We silently agreed. No wit, no jokes, it was best to get this problem out of the way.

To our surprise, my uncle dropped Simon off at Jenks. He said that if he had more trouble from him he would insure that he would be in jail.

We returned to the square, headed for the police station and he drove past it. I knew where I was going and that I was under family arrest.

My voice cracked from exhaustion, "What is the meaning of this?"

"I am dropping you at your mother's house. I am telling you you need to stop drinking. Your bartender friend fabricated the story to protect you and I can't charge you at this point. I have hired the man you attacked to work for the town. He won't press charges and he is forgetting it all. Ignore him, avoid him, and no more fighting." He seemed somewhat supportive, but it seemed odd to me.

"This is it, Harry. Clara convinced me to give you another chance and I will but if you continue to drink, I will have you arrested." My uncle's authoritative voice reappeared.

"Fine, please just stay away from me." I spoke up but it did not resonate very well with my uncle. He shook his head in disgust. I immediately thought of my father. He would not have been stern. His voice would have spoken of hope, not anger, but simple support.

I hated my uncle.

Chapter XII

It was the first day of our last year and the excitement and joy of school beginning was an emotional conflict for our class.

The thought of the end seemed to create a more joyous celebration of each passing event.

Our decorating *Sally* for the holidays, pep rallies, dances, and arduous studying had become rituals. It seemed we were more serious, our ideas were thought provoking and arguments on who had won *Nickel Spin* during snow storms were peppered with eloquence and computed evidence.

Our first discussions at the Franklin flashed in my mind, the sheer bravado, failing to recognize we knew nothing about what we were saying. The only true statement was our prediction of the Volstead Act, which now gripped the country and made us criminals by our receiving whiskey from New York. I drank in secret and when we all drank I consumed more than anyone realized, including myself.

I stood at the pillars as I had done the day I was meeting Simon for the first time. I did not know what to think, I virtually only thought of the end. I seemed never to stop thinking about our graduation, of not seeing my friends until weddings and reunions. I looked over the vista to the changing leaves. One more fall, one more day to see the leaves fall from their branches. The departing leaves still had beauty. They seemed to fall and wherever they hit caused no harm. It was random, but the leaves seemed to float, to softly change direction, trying to land with a sense of purpose.

I seemed to be emotionally floating as well. I had responsibility for the farm, but was still insulated by the manager who was operating at a tidy profit. My sister was content in marriage, my mother growing older but consumed with her civic duties. I was alone on campus despite my house being just a few miles away. I was scared, not happy, gray inside, and it revolved around graduation and the return to my mundane existence in a small town.

I looked to my right. I thought of the the morning I walked down the steps to see Simon. The bells began to ring just as they had then. It was later in the day, but I thought of the fog, the Franklin, and our first day as roommates. I still can't fathom how many times I said "study area" to the dean. We had been the talk of upperclassman and now we were the ones scrutinizing the scared and nervous freshmen. It physically hurt to think about the end, but I always rationalized that it was the tackles I took during practice that made me feel that way.

The freshmen asked questions, excited at their new surroundings. I could not fathom how they handled the fear and anxiety I had felt and still felt.

"You owned the Titanic of cars?" It was a routine question, not my running records or broken collarbone that ruined the biggest game in the school's history.

Barnes was consumed with the baseball scandal, reveling every article he could get his hands on. He reported to Simon and I the happenings of the players whose reputations were being trashed by the press. There was no hack of a reporter to bail them out. Barnes had a picture of the ringleader, Rothstein, hanging on his wall. In a picture, Rothstein looked unthreatening. It did not resemble the man I met at Saratoga. I chalked it up to my hazy, fearful memory and a bad photograph.

The photo of Eddie Cicotte, the lone player to admit the scandal, seemed to be a villain to Barnes. I had seen Eddie at Saratoga and the pieces all fit that the players were smart to have fixed the games. The new commissioner of baseball had banned the players for life despite a trial that had exonerated them. Eddie's nickname was "Knuckles."

Simon always said he knuckled under the pressure, the gamblers had not. It was a character flaw, plain and simple. I never thought of who he was actually referring to, but his repeated comment always provoked a hearty laugh from Simon and Barnes.

It was odd. Despite the overwhelming evidence, there was an undercurrent of rationale by the players because the owner was cheap. Fennimore was cheap, and their dislike seemed appropriate. The Black Sox moniker was actually a reference to their jerseys and not the true scandal. The underpaid players had to pay to have their jerseys washed, something they opted not to do. They were all filthy. The country latched on to the story and most felt that they had betrayed a moral code of sportsmanship. I did not compare it to my forthcoming game where I was helping Simon. I was not going to play so there was no moral misgiving.

Barnes would receive a commendation from the president of the University on his social science paper, *Corruption and Greed on the Infield*. It was published in the campus paper and reprinted in the daily paper in New York.

The professor stated during the honors ceremony, "Mr. Barnes' thesis offered an insight that captured the spirit of corruption and the destruction of sportsmanship. It was as if Mr. Barnes had viewed the games from the dugout or outfield."

Barnes received a check for $100 for the publishing of his paper. Only Barnes, Simon, and I knew the truth about assisting in the fix. Barnes received a scholarship to attend Harvard after graduation to continue his education in writing. It was amazing—Barnes had gambled, won, and players had been banned. Their reputations were ruined and he was going to Harvard in the fall of 1921 for free.

It was typical Barnes. Every so often, he held his hands in the air, speaking mythically, "These hands that saved lives in an icy crash and raised the bar with literary excellence."

The line always provoked laughter, even to those who did not know the actual truth of our drunken car crash. We had raised the bar alright. Fennimore gave Barnes the Harvard sweater as a gift upon his acceptance. I did not know what to think but Faf bothered me by being so clueless and thinking otherwise. Fennimore, being the cheapskate that he was, did not realize a gift of a used sweater was an insult.

It was two weeks before the Yale game and Simon pressed me to feign an injury, "Do it sooner than later. This can't fail," was a common comment every afternoon as I left for practice.

We were playing our cross-town rivals and I had misgivings about missing the game, but they were far different from the game I had missed due to the violent storm and Jacob's death.

Whiskey came every two weeks. the last few days before the shipment we tried to ration as we were always running low. Everyone seemed less involved as the semester went on, I still relished the opportunity and Simon and I would disappear into heavy drunkenness several times a month. I avoided going into town and we sometimes drove to Watertown to avoid the scrutiny of my uncle.

Douglas knew the auto parts shipments were illegal contraband, but free tickets and access to the news of the sidelines kept him quiet. He was gambling his job and knew that we had a great deal to lose as well. His promotion to station manager had insured us we would have no problems.

The last game in September was a huge win for us. I had run circles around our rivals. Douglas was euphoric that I had evened the score against our arch rivals.

"We would have won last year if not for the death of your worker," Douglas would repeat every time we would pick up the auto parts.

His comment would become annoying, but he was our easy link to alcohol. I always mumbled that I had wished we had lost just to shut him up.

The week leading up to the game, I began to feign a leg injury. I was coached by Doctor Sheldon and fed the lines to Coach Kinnon as if I was the hack of a reporter describing the sinking of the *Huckster*. I played the part and was excused from practice on Wednesday.

The coach would visit my room on Thursday where Simon had instructed me to be in bed. Coach Kinnon was not happy to say the least, but I followed the script. Simon was on the phone with Arnold several times on Thursday morning and assured him that I would not be playing.

It was raining badly on Thursday afternoon when the hall phone rang. It was Douglas.

"Your box broke open, I have to call the police," Douglas fearfully shared. "I can't lose my job, my reputation," he yammered.

"Douglas, give me ten minutes, I will come and remove the box," I yelled into the phone. The car was in storage, Simon was at class. I had to run.

I left Jenks and sprinted toward the the county road. Despite the rain I was in full stride and was at the train station in time to retrieve the box. Douglas was relieved. I, however, was greeted by Coach Kinnon at the entrance to the campus holding a taped-up box concealing illegal whiskey.

"Thank god, you're feeling better," He seemed distrustful. It seemed to me to be more a question than a comment.

"I felt the need to test my leg. It's fine," I lied and the rain hid the concern on my face. The coach drove me and our beloved whiskey back to the campus. Douglas was relieved.

"Hope your car is alright." Coach Kinnon looked at me sternly, fatherly. He knew something was not right, but seemed to have no interest in finding out. He looked the other way as he had no interest in losing to our rivals, deprived of his star running back.

I had made a serious mistake and was now forced to play. I would not practice on Friday spending the entire day being berated by Simon's sarcasm and anger.

"Was the whiskey worth what could happen to us?" he mocked.

"This is going to be one bad hangover." He somewhat backed off his anger as he spoke later in the day. Simon had an alternate plan. He called New York and stammered his sentences into a way out.

Friday morning arrived. Simon was drunk and had not slept the entire night.

"Harry, these are bad people, not the type to double cross." Simon was lucid as he talked, his adrenaline made him speak with clarity.

"They expected you not to play. The money has been bet and you agreed to this in Saratoga." He was pointed but resolved as he spoke.

"You're involved, and if they lose we will be visited by Rothstein's associates. These visitors won't be here for a campus tour." He was stern as he spoke evoking fear in my thoughts.

"What about the $5,000 you gave him?" I asked.

"That is a fraction of what they will lose. We will be in trouble, serious trouble." Simon spoke with a soft, ominous tone.

His response jarred me.

"But I have to play. I would be finished with Coach Kinnon and everyone would know something is wrong, especially if the fix becomes public knowledge. My reputation would be ruined!" I was defensive as I spoke but knew I was on shaky ground. Oddly, I thought of Jacob, the lumberjack Croteau, and Douglas's comment on the phone.

Simon was blunt as he laid out the plan. This, too, seemed rehearsed, unlike the calls he made to New York.

Methodically, he spoke in a low tone. "The syndicate bet Yale to cover by six points, our team can't win by more than five points." He seemed relieved as he finished.

"That's it?" I questioned, thinking the result would be easy to obtain.

"Harry, don't be a fool. If things get out of hand, you might not be in the position to control the outcome. This is not a stacked deck where you can deal from anywhere." Simon revealed his *Bone-Ace* skills as he spoke.

"Simon, I can run into the line, I can fumble a few times. I will keep the score close." My ease of speaking seemed to calm Simon down.

"So you cheated in *Bone-Ace*?" I laughingly questioned.

"It wasn't random who won, let's look at it like that. Stay focused, Saturday will be a difficult day." Simon now was back in control.

"I will assure Rothstein that we will not cover the points, or lose. Just a pep rally and fixed drama to be off the hook," Simon said resolutely.

Saturday could not have come any sooner. Simon made quick work of the crate stored across the hall and was consuming early in the morning. He offered me a glass. I wasn't sure if he wanted me to be in no condition to play or to just calm my nerves.

"That's for later. We will celebrate losing a big, fat, sturgeon Rothstein off the hook!" I laughed.

Simon was not amused.

It was a beautiful day, stunningly bright for October the trees still adorned with a majority of their leaves, copper in color and not a wisp of wind in the air. The sound of the band was crystal clear as we ran onto the field. The stands were packed and cheering in anticipation of a big blow-out win, unaware that the game would begin with a fumble and a Yale score.

The game started at one o'clock. By five minutes after one, Yale was leading 6-0. My fumble looked legitimate as I ran into the Yale line with the greatest of speed and force. I glanced at Simon, he was relieved and smiling. It seemed ironic Fennimore had our team's sweater on. The fix was in and he knew nothing, as always.

The game was half over and Yale was throwing the ball, something we could defend but Coach Kinnon was a purist and felt it was not football.

Yale was leading 20-6. I had scored the lone touchdown and I was still confident we could win and the syndicate would win as well.

There were fourteen minutes left. Yale had kicked a field goal and scored after our quarterback fumbled. We were losing 28-6. I had read that Walter Camp from Yale had created the scoring rules in 1889. Little did he know I was calculating what had to be done to win twice. People were leaving the stands, disgusted by our team's effort.

Coach Kinnon grabbed me. "Son, this is about character, this is about doing the best you can in the face of adversity, this is a test of who you are and who you can become." He didn't yell, he spoke with command as if he was my father.

I said nothing. I told my teammates to start moving to the right on every run. Several plays were just a pile of bodies. I then ran right on the third play and I ran the length of the field. We were closer, just 28-12. Yale fumbled on their next possession, I made easy work of the short field and again ran right into the end zone. It was less than nine minutes to go, we were trailing 28-18.

Our defense had come alive. We received the ball back on the 40-yard line of Yale. I ran right again, scoring with no one in pursuit. We were losing but we had time to win. It was 28-24.

Yale tried to throw the ball with no success. They fumbled again on their side of the field. In one run, we were leading and I had scored five touchdowns. There was less than five minutes to go and we were leading by two points. Perfect I thought, now I can simply run into the line and then whiskey to be drank.

Yale tried to score. They were at our 16-yard line and could not convert, the ball was ours. Our defense had been emboldened by our scoring and with less than a minute and a half, Coach Kinnon simply said hold the ball and be careful and run the clock out. It was 30-28. Simon seemed nervous on the sidelines, I would be getting the ball.

The first two plays I simply ran right, Yale had figured my best side and seemed to collapse on that side every time. The Yale sideline, to my left were dejected.

The Coach was pacing. This game was one for the ages, I thought.

It was the last play of the game. I was handed the ball, moved right as the entire Yale team converged and I tripped. It was surreal, as if it was the last step of the walkway where I had broken my collarbone. I knew what to do this time to correct myself and in an instant, I was running left and passed the line with absolutely no one chasing me. The entire Yale team was on the ground and I was 60 yards from a sixth touchdown and absolute peril. It was utter slow motion. I could see Simon frozen, I could not hear any sound. I saw Barnes' pictures of Rothstein, Cicotte. I was 40 yards from the end zone and saw the Yale Coach to my left. He was dejected. *Thank God*, I thought.

I suddenly stopped. I turned, walked out of bounds, removed my leather helmet and handed him the ball.

"This was an epic game that needs to reflect a score worthy of the battle it was. Thank you for a great game." My words were a lie, staying in bounds was what I had been taught by my father.

The sound returned to my body and instead of a roar of approval there was now confused silence.

I had no idea what to think. The Coach reached out his hand and shook my hand, with a smile on his face.

He softly said, "You are a sportsman and it was an honor to watch you run, well done young man. I am proud of you." Instantly, he sounded like my father.

The fans could not hear what he said or I had said, the sound from the stands was an applause that seemed to build as our team celebrated the win.

The fans were stamping their feet and those in the first few rows ran onto the field as the game had ended. The applause seemed to resonate with a feeling of pride as people took what had happened as a sign of courage, character, to not to have scored a sixth touchdown.

Arnold had won, Simon was off the hook and I was heralded as a gentleman of character. Coach Kinnon hugged me and said, "That was honor my son. Taking advantage of a blunder when the game was over is true character."

The front page of the paper called it an epic comeback, with the headlines reading, *Charles Scores Five Touchdowns in Greatest Win!* The second line in smaller print was, *He Demonstrated Character Worthy of The Charles Family.*

Every paper across the country published the ending, I received an article from California with the headline, *College Athlete Gives Up Record to Honor Yale.* It turns out my sixth touchdown would have been a national record.

My uncle sent me a telegram. He could have called but knew I would not have spoken with him. He stated I had showed the Charles's character, he had taken it from the front page of the paper. I could only think that he was encouraged to send it by Aunt Clara, or perhaps trying to right the wrong of my uncle, she sent it herself.

I was summoned to the president's office as instructed to by Coach Kinnon.

"Mr. Charles, I want to personally thank you and congratulate you on your conduct and selfless courage to forgo another touchdown to illustrate that sportsmanship is at the core of college sports," he pontificated, but it was a great deal better than how the dean had treated me when I first arrived on campus.

I didn't see Simon until I was back at Jenks. He smiled, signaled victory and turned it sideways as he made me a double from the bar. The deluge of visitors would finish the box of auto parts before midnight. Two thousand dollars showed up later that week in an envelope to Simon. He gave me $1,000 and an extra hundred.

"Your character earned it," was his only comment. I laughed, he smirked. It was his approval for our friendship, my repaying loyalty.

Part Three

Chapter XIII

It was our quintessential party, our 1920 Christmas dance. The end of an era. The end of our biggest parties. The fraternity had planned all the arrangements with the best decorations crafted by the undergraduates, festive garland on all the mantels, and as usual the irritating display of concern about money by Fennimore. Simon and I were given the highest honor to cut down the Christmas tree. Walt tagged along to help.

Simon secured auto parts to be delivered in two shipments. We never noticed the Farmer's Almanac said, "A storm's a brewing."

Simon and I drove to the clearing, the site of my sister's wedding, and cut trees to accentuate *Sally the Sturgeon* in the dining room. We drank while we cut, we drank on the way back to the fraternity. I was greeted at the door by Appleton.

"It's snowing, bad." he muttered with concern on his face.

"What are you talking about, it's just a dusting, festive isn't it?" I smirked.

"Harry, I just spoke to my mother. It's a blizzard south of here and it looks like it won't let up. The railroad is closed in Albany." Appleton was exasperated as the

Sergeant of Arms was responsible for clearing the walkways and general safety around the fraternity.

Our efforts to contact both Rebecca and Beth were stymied by the phones which had gone dead.

The dependable train, the *Creeper* crept to a halt as the state was gripped by a blizzard. We sat dejected in our room. The straps that hung on the wall, that once stabilized my broken collarbone were a subtle reminder that our time on campus would soon come to an end.

It seemed odd that a flip of a calendar page would signal our final few months. The straps that had eased my pain, whose date seemed unimaginable when we arrived, were now tattered strips of cloth whose time had passed. I thought of how long ago it seemed when we stole wood, the straps once hidden under a teepee hut, out of view from the dean, and which were to become relics, souvenirs that had little worth but had provided comfort from my errant step.

We tried to make the most out of our sparsely-attended Christmas soiree. We were a joyful lot by midnight and without our dates we simply drank. I made fun of Fennimore all night.

Fennimore's girl had taken the train earlier in the day from Watertown. Ironically, her name was Sally but she went by her middle name, Fannie, and from afar she looked like a sturgeon, pale, and her proportions did not yield a very attractive woman. Her hair was in a tight bun, unflattering and dowdy. Luckily, Fennimore had filled her dance card with himself as the majority and a few lower classmen to make sure her card was full.

Barnes would mock, "Dear God, nobody give me a pencil with an eraser!"

The storm was a contradiction in colors at night, the horizon black, the snow highlighted by the lights seemed to fall in gusty swirls, but the ground was uniform, perfect, a bright white with only a smattering of shadows created by little flakes. The ground was crisp and orderly. It made me feel hollow, it made me introspective. It was not what I had anticipated for the evening that once was full of anticipation and excitement. I reminded myself that I had taken a bottle of whiskey from the pantry and stashed it in our hidden lair across the hall. I was prepared to survive the early morning fears of loneliness. I had planned like Simon.

Beth and I had planned to make arrangements for our wedding on August 26, 1921. With the phones dead, I imagined and filled in the details to what was going to be a wonderful day. My verbal invitations to my brothers were a topic and several worried if they would make the grade. I don't remember who I invited and really had no concern.

Appleton lost another 'S' from a sweater his mother had sent him. He vowed that he would solve the mystery and put to rest his suspicions of everyone that had started the drunken night Simon had introduced the class song at the Franklin.

We all knew it was Barnes, but the delight in his anguish was too much to spill the beans. We all feigned ignorance, we all cherished the joke.

Most of the campus stayed still, venturing out might mean not getting back to the dorms and it simply left us to our own devices, drinking.

A few town folks, in search of excitement, joined the festivities. They stayed only long enough for Fennimore to shoo them away with the advisement, "private party, sorry."

He was not sorry and failed to see that there was no harm. It was all about the cost of food and drinks and not human kindness. He seemed to lack empathy, just the opposite of Simon.

Fennimore began to assert that we were a bottle of whiskey short.

I drunkenly blurted, "You're lucky it's gone. I would have smashed it over your stingy little head, right in front of your sturgeon of a girlfriend."

Fennimore was not amused and instructed Appleton to initially detain me as the Sergeant in Arms. Appleton was hardly a match for me and I immediately found it funny. I then pushed Appleton, and said my goodbyes in a hostile gesture.

"Transitional, it's simply transitional," I philosophically mumbled. I had never thought of it until that very instant, but it seemed to resonate with me.

The snow continued to accumulate. Easily three feet had fallen and it was as high as the fraternity windows as I left. Simon followed me as we traversed the campus back to Jenks.

I imagined I was still a football star, burrowing into the snow like it was the defensive line of Yale. The snow was no match and Simon just followed in my footsteps, like two explorers looking for refuge. I was looking for a glass of paradise.

I swung to the entrance, ahead of Simon. I stopped and looked at the cattails submerged in the snow. The faint outlines allowed only the top parts to show, the brownish tips were perfectly vertical and had not succumbed to the mounting pressure of the snow. They stood guard to the frozen pond.

I thought of falling into a hole in the ice, not like the languishing *Huckster*, but falling to be entombed until spring, perhaps not to be found until the summer when the campus was empty. A groundskeeper, cutting grass would discover me and my uncle would be the first to arrive, just as Jacob had discovered my father, a gruesome sight worthy of a Charles. No betting board, just quickly falling to my demise.

Despite the now waist-high snow, we made it quickly, a bit frozen, but no worse for the wear. We changed into dry clothes.

"What an embarrassment, that party," I said.

I never really heard what Simon said as I fell asleep.

"Harry, it was embarrassing, you need . . ." Simon's voice had trailed off.

I awoke before daybreak. Simon was gone and I instantly remembered the bottle, my savior was hidden across hall behind the bar.

I stumbled a bit, grabbed a lantern and crossed the hall to find the door ajar. The bar was moved and my bottle was gone. A note was on top of the bar. The last of the whiskey within 300 miles had been taken.

It was a note by Simon: *Appleton's room—don't be late.*

I quickly walked down the hall turned to the adjacent wing and saw Appleton's light on.

"Harry, you're late," Simon said in his customary sarcastic way.

I was still drunk. I mumbled the words, "How's about a drink?"

Robinson, sitting in the study chair near the corner spoke for the group in a dictatorial manner, "You need to slow down."

"Yea, Simon, cool it, leave some for the real drinkers," I laughed, but the room was oddly silent.

Robinson, the president of our fraternity, was stoic as he admonished me. "Harry, this is an actionable offense by the fraternity. You stole this whiskey."

Defensively, I interjected, "I delivered the whiskey and many times paid for it because the fraternity would not. It's hardly stealing if it's my own hooch. Besides, Fennimore is the stingy thief, stealing fun." I began to realize that drinking was not the intent of my requested visit.

Barnes was quiet, sitting on the opposite bed. He said seriously, "Simon, you win a full moose. You were right, he would arrive before dawn."

Barnes hated to lose and always played it safe when he gambled.

"Hey, half moose to me," I laughed as my quip was perfectly timed. But Simon, Barnes, Green, Appleton, and Robinson were not laughing.

Robinson stood up as if he was my elder, and spoke loudly, "You will be sanctioned for this offense. Sixty-days suspension from the fraternity events, functions, meals, and meetings."

I didn't like what I had heard. I was confused why my friends had not supported me. I slammed the door and went back to bed. Robinson occupied the President's Suite at the fraternity. Obviously, his title had gone to his head. His suspending me would save me a stamp for the invitation I had planned to send him for my wedding. I would not ring in the new year with my friends. I was banned.

Several days later I received a letter from the fraternity stating that due to my transgressions against my brothers I was barred from the fraternity until March 1st. I saw Simon and remarked that I was *bar-ed* for drinking my own whiskey. I called Beth and told her to remove Robinson from the invitation list.

Simon seemed distant. He was not a fraternity rat and he seemed to take no sides. He shared that he did not agree to the penalty, but the words of support seemed short of supporting me.

"Harry, just slow down," was his constant reminder.

Whiskey was in short supply. The semester rambled on and I began to fall into a fog that we would be graduating. My suspension was lifted but I spent little time at the fraternity and avoided Robinson. I simply hid the whole spring, focused on studying, and the self-inflicted hangovers using the copper key made the last few days palatable.

It was the day before graduation, I stood next to the pillars, the adjacent area was being prepared, readied with chairs, and podiums for the final day. It was a day of brilliant sunshine, only a few puffy clouds, and all I could see was the day Simon arrived.

Puffs of steam, fighting the early morning storms, a telegram in my pocket, fear, shallow breaths of concern and anxiety seemed to engulf me. It had been four years of jocularity, bootlegging, fights, touchdowns, and the deaths of Jacob, Croteau, and my beloved father. All three did not make sense.

Simon's words to me at my sister's wedding, saying that I had no plan, came back to me. My fellow friends and classmates seemed destined for positive futures and in a day the trains would take them back to their new lives. My saving grace seemed to be that I would see my closest friends again in just a few months. It was the only thing that seemed to make the next day possible for me. I did not want to say goodbye.

Each year when the trains departed for the summer, I knew they would be back, but I just could not understand why it was transitional. Why the constant angst? Why was this a part of life? Why was it unanswerable in my mind?

I could not stay. I was not headed to New York, I was headed to hide on my father's island. I walked down the steps as I had done so many times, not taking the time to look back. I paused at the last step, the step where I had broken my collarbone. I leaned over and picked up a small rock. I was graduating, something my uncle, my father, and my mother had not accomplished and I did not want to see my uncle, aunt, sister, and the throngs of parents and dignitaries who would comprise the audience.

I retrieved my car, used the copper key, and rowed majestically across the river. It was calm, no wind, and my oars seemed to glide effortlessly, as if this was a destiny for me, a place no one would find me. I doubted anybody would look and was certain no one would care.

I rowed back two days later, somewhat at peace. The last train was leaving, my timing was calculated and lucky, I thought.

I drove through town, and circled the empty campus. I was fragile but all I could imagine was a fall day, orange leaves comforting my feet, the football stands filled, the *Huckster* making the *Awwwooggaa* sound.

It's rhythm, cadence, was repetitively completed by Simon as if he was leading a finely-tuned orchestra to insure the greatest attraction. It was one sound and it seemed just right. The camaraderie, the sense of a true family was now gone. Returning to Jenks was a walk I will never forget.

The door softly closed and the echo seemed to linger. Everyone was gone. My footsteps seemed to create the frenetic pace of us getting to class on time. I closed my eyes and for a moment it felt like the halls and vestibule were full. I peered into the center room. Chairs were covered, the room was cleaned, and I could hear Fennimore complaining about the results of a *Nickel Spin* contest.

I stopped at each corner of the stairs. The worn woodwork now was etched with the exuberance of our class, and I was now faced with the mundane task of running the farm.

It seemed I had inherited a future, I didn't need plans. My destiny I could not change. I was now just Harry Charles, farmer.

I pushed the door of our room open. I thought for a second Simon might be holding court and making drinks.

Everything was gone, our bar, the straps, my clothes. It was just as if I had just arrived, only four years later. I walked to my bed, which had just a mattress and uncovered pillow. I laid down and closed my eyes.

In my mind I could hear the dean knocking and whispering. I still don't remember where we gathered the fencing, no one from town had ever complained.

"Mr. Charles, open the door," he had commanded, asking about the mess of our first night at the Franklin.

I was retrieving memories faster than I could handle—the pants on the bar, a successful experiment with salt. It physically hurt, even when I laughed, recollecting a singular moment, a flash of my repeating "study area" to the dean.

Why was it over? I had not said goodbye. For just an instant it felt like I was not in transition. I had not graduated emotionally, I was deeply sad. As I turned to my side, I glanced and saw a bulging envelope under Simon's bed. My hands shook as if I was struggling with a hangover. On the outside it said, "For Harry."

Dear God, just like the envelope my father had left Jacob to give to me, I thought.

It was his derby flask. I felt the horseshoe and laughed at how Barnes had been taken by Norman under the tutelage of Simon. I turned it over. Simon had engraved three words on the flask: *Credo in Veritas.*

It was Latin for 'Believe in Faith'—the first class Simon and I had skipped while playing cards with the Canadians. I glanced out the window at the cattails guarding the pond, I turned and left Jenks.

I could not imagine that I would ever return. I would think of the pond often.

Chapter XIV

It was hard to think. My mind drifted for what seemed like an eternity. It was a mere 10 weeks and Simon would be returning by train to escort me to my wedding in Ballston Spa.

I missed my friends, my daily life of interaction with people I respected. I had yet to accept that I would was now alone in my town, without the camaraderie and excitement of being a college student. Every trip to the feed store, every time my car flirted with the edge of campus, I would close my eyes to protect myself from memories that evoked sadness, memories that should have evoked happiness but that were now painful.

My spirits were buoyed by my daily conversations with Beth. Our plans were in place, her father was working on the farm to accommodate guests with dancing and frivolity. My mother wanted flowers. I wanted to exclude my uncle, but was overruled by her threat that she would not attend. We were having flowers, my uncle would be a guest as well.

Simon was coming the Wednesday before the Saturday wedding. Rebecca, Beth's maid of honor, was meeting Beth to help with her arrangements and dress. Simon was my best man. It was perfect.

But I continued to feel hollow, perplexed that my daily routine seemed so meaningless, mundane. I had studied principles, ideas, Latin, philosophy, and I was carrying bags of seeds and feed while directing my underlings to complete tasks that for them were a challenge. I could not speak about what I had learned because they could not understand me, as if a two- and three-syllable word was a distraction from their work.

I was, for all intents and purposes, a farmer. I thought of my classmates heading to other schools, jobs where they would feel accomplishments. Barnes was heading to a career in writing, Fennimore had taken a job at a bank in Watertown. Appleton was a teacher. Everyone was now deciding where their life would go. I watched corn being picked and fretted if I had planted too early for the fear of frost. I suffered as pigs if being slaughtered was not the lowest point of my day.

I sought refuge at the River Hotel. There was little alcohol available and Norman was relegated to cleaning and cooking. A man of his ability, my future boat navigator, was subjected to the rigors of hospitality in the kitchen and cleaning rooms for tourists with little regard for cleanliness.

He was able to secure whiskey, however. It was not much, but it sustained me for the four weeks before Simon shipped auto parts in advance of his visit. The letter inside the crate said: *Behave yourself.*

Time seemed to move faster and Norman and I were the only people in the tavern having any inkling of fun.

Beth called a week before the wedding date. I was excited to see my friends again and her wedding count included Fennimore and his girl.

"What? Fennimore's is coming? I thought we discussed this and I did not want him at the wedding," I sternly admonished her. I leaned closer to the circular speaker box to intensify my angst.

The sound crackled as she spoke, "Simon called me and I thought you knew?" she defended with the same intensity. She was strong, I loved that about her.

"I am not happy. What is his girlfriend's name again?"

"Fannie," Beth giggled as she said it. *Sounds just about right*, I thought. We laughed in unison as we both were in sync about his guest.

It was Sunday, just a few days until we would leave for Ballston Spa. Norman requested my attendance at the hotel very early. I had no qualms as he had been cautious about how much of the whiskey we should drink until Simon's visit.

When I arrived at the hotel, a shimmering new car was in the parking lot. A new 1921 Pierce Arrow. It was superior to my car, polished to perfection, simply out of place for the hotel as most tourists came by train. The car had a simple ornament, a wheel with an arrow through it. The days of his ostentatious jockey were gone. This was an elegance unseen at the River Hotel. It flashed in my mind that I was now looking through the porthole windows at the Franklin. I looked for Simon and he was here, and I was certain he would point out I was late.

I walked into the hotel tavern, Simon had indeed arrived, clad in his gambling jacket. He was early. His hair was a bit longer and he seemed older. I didn't need to relive the morning at the Franklin. I knew what was next.

"Harry, you're late!" he sternly proffered.

Norman laughed, and quickly reached under the bar to freshen Simon's drink and pour me my usual stiff whiskey with ice. Norman did not make Manhattans. It was whiskey, nonetheless, hidden so the owner would avoid trouble and still prosper despite the laws governing our happy, illegal behavior.

"You are early!" I laughed.

"I have no telegram to evaluate your true arrival time compared to your actual arrival time," I said and realized that I sounded like the science class Simon and I had suffered through our freshman year.

"Well, Professor Sheldon, somebody took notes!" Simon laughed. He was right. I had taken notes, which he absconded with near test time. Simon had missed a fair amount of classes, but he seemed to dig down when things were difficult.

We drank for a few hours, Simon updating me on a few classmates new jobs and where they were living. Simon looked at his watch rhythmically, Norman was content and happy to be among friends. There was no ruse, no false grumpy behavior, money was plentiful as always.

"We are going where?" I asked as Simon had spoken directly to Norman.

"Canada," Simon critically answered.

"You must be joking. Swimming across the channel? I am no *Huckster*!" I laughed.

I realized then that he was serious. "I am not swimming," I sarcastically blurted out to see if it was really true.

"Norman will be our navigator, our friend, and pilot. It is time we sent this boy off to married life and the owner has given you a paid afternoon," Simon shared.

"Horseshoe is up! My luck is saved!" Norman paid homage to Simon's greatest con on Barnes.

I was numb with excitement. It felt like going to New York. I would be leaving town and again in an element that I now felt worthy.

Norman was stunned at the opulence of Simon's car. I now was simply the Franklin, Simon was the Astoria. Simon had the biggest toy.

"It is time he had a ride over Queen Victoria!" Simon shouted. Rarely did Simon raise his voice, but a mixture of the sexual tone and his consumption made it a timely delivery. Clearly, Simon was excited as well.

"Exotic dancer?" Norman quizzed.

"She is beautiful, she can rumble, and she is a very fun ride," Simon continued in his provocative tone.

"We're heading east along the river. It's a bit of a ride but she is worth it, boy is she built," Simon informed our dumbfounded expressions.

"She is the just-completed Queen Victoria Bridge," Simon concluded his tawdry joke with a smirk.

We drove through town and passed the college. Simon gazed at it with deep thought, I glanced away. It was a brilliant summer day, and in a few minutes we were deep into the countryside watching the river widen, our distance still close enough to view the islands. Once again I was reminded of the day we crossed by ice, the day that a man drowned trying to go yards, not miles, to return to Canada.

We were taking the safe trip, without any concerns, and it was just what Doc Sheldon ordered—opulence, and a time to be with friends.

It was a mirage of simplicity. My friend Norman, sober, and handling the lengthy drive as a friend, navigator, and protector.

We bumped along, then rain, driving rain slowed our progress as Norman navigated us closer to the river. The Queen Victoria Bridge was in sight. The errant storm had now cleared and the bridge glistened. I felt scared as if it was the storm that had taken me to the Canadian shore, my father battling currents to reach me. I was with friends, but I had fear, fear that only my father could cure.

Norman rumbled over the bridge. I realized I had never seen the river from above. Even the trees I would climb as a child did not come close to the height of the bridge.

We turned to travel west. I had lost my bearings. We had traversed bad roads, a horrific squall, and now I had no idea where we were heading. The river disappeared, my concerns nullified by our depleting bottle of whiskey.

We had crossed into the dense forests of Canada. I thought of the moose my grandfather and father had once chased across the frozen river. A moose could cross to our country in less than a few hundred strides, a half moose at a time. Our previous foray during college was the path of a moose. We saved time. Had we hit a larger hole in the bay that day, we would not be traveling now, days before the biggest day of my life. We had opted for safety and a four-hour drive.

We continued to drive in solid forests. The river was again gone, my familiarity had stopped, though my fear continued. The river was our compass, now lost again, our whiskey was gone as Simon completed the last sips.

The wind seemed colder, the light diminished in intensity. I was lost, lost without our whiskey savior, lost and sadly drunk with confusion.

"Well, we need to find whiskey," Simon announced. Barnes would have been amused.

We rounded a corner and there it was . . . the Evergreen.

"Well, isn't that lucky," Simon laughed. Norman had done a perfect job.

I could barely comprehend what I was seeing, a memory of our time in school. Our pledge pins had been lures of trouble, my Franklin combatant, Jacques ultimately becoming our friend, our bootlegging partner.

The Evergreen was surrounded by cars, no horses, time had made them obsolete, Even so, Simon's car was out of place.

"Why?" I spoke with angst. "Simon, dear God what are we doing here?" I spoke loud enough to drown out his laughter. *Drown.* We had never known who else might have drowned during our short bootlegging operation.

"I wanted to see the bobcat." Simon was not sarcastic when he spoke, but he knew what I was about to say by the smirk on his face.

"Lynx, it's a lynx," I retorted and our minds turned to getting strong drink.

We reached the door. The horseshoe was still positioned wrong, it's luck long extinguished. I opened the door and froze. To my left was a plaque, hung with great care in the most prominent spot. Unlike Jacob's plaque, it paid homage. It was framed and the copper screws had been meticulously placed around the frame in perfect symmetry. It had been hung with care.

Simon began to read, "To our dear friend, Jean Pierre Croteau, whose courage and friendship will be missed by all who loved you."

"Harry, I did some research in New York, it was Pierre who died," he gently shared.

"I thought it was a lumberjack?" I questioned in a state of confusion.

"We thought he was saying *LaGrow*, he was actually saying *Croteau*."

I thought of the first meeting, Pierre animated over his card losses and Simon taunting him with the horse's name while predicting the next card in the deck.

LaGrow, let's get that stack to LaGrow was what popped into my head, and now, I had found out he was dead.

Simon led the way, confidently entering the sparsely-occupied bar. The stuffed animals seemed to focus on us as the patrons seemed undisturbed by our entrance. We had aged since our first visit. We were now adults, we were not noticeable.

"Simon," was yelled from our original drinking lair. It was Vanier, card nemesis, bootlegger, and he knew we were coming. Simon had been checking his watch at the River Hotel. This was a plan that included meeting Jacques.

"Thank you coming to visit me," Vanier said while shaking Simon's hand. Reaching out to me, as I shook hands with him I said, "Jacques, this is our good friend Norman. He works at the River Hotel."

Norman shook hands and it seemed like Alban's familiarity with my rushing record., It looked as if Jacques knew who he was.

"We are sorry, I liked Pierre," Simon spoke for the group in a gracious and respectful tone. Jacques signaled for the bartender with the identical wave that Simon's bravado had shown at the Franklin.

Simon pulled an envelope from his pocket. It was as thick as French toast.

"This is for his widow. If we had known the peril of moving it in the fall, if we had known what would happen . . .," Simon stopped, reassured by the intense emotion of Jacques' face that what he had said was enough.

Jacques put his hand on Simon's shoulder. "Thank you" was spoken through tears trickling down his face.

"He was a courageous friend. He injured his leg helping me during a robbery and he could not swim very far. That is why he drown." Jacques wiped his face with his sleeve as he spoke.

Jacques waved to the bartender and then pointed to a door on the right side of us.

It was a private dining room. Vanier had planned dinner. The room was completely different from the tavern. Two colorful hutches were adorned with china and crystal glass and drinking mugs for beer. It was a small Waldorf Astoria—a beautiful tavern table, seating for eight, Windsor chairs of the finest quality, elegance seemingly out of place.

We drank and ate courses of steak, chicken, fresh vegetables, corn, and apple pie with ice cream for dessert. We toasted Croteau, and when we did the room would fall silent for a moment. Life would then come back in collective, respectful banter.

Vanier spoke to Norman when Simon and I would be loudly, very drunk, recalling our college follies. I would have very little recollection of what was spoken. I slept the entire way home to the River Hotel. The Queen Victoria had done her job. Simon was right, she was a great ride. Our Canadian excursion had been perfect. Simon's car was now also stocked with whiskey. It was Jacques' parting gift for my wedding.

It was a whirlwind from that point forward, a blur of time, people doting over Beth, shaking my hand. It was a simple Methodist wedding, the beginning our life together, a gala reception worthy of a Charles, a gathering for our journey together.

Beth had borrowed white horses, adorned them in purple halters and saddle clothes and they were the center of attention as people would tour the stable. The cherry doors glistened, the friendly horses stayed, the ones with a tendency to nip were relegated to an adjacent paddock under close guard by one of Mr. Day's many stable hands. I thought it might be appropriate for my uncle to be under guard, but my mother was full of smiles. I could tell that she was emotional, I could see emotions that could create tears without crying. She missed my father. My uncle seemed to avoid me, I purposely avoided him.

Mr. Day had worked with his daughter to complement her plans. Purple flowers adorned the stables, smaller purple carnations adorned the race horses' manes, copper name plates spoke their name and that they were worthy of great efforts. When summoned from their stalls, they would poke their heads out. Their noses were beautiful, always reminding me of a chance to make money off their herculean efforts that would sometimes result in a fraction of an inch, just enough of a margin, to win a race.

Simon was constantly by my side, shielding my uncle from conversing with me, doling out whiskey in amounts to meet the criteria that Beth had implored upon my best man.

"Behave yourselves," she would instruct Simon. Her reminders were thrust in my direction and ear shot. It was as much a warning to Simon as it was to me.

My fraternity brothers were in fine form, a bit older now. They seemed to mingle with ease and lacked the frivolity of our parties on campus. Appleton was not wearing a sweater with a nostalgic 'S,' thus there was no culprit to seek vengeance in the morning despite Barnes, his sweater nemesis, being in close vicinity every time I saw them.

I stopped in my tracks. "Simon, what is Rothstein doing here?" I spoke, but the words barely came out.

"He is friends with Mr. Day. Since he was in town Mr. Day asked him to stop by, and he gave me an envelope as thick as French toast for you and Beth. He knows how to repay loyalty," Simon told me. Once again, it sounded if it had been rehearsed.

"Harry, the Travers Stakes on Tuesday is fixed,"

Simon said quietly. His traditional Cheshire smile appeared as he spoke.

"Seriously? I thought the race was maybe one or two horses?" I said, not realizing I was actively following the horses. I was now astute to the subtle happenings around the track.

"Rothstein is betting on the underdog, his horse *Sporting Blood* is entered with the idea he can't beat the heavy favorite *Prudery*. The bookies don't know that Sam Hildreth will enter *Grey Lag*, utilizing the same-day entry rule. *Grey Lag* would be a huge favorite and the odds on *Sporting Blood* would go way up, maybe three-to-one," Simon detailed in a whisper.

"Nobody can beat *Grey Lag*, and frankly *Prudery* would crush *Sporting Blood*," I countered.

"Finally someone understands what I have tried to teach them each summer!" Simon laughed as he spoke.

"Harry, Hildreth hates the owner of *Prudery*. Later that morning after Rothstein has placed $150,000 on *Sporting Blood*, Sam is going to scratch *Grey Lag*." Simon was in the know and spoke with utter confidence that the plan would work. It was classic Simon, one-upmanship and clearly on the inside.

"How can he be sure his horse can beat *Prudery*?" I quizzed.

"He is going to hand the coach a football," Simon burst into laughter as he finished his Barnes-like quip.

"Very funny, let's not forget we got lucky that I was so quick thinking," I responded sarcastically, not realizing

I had mocked myself.

"I have the envelope that Rothstein is giving you for your wedding. It's going on *Sporting Blood* Tuesday. Check the paper on your honeymoon!" Simon spoke as if I would not object to his taking my money, like he did on the baseball bet, one also orchestrated by Rothstein.

"My best friend Harry, married, betting a fixed horse race, with plenty of auto parts, *Omarkayham* what a weekend!" Simon announced with glee.

The horse's name, a punctuation for a card at the Franklin that resulted in our notoriety on our first days on campus, the times we benefitted from knowing the results—it was classic Simon, who was destined to be a doctor. He had a plan, but I was still concerned that I would be destined just for making decisions like when the corn should be picked.

"Hey, before I forget, Fennimore needs your help. Bring your attorney, Quinn, when you go to meet him. He is now a junior officer at that bank in Watertown and needs to sign up some new accounts. He wants your farm accounts and you are *Sally*, the big fish!" Simon spoke as if he was not asking me but telling me.

"I don't know," I spoke with little defense as I knew I was going to overruled.

"He will call you. Simply do it—it will be beneficial for both of us," Simon directed.

Simon was plying me with whiskey and my defenses were down. We sealed the deal. I was in great spirits. Fennimore spoke to me during the day with a subservient voice and for once he was not bothering me.

The party continued for hours. The horses slept despite the country band playing into the night. Beth hugged all and all hugged her. She was radiant and sensitive to all the guests. She hugged my uncle on several occasions, which made me grimace a bit.

My uncle shook my hand, congratulated me, and spoke with all the sincerity only he could muster. "Congratulations. Your demonstration of character and selection of a bride of such warmth would have made your father proud."

All I could do was think of vomiting like I had at the Franklin the night I set the school record.

"Uncle, I did not want you here. My mother insisted, so let's agree to keep our distance." My whiskey voice of disgust enhanced my disdain.

"How dare…," was all my uncle could muster as Simon pulled me away.

"Harry, forget it. Forgive, move forward, believe in faith. He is your family," Simon instructed.

"Hogwash, I hate him," I blurted out, making certain that my uncle could hear what I had said.

Beth and I left for Vermont. On Tuesday, while sitting for breakfast in the magnificent Walloomsac Inn, the paper arrived.

The paper contained a prominent line, 'Sporting Blood Wins 1921 Travers Stakes.'

The elegantly-appointed waiter, doting on us as the notable newlyweds, celebrities in the exclusive enclave asked, "Sir, what can I get you both for breakfast?"

The answer was easy. "French toast, thick French toast," I smiled as I spoke. I was rich.

Beth smiled, she knew the plan.

Chapter XV

Beth fit naturally into our town. My mother was grateful to have a new addition to her garden club, quilting team, and church supporter when she needed youth and energy for a worthy cause. I was content to isolate myself from the townspeople, the River Hotel was my home when Beth was engaged by constant activities. Norman secured whiskey, I was continually grateful.

We seemed to have a rhythm—the seasons of work, the summer my challenging time, our refuge a few weeks in Saratoga helping Mr. Day manage his racing stable. Our yearly trips to Saratoga were by car, the aging Pierce Arrow held up suitably and continued to look the part of the high-class society that was created each August.

Beth was not interested in impressing people. She loved to work with the horses with her father and it became easier as Mr. Day was training less horses each year. It was my chance to gamble and I did not need to send a telegram to Alban's or send my regular bank drafts to cover my losses. Simon was busy, medical school consumed him. Beth and Rebecca stayed in touch by mail, I tried to call Simon often but rarely connected.

I seemed to lose touch with my classmates with the passing years. Like clockwork, Fennimore asked for my help to secure accounts. Quinn joined the bank's Board of Directors. I was not asked despite my doing a favor for Simon. It seemed that Fennimore failed to see my contributions.

I craved a simpler time. I rarely passed the campus. I would add extra miles to my farm's errands so as to avoid Park Street. There seemed to be little transition from year to year, it seemed like time had stopped. I would run the farm, drink when I could. It was 1925. Happily the phone rang on a dreary winter day. It was Norman and he had news.

"Gold Cup Boat Race has been announced, $5,000 for first place!" I had to pull the phone from my ear as his exuberance was far too great for the speaker.

In an instance I spoke like Barnes, "Let's buy the fastest boat."

I was out the door. January has been cold but with little snow. My car made it to the River Hotel in record time and Norman and I were on our way to the Clayton Boat Builders. The racing route ran along the river and the actual racing course was viewed every time we trekked to the builders to see the progress. Norman and I were splitting the cost and we were not sparing any expense. Our frequent trips were always concluded with revelry and strategy at the hotel.

The course would begin three miles from my property, the finish just a mile from Visger Point to the town dock. It was easily navigated, yet we spent hours reviewing depth charts and issues that might arise from 30 boats trying to secure safe passage. We were confident and my knowledge of the narrows that ran along my property made our belief that we would win by sheer expertise. Norman was the navigator, I was the pilot. Norman took his task with great duty, charting the areas of the river that were not as familiar. The final mile and the first portion of the course were studied as if he was a student at college. We looked at the harbor from the hotel often, the home of my sunken, legendary car, and we would drunkenly vow to stay clear of the harbor.

The boat was completed in April, just as the ice had given way and the river began to flow strongly. It was 26-feet, with ten mahogany strips glued together created the front of the boat. It had been built with the utmost craftsmanship. The first eight feet were precision, the hull narrowed to the front forming a perfect point. A steel blade ran down from the point to the base of the boat, and it equally distributed water to both sides causing little friction and utmost speed.

The glass windshield arched across the entire boat, the cockpit was built to allow two passengers to navigate while not extending above the few inches where the windshield began. Sixteen feet of crafted cherry and mahogany had created a narrowing back. A large square box covered the engines, which were state-of-the-art, created by a company that had provided engines for the government during the war. It gleamed with varnish, reeked of expense with its brass adornment rails that ran both sides from front to back.

We would launch in early May. A ceremony worthy of a champion was planned so as to give time to practice and gain the notoriety I silently sought.

Norman and I practiced the verbal rhythmic cadence of moving left, port and moving right, starboard. I regaled him with the knowledge that the word posh was a reference to traveling in style when going to Europe. The best was going traveling port out and starboard when returning. It was the best light while on the ship. Norman would bark the commands behind the bar, I would remark on the rare occasion when he made a Manhattan, that it was just starboard. The boat was a perfect place to drink, Norman was the *navibartender*, part navigator, part bartender. We were so confident that Norman built an assembly of ingredients in the circular spaces below the windshield to masterfully create perfect Manhattans, even at the highest of speeds we would reach in our practice runs. Norman never made Manhattans at the hotel, but the boat's opulence warranted the need for a beautiful cocktail.

It was as if a racehorse was swimming, the front neck of the boat cutting through water at 35 miles per hour, like the perfection of a thoroughbred running into the wind. I was the jockey and I relished the chance to compete on a large stage once again. This had not gone unnoticed by Beth, who seemed to see a difference, more buoyant, in my daily behavior.

Beth was designated to name the boat. My constant ideas were shot down with her smiling stare, saying that she was capable of a coming up with a moniker suitable for a Charles. It would be unveiled the week prior to the race and unbeknownst to me she had arranged for Simon to attend.

I finally connected with Simon. He played coy that he would be in town during the christening and staying the week until the race. He was planning his wedding for August, I was his best man and he was regaling me with the jazz music that had engulfed New York. The taverns we had visit when we had gone were now speakeasies, places to drink and dance the nights away. Our fifth reunion was planned for late June. He seemed perturbed that I had not contacted Fennimore about the festivities planned. I had thrown the invitation out, not willing to reunite despite it was the week after the Gold Cup.

The light of April and early May gave way to summer, the boat delivered to the point by the proud builders. It was their Fay Bowen model. Only two had been built, and mine was the most costly of the two. Norman and I would traverse the entire course, never venturing at top speed. Occasionally we would see others practicing, Norman made drinks while we slowly glided along and watched and then when our drinks were empty, we began our run, illustrating that we were the class of the river. I would cut a wake just high enough with angled turns to slow the others practicing who could not traverse across the rippled waves.

I was anxious as June approached. Like clockwork I was summoned to the River Hotel, greeted by a new car, more regal, more elegant than the ones parked years prior. Simon had arrived. I was stunned that he was in town. Our ceremony was the following day and I was now joined by my roommate to share the christening.

"I hear your boat is getting a name tomorrow. And by the way, you're late," Simon laughed as he spoke.

"I can't believe you are here, did Beth arrange this?" I was trying to make sense of his arrival.

"I have my fingers crossed it will be *The Sheldon*!" He seemed serious as he regaled those in the bar with his idea.

"Beth is in charge!"

It didn't matter how long we had been distant, it was if we had been drinking together the day before. We had grown up together, survived dubious behavior and no matter what had transpired, a deluge of memories simply morphed into a new bond of friendship. We spent the day and night catching up and conversing of all the news. He would interject about my attending the reunion. I would avoid answering. Simon was talking with the owner of the hotel about running a pari-mutuel betting on the Gold Cup. It was a the new thing in gambling, creating odds based on what people bet, with simple math and a cut for the house. Norman was dispatched to gather 30 planks, a chalkboard large enough to place all the boards from top to bottom, leaving room to write and rewrite odds next to the boats' names. Simon was studying the entries published in the paper and it was if he was calculating the demise of the *Huckster*.

"The town will be filled with tourists, vacationers, and people will love to bet on the race!" Simon was energized as he spoke.

"Easily $5,000 in bets, the house takes a portion for running the betting, all profit and when Harry wins, I win!" Simon boasted.

In a matter of a few hours, cherry boards had been painted with the utmost care, boat name and owner majestically written in gold beckoning a wager I thought. The hotel used stationary to provide receipts for wagers and in a mere few hours odds were being posted. I realized the paper had published Beth's selection of a name. Her surprise was gone and my boat was now named *Running Back*. I hid my excitement, I knew I had to hide that I knew.

It was Saturday, a week before the race, as we stumbled to Visger Point, Norman was granted time off for the festivities and race. The owner, knowing he was making a tidy profit off the race visitors and a portion of every bet on the race, was in high spirits. Beth had arranged for the name to be hidden. She hugged Simon, scanned to see how time had treated him. It was if it was 1920. Time had been good to him. He was a bit heavier but he still radiated charisma and kindness when he spoke to everyone.

Rain clouds began to appear. Good drinking weather was on the horizon, Simon brought a bottle of champagne from New York, townspeople had gathered to watch from the shore and edge of the dock. My uncle, luckily unaware of the event, would have not approved despite the future demise of the alcohol. It would have sent him into a lengthy discourse and reprimand, and I am sure he would have enjoyed arresting Simon.

Beth began a short speech, saying that the endeavor would be a triumph for the town, the boat a simple marvel of pride. She pulled back the tarp and in Victorian script, *Running Back* gleamed in the summer light. The cherry background was identical to the betting boards.

Simon leaned over and whispered, "I need to place a bet on *Running Back*!"

The gathering applauded. I hugged Beth, not letting on I knew the name but she had created perfection.

Simon handed Beth the bottle. She approached the front of the boat, planning to swing the bottle to collide with the silver strip.

"I christen this boat, *Running Back*!" she majestically spoke.

The bottle hit with a loud thud, the bottle broke into a frothy explosion, the water rippled with fizz, fish began to taste broken glass, immediately spitting the small bits out. Those smart enough were enjoying expensive champagne.

Simon applauded along with the gathering. Catching me at a festive time, he demanded, "Now won't you attend the reunion? You can bring the Gold Cup for a really big drink!"

The week leading up to the race was a never-ending party. Visitors from Boston, Connecticut, New York City—people were coming by full trains each day. Townspeople had rented rooms and the advertising and prize had made the race the event of the summer. Simon was greeting people he knew from New York as if he was the mayor of town.

The betting had been furious. The owner indicated it would top $25,000. He and Simon intended to take $5,000 for their efforts and Norman was doling out whiskey to those who had not brought their own to the River Hotel. Everyone was making money and good times had arrived.

Running Back continued to be bet heavily, our boat was eight-to-one, many were a hundred-to-one. Everyone had an opinion and the chalk odds changed hourly. Simon was calling me the chalk, the favorite, a moniker that bookmakers used to describe the chalk residue that fell to the floor each time the odds would change and would be erased and replaced. The wagers were not the *Huckster* $2 bets, people were wagering hundreds. The owners of the boat builders from Clayton were betting on Norman and I, knowing that we spared no expense. Our closest betting rival was twenty-to-one. It was fascinating. People's convictions were backed by bravado and that they knew the owner and drivers. It was Saratoga in our small town and I was *Man o' War*.

The night before the race was as if the *Huckster* was seeing it's demise. Cars jammed the parking lot, men of caliber and women dressed as if it was a wedding. People were betting and secretly drinking in the open. Simon did not need to bet but he did. *Running Back* was five-to-one and it simply encouraged others to invest elsewhere seeking a better return. It began to rain after dinner, violently. It reminded me of the night of Jacob's fire with thunder, wind, and rapid downpours among lighting strikes that crackled with the warm summer air.

Dinner was mostly drinks. Beth left knowing it was futile to try and get me to leave. She reminded me to behave myself, but her repeated efforts simply transformed into more revelry. There were no rooms at the hotel. Simon, Norman and I stayed until there was no one left in the bar. I begrudgingly left a few hours before daybreak to try and sleep. Beth roused me at 11:00 am with coffee, a mere few hours before it was time to prepare. Energized, I was off to meet Norman for the race. We had planned each minute to the starting gun at 1:00 pm, meeting at noon to review our plans and repeated tactical maneuvers. Norman was at the boat looking at charts. There was no second guessing for Norman, he was prepared.

The day was mixed, with storm clouds that dotted the horizon and different parts of the course. It was still sunny, with small air-swept waves, but conditions were generally good. The start at a narrow part of the river was calm as we glided past the start and headed upriver for final discussions and for me, planned drinks. We navigated strategically to stay to the far part of the river most would avoid, not knowing the actual depths and potential for submerged rocks or impediments. We knew better and would avoid the chaotic start that would cause loss of speed as boats traversed the choppy wakes of the other 29 boats.

"We are seven-to-one Harry, I bet the bar!" Norman laughed as he confidently spoke.

"Starboard Manhattan, *navibartender*!" I commanded.

Norman's face spoke that he did not want to see me drinking before the race.

"We have time, just a couple, a bracer for the jockey," I instructed, but was perturbed that he was giving me instructions.

The shores were lined with people, thousands at the start, I could only imagine the throngs of people at the town dock. Plans had included a band, a ceremony stand for dignitaries, a place for the winners to pose. Reporters had had camped out even before the rain had stopped while it was still dark as they wanted the best place to take pictures. It was epic and the starter sounded three preparation shots to arouse the boats it was time to assemble the start. We were four miles from victory, a $5,000 bounty, and a gold cup. It was if I was being handed the ball again, breaking through tackles, piling up touchdowns, being interviewed as a football star. The boat's name said it all. Two shots were fired, five minutes to the start, I gulped a full glass of whiskey and was ready.

I guided us to the far outside, while everyone was clustered near the starting point to the right. *Fools*, I thought.

Time froze, a nautical flag was raised, it was a five-flag configuration designating the start, the next shot created chaos, a thunderous roar of engines. I was in sync with the gun and we were in a perfect spot. It was a carnage of water, spray reaching above many of the boats. Goggles were in place, heads tilted down, as we forged to the lead in the opening of a football field. Our work had paid off and many boats were slowed as boats swerved to avoid the lack of sight. Norman began to bark starboard, port, slight port, hard starboard. We were leading and I was still only three quarters speed. We centered in the channel, without any boats around us we had complete command of the river. Norman would turn to view the chasing boats and simply remark, "Stay the course."

It was surreal. We passed the River Hotel. A mass of drinkers had stayed at the Hotel to view the slight turn toward the final mile. Partly because there was a strong spring shower, the somewhat calm water was now a wave ridden and slightly choppy mess. Norman continued to yell slight starboard as we eased toward the last half mile. Victory was ours.

I knew the next commands as if I was running toward the Yale coach, slight starboard from here on toward the town dock.

"Port, hard, port, now!" Norman yelled. It was muted by the rain and whiskey. I had no idea what he was saying or doing.

I continued to move slightly starboard, "Harry . . . PORT." It was the last thing I heard before the tremendous thud. I went black, my mind thinking it was Beth hitting the boat with a champagne bottle.

I awoke in tremendous pain. I could not comprehend the room I was in. White, everything was white, except the slight coloring around the tiles on the windows. I could hear Beth's voice, and another voice that seemed familiar, I could not place it but could hear the rustle of leaves and the flowing river. The air seemed odd. It was not June and the slightly open window filled the room with cool fall air.

What is going on, I thought. My head hurt, a bandage was tightly wrapped around my temples, my right leg was lifted into a sling. I felt sick and was perspiring despite the cool air. The voices were muffled, I heard nothing well and stopped trying to make sense of my surroundings. it was if time had stopped. I could only remember the start of the boat race. I was shaking, I was dreadfully ill and wanted a drink.

A doctor walked in and softly spoke, "Well, this is a good sign, how are you feeling, Harry?"

I could not talk. I knew the person's voice. I knew him. Dear God. "Walter?" I whispered.

"I am sorry I did not invite you to my wedding," I stammered, not knowing why it came out of my mouth. Beth rushed in, tears streaming down her face.

All she said was a comforting, "Harry."

"Harry, you have been in a coma. You struck the windshield with your head," he explained.

"Your leg will take time but the worst is over and you should be okay in a month or two," he clinically laid out.

"Dear God. Norman?" I questioned.

Beth smiled. "He saved your life. He was thrown clear from the boat, swam back and as the boat filled with water he pulled you out."

"Well, maybe I will go to the reunion, great story to tell," I managed to speak more strongly.

Walt looked up from the medical chart. "Harry, you have been unconscious for two months. It is September and you are lucky to be alive."

"Did you go?" I sounded like Barnes.

"We can talk about that later, you need to rest." Walt walked out of the room. It was just Beth and I, and I could not ask her for a drink.

I healed sufficiently, but it took time. Many months later, I found the courage to read the newspapers Beth had saved. The headline read, *Charles Critically Injured in Gold Cup. Norman Johnson Saves Harry Charles* was boldly written under the caption. I felt bad for the actual winners who were simply a footnote. They had been from Canada and the editor felt that they did not warrant the notoriety after the terrible accident.

Norman was heralded as a courageous hero. We were destined for victory but the boat had been crippled by a submerged log that had fallen by the errant storm the night before. Norman said it was bad luck. I knew otherwise and received condolences for our perceived bad fortune.

I had missed Simon's wedding. Rebecca's brother stood in as my role as best man. Prayers had been said at the ceremony for my absence, their honeymoon traveling to Europe and the large wedding at the Waldorf could not stop for my unconscious state. I profusely apologized. Simon would have none of it and simply was grateful that I had not been killed. The winner of the race had paid 50-to-one, Simon would often joke that I cost him "*a boatload.*" It would be a running laugh in the coming years, but a painful reminder that I could not understand a simple, one-word command by my navigator.

The owner of the hotel paid for the boat's repair from the proceeds of the betting pool. The new betting formula spared him as a true bookmaker and he skimmed off the top. No risk and the house always won. His profit far exceeded the cost of the repairs. I gave my share of the boat to Norman. He asked to keep the name but despite the concern for bad luck associated with changing a boat's name, I demanded he rename it. Beth was displeased as she felt the name was a testimonial to me, accident or not.

Norman changed its name to *River Hotel,* both as advertisement and thank you to the owner who had paid to make it river worthy again. Once it was returned to the town dock, people would ask if it was the boat that was crippled in sight of the finish line of the Gold Cup? Norman had saved my life and my errant whiskey mistake was now a spectacle, subjecting Norman to questions, and somewhat unwanted photos. Norman asked me to drive again the following year. I declined and to my good fortune aluminum racing boats would dominate the race.

The River Hotel was a beautiful sculpted piece of art, and also ran against the advancement of metal and design. Beth and I watched from the dignitary stand at the finish line and she remarked that the boat would have won had I been driving. They would race one more year in 1928, but it was the last Gold Cup, as litigation about the eligibility of boats would simply clutter the initial concept. My chance at victory came in one simple word, 'port.'

It was the fall of 1928, but my mother, tireless in her gardening efforts, had fallen ill. She died just after the second Gold Cup. I could never connect any joy from those days. I had been almost crippled and killed and now my mother was gone just after the last race. My aunt, beset by grief, passed just a few weeks later. I was able to avoid my uncle at my mother's funeral, forced by attrition I had to participate in Aunt Clara's burial. I was now left to care for Beth, and watch as a spectator over my married sister.

The phone rang in November. It was Simon. "Guess who died?" he exuberantly spoke. I was stunned.

"Simon, my mother and aunt passed away just a few weeks ago," I said.

"What? Harry why did you not call?!" His tone and concern were now evident as he spoke.

"I tried," I pointed out.

"Harry, I am sorry." It sounded as when my father had shot himself.

"Thanks, Simon, who died?" I was making sense of his initial question as I collected myself.

"Rothstein, he was assassinated," Simon almost gleefully informed me.

"Please tell me it was not you," I queried.

"I only shoot lynx and bobcats!" Simon quipped like Barnes.

"Harry, Albans says your losses on horses were far too often and all too frequent. I called Fennimore. He is going to allow you use your farm account to buy stock with Albans," he spoke knowing I would not object.

"I will send you a telegram, simply buy what I tell you." Simon sounded like the guiding puppeteer who had once saved Albans after *Man o' War* had lost.

I followed what he said to the letter. Fennimore loaned monies against my farm accounts, I bought numerous stocks and for once, Albans began telling me I was winning. Beth knew nothing about what I was doing. She felt the strains of my mother's passing. I still listened to the radio when races were broadcast, always after I had gone to the train station to telegraph my wagers to Albans.

I had to endure the winter, Fennimore commenting that my personal accounts and commercial accounts were at levels lower than in previous years. I detested his interference in my matters. I knew monies were owed to me by Alban's. I was ahead and continued to invest in the market. Whiskey was plentiful at the hotel, Norman had taken a greater role as manager and the owner was rarely visible, which made the bar's drinking less stressful due to a lack of secrecy and oversight. Norman knew who he could trust, those he could not were shut out of the good times.

The summer of 1929 came quickly. The farm's harvests were bountiful, tourists were plentiful, and I continued to benefit from my uncle renting cabins to city dwellers. I asked Simon to visit, a chance to drink and fish on the river, but he was consumed with his forthcoming trip to Europe with Rebecca. He was a full-fledged doctor now, inundated with the well-being of his rich, famous patients as well as the indigent patients he quietly helped. It always bothered me when I would hang up the phone and invariably one of my farm hands would topple a cart full of produce.

It was October, the trees were turning a fire-engine red. The phone rang.

"Harry, you are in trouble," someone spoke softly into the phone.

"What?" I was startled, as when I had heard Jacob had died.

"It's Albans. Listen to the radio. The stock market has crashed. It's chaos! You have lost everything and I need $40,000 to cover the remainder of your losses." He was sympathetic, but I was in shock.

I hung up the phone. Instantly it rang again. It was Fennimore.

"I am trying to stop a run on the bank. I have frozen your accounts. Your loan is being called in, which will take the majority of your assets," he told me.

"I have a margin call to Albans. You need to allow me to pay him." I still did not fully understand what I was saying as I spoke, not knowing the realities of a market crash or why I owed monies to Albans.

"No," he replied.

"Faf, we go a long way back. I need you to cover this and I will pay the bank back," I angrily responded.

"It's Francis, and it's not my decision. It's the board and I am doing as told." He spoke with no kindness, no allegiance as to what I had done to help him.

"The only thing I can do is try and allow you to borrow against the narrows and island. I have received multiple inquiries over the years acting as your banker." It reminded me of the times I had told him unequivocally, to say no to any sale.

I would cling to the radio for the entire day, as if my horse was way behind. Every word seemed like he could never win, every decibel of the news was the sound of defeat and carnage. People were frantic. New York City was in turmoil.

I was broke. The Depression set in, and I now was making payments to the Canadian Coal & Barge Recovery, a Canadian firm that happily held a note to finance my losses. I was told they needed deep water for their barges and were speculating that the land would go up in value. The country plunged into darkness. Our small town, insulated to a degree, survived. Tourists dried up, the only thing plentiful was whiskey. My island hung on a narrow strand and I was reminded each day as I tried to salvage monies from an unprofitable farm.

Norman bought the River Hotel and I was his best customer. I never asked how he could afford it. Simon returned from Europe unscathed, he had simply sold his stock before his trip to invest in property in Europe. Fennimore was heralded as a hero and was made president of the bank, the board of directors commenting in late 1930 that, "His courage and foresight helped minimize losses, kept people in their homes, saved a community, saved this institution."

Due to the Depression, happily for me, our 10th reunion never took place in 1931. Prohibition would end a few years later. I resorted to investing on slow horses. Albans survived the crash and continued booking my losing bets despite the advent of pari-mutuel betting at tracks on the East coast. Beth spent more time in Ballston Spa. My sister and William, Jr. simply existed. I spent little time with their children despite being less than a three-minute walk to my mother's house. I managed to hold onto the island and narrows despite the Canadian firm offering increasingly larger amounts to forgive the debt and to provide a substantial amount of money in difficult times. I could not sell, it was something my father had told me not to do. My uncle caught wind of the bank-arranged note and berated me that I had not come to him first. He was angry at me as if I had jeopardized what he thought rightfully belonged to him. He had won the coin flip and was still unhappy he had won. I watched my sister from afar have children, the devotion of my family squarely on her two sons named after my grandfather and uncle.

Chapter XVI

Simon invited me to Saratoga in early August 1940. I left the remoteness, the solitude of my existence to try and see Beth. She had begun to spend most of her time in Ballston Spa to care for her father. It was an excuse. She had resolved herself that I had changed. I was distant, angry, anguished, and always sad. I tried with so many words to convince her to stay. My diminished spirit, my redundant words had no meaning, they were simply things she had heard too many times before.

The beginning of our life, full of joy, had morphed into predictability. There were things I should have remembered to say, knowing what not to forget but they were now dull, old, and untruthful contrived pleas. There had been so much promise, so much of a future, time to cherish our lives together and now it was a six-hour train ride to have a chance to see her.

I wrote to her often about returning. It seemed autumn was my time of desperation, watching the leaves fall. The remaining leaves on the trees always seem to whisper to me as they rapidly fluttered from the wind. I thought of them as Beth, trying to speak but knowing they could only wave goodbye. I would experience many days like this. I drank alone, not wanting to be with anybody. I had begged her for renewed chances but squandered them like the bank drafts I would send to Albans. I had stopped dreaming, joy seemed like the river passing, my emotions only freezing when subzero days drove me to over-indulgence at the River Hotel.

I arrived at the Adelphi. No Albert, no McClennan, no fanfare, no charming introductions. My confidence and belief in myself was gone. I was the old man avoiding conversation, the bartender now waiting for me to leave. Simon's arrival was subdued. He tried to buoy my spirits by discussing his sure thing. His racing paper was marked with precision, identical to our first trip to Coney Island, just watching and not being watched. We spent little time in the bar. He whisked me away to another restaurant where we were without others. We tried to mingle at the hotel, but no one seemed to know Simon. His life had changed direction and he was now dedicated to others.

I had brought what I had left for money, my jacket holding my last $5,000, the remainder of my farm accounts. It had little meaning. I knew in advance I was going to bet it on something and Simon had given me my chance to place it on his cinch in the United States Hotel Stakes. Unknown to Simon I was going to change the odds for once.

Simon's new car had air conditioning. It was a Packard, a top-of-the-line model, but unlike his previous cars, it did not stand out. There was no George to drive us. It was an expensive car, but blended in among others more ostentatious. Simon was wealthy. He profited from avoiding the market crash, was an esteemed member of the elite in New York, and no longer needed to show bravado. He demonstrated class and was quietly successful. He was dignified.

It was August 3rd. There was no Mr. Day. He had been bedridden for the last few years. There were no bookmakers. The betting system Simon had introduced to the owner of the hotel on the Gold Cup was now a reality. Everyone bet into a pool, betting against each other with the track profiting and having no fear that they would end up drowned in a lake.

"Are you sure he is going to win?" I asked as I consumed another Manhattan.

"Mr. Longtail, this is a race horse!" his voice was entertaining as he spoke.

The waiter, dutiful in his service, arrived with a message for Simon.

"Harry, the hotel received a message for you to call Beth." He caringly read from the slip of paper. He seemed concerned, as he knew I was distant from Beth. It had not occurred to me why she had contacted him as opposed to calling me.

"That's odd. Speaking of odds, what do you think the horse will go off at?" I asked.

"Twenty-to-one, maybe more. Don't you think you should call Beth? Sounds important," he sternly retorted.

"After the fifth. When do I get a chance to win a boatload and spend the day with Dr. Sheldon!" I laughed as I spoke,. Simon's reaction seemed uneasy, his face not whimsical as in previous visits to Saratoga.

After the fourth race, I began to place bets on the horse *Whirlaway*, his odds dropping every time I bet, the size of my wagers startling the tellers who were simply hourly-paid runners. I would wait, leave the table, plunge on the horse and return. In the 30 minutes prior to the race the odds would change dramatically, and Simon knew something was up. Instead of 20-to-1, I had made *Whirlaway* 14-to-1, a chance to net $75,000 dollars. If he won, I would have enough to pay off the note on the island and land. I would be rich, successful again.

I began to look like Albans, disheveled, perspiring, desperate, delusional. Simon was concerned.

"Harry, are you okay?" He spoke like it was the fights in New York when I envisioned the terrible suicide Jacob had encountered, as well as my dear father's death.

"I need to win," I somewhat gasped. I drank the entire Manhattan sitting in front of me.

"Dear God, how much did you bet?" It was not concern but anger in his voice as he spoke.

"Five thousand, thought you would be impressed." It was a Barnes-like quip that fell dreadfully short.

"Harry, this is no fix, no sure thing, have you lost your mind?" Simon angrily berated me.

"You're late!" I drunkenly retorted.

He spoke like my uncle, a condescending adult, "Shame on you, Harry."

They were now at the starting gate,. Horses were loaded, no errant beginning to decide the outcome.

The race was off. Simon's $50 ticket sat on the table. He could have cared less about it. The wind could have blown it off the table and he would not have noticed. He used a pair of binoculars to watch the horses run down the backstretch. It was a short race, six furlongs and everything I had, my dignity, was on the race. Sadly, Simon knew it as well. I watched Simon and quickly realized *Whirlaway* was last. All I could think of was *Man o' War* losing.

The field of horses were turning for home. It would be like the times Beth would look at me. In less than two furlongs the race would be over. It was all the times we had been at Saratoga and *Whirlaway* was moving, fifth on the outside and closing, his jockey, Johnny Longden, pushing, whipping. It was *Indian Scout*, *Upset*, and the myriad of horses I had bet over the years. He was second, chasing Mrs. Parker Corning's horse *Attention*. Her table was situated next to Simon and I and she was cheering without an absolute care in the world. I was betting everything and she was simply hoping to get her picture taken.

The race chart would be published the next day, *Whirlaway*, "closed fastest but second best." I had lost. A mere head, the length of a football. In a minute and eleven seconds I was fully destitute. The distance was charted as a neck. It separated me from $75,000, a fortune, and all I had was a stack of colorful tickets, confetti that would be thrown to the ground as I went to get a drink. It was uncomfortable at the Adelphi bar, in part due to my drunkenness and sullen, belligerent behavior, but mostly because of Simon's disgust.

I did not call Beth until the next morning despite Simon's urging. I repetitively taunted Simon by calling him by the jockey's name who rode *Whirlaway*, Johnny Longden. He was frustrated with me and not amused that I would not listen to him. I told him no matter how hard he tried, "Old Johnny ain't going to get there."

I reached Mr. Day. He was distant, resolute, uncaring when he told me that my uncle had died. Beth did not call back and I was on the train that afternoon. Somehow I felt relief. Perhaps he would do the right thing and I would inherit the land that once belonged to my grandfather, that somehow his death would bail me out. I was dead wrong.

Beth attended the funeral. I tried to talk to her but she was there to console my sister. She stayed at the River Hotel. Norman did not make her pay for her lodging. I did not speak at the service. William and my sister acted as the head of the family. I stayed for most of it, treating it as if I was a former friend of Jacob. I retreated to the island to drink and simply avoid everyone and anything. A week later I was summoned to my attorney's offices. It was a brief stay, as Quinn told me that my uncle had gifted most of his valuable land to the town to build a hospital, a small portion of pristine river property to my sister for a cottage, while his monies were gifted to the college. I was handed an envelope containing a note, it said, *For Harry.*

It was the gold coin that determined the outcome of the land separation. I should have laughed but my uncle had made his point. It was evident he cared little for me. My condescending relative, his grating voice seared in my memory, must have enjoyed provoking me with his last words. I remembered my father's words, guiding me to not sell the land, and my decision to offer him a ridiculous amount so he would not buy.

It was summer until late November in 1940. Leaves normally brown and red were green as they fell to the ground. It was hot and terrible drinking weather. I spent days on end drinking, begging Norman for whiskey. I was in despair, deeply troubled and I needed money. I could not reach Simon. Fennimore rejected any help. I called classmates hoping to secure a loan but nothing transpired after our conversations turned to my desperate failure.

In February 1941, while the war began to rage in Europe, I was incoherent, unmanageable, and alone. I was found unconscious outside the River Hotel. I awoke in a car, a car I had been in before. I was in the backseat, despite it snowing outside. I could feel the air conditioning fans blowing. It wasn't a trip to the Evergreen. I was covered in blankets, shaking, trying to comprehend what was happening. It was if I had hit a submerged log but there was no thud this time. My religion told me of heaven, it also told me of hell, and I was now trying to figure out if I was dead. Each turn of the car reminded me that I was not. The pain was unbearable. I was disoriented, sweating despite the air conditioning, and I could only muster enough strength to lift my head.

"Simon?" I moaned part question, part prayer.

"Harry, it's going to be alright," Simon spoke and his tone was trying to beckon my spirit.

"Don't talk, close your eyes, believe in faith." I did as he asked and pondered if he had said fate or faith. Our meeting at the Franklin, his jocularity about the college motto, *Believe in Fate,* flashed in my mind.

When I awoke days later, it was surreal. I was thirsty, I craved whiskey. It was as if it had been the Gold Cup accident, same room, same coldness, bleak, stark white, the only thing different this time was I could not hear Beth's voice. The only voice I heard was Robinson.

"How are you feeling?" Walt was blunt.

"What happened?" It was all I could think to ask.

"You had a seizure, you are lucky to be alive," Walt said, identical to my previous visit.

"Boating accident?" I knew what had happened, I knew that I could not admit to it. I quipped like Barnes and realized it was a mistake.

"You are very sick." He was scientific and had no empathy. He seemed disgusted but the cadence of his voice was deliberate.

"Does anyone know?" I asked.

"Of course, Simon drove the entire night from New York to bring you here. Your family has visited each day, a stream of visitors praying for your recovery."

"I didn't think anyone cared." I was ill at ease when I said it.

"Nonsense, it's an issue you need to deal with, your living depends on it," Walt summarized while looking at his medical papers.

"Am I dying?" I said and for a second I felt relief, that death would cure my intense sadness.

"You will if you continue drinking," his voice rose not in anger but more of a friend telling me what to do. He was trying to save me again, the man I had vented anger and ignored in a time of personal celebration.

Walt left the room. I felt nauseous, I was thirsty, I felt dark. I needed whiskey and I was so weak I could not raise my hand to protest.

A nurse came into the room, "Simon called and wanted me to make sure you listened to the horse race. I am not sure what this means but he said he put a full moose on your horse." She seemed confused as she talked.

I realized it was May. I had been in the hospital for three months. It occurred to me that I had lost my land, the note had not been paid.

The announcer voice crackled from the radio, it was a brown Philco model radio, the size of a chest of drawers. Evidently Simon had bought it for my room and had to argue with Walt to let me have entertainment.

I was trying to figure out what horse. It was the Kentucky Derby, and it reminded me of the flask Simon had given me. The names were being read, 11 horses. Number four was *Whirlaway*.

I laughed. I thought of my last bet at Saratoga, my loss and the financial peril I now faced. I can still hear the words, "It's *Whirlaway* closing the gap," just like the day he lost.

I closed my eyes, envisioning just what the horse looked like as it galloped down the stretch. The announcer blaring the words, "It's *Whirlaway* setting a track record, the chestnut colt with the long tail is the Derby champion."

I had closed my eyes, not realizing many of the hospital staff were at the door listening.

My nurse asked, "Did he win?"

"Of course, $10 to win!" I gleefully retorted, not thinking that for many of those at the door it was more than a week's wages. They dispersed, seemingly unimpressed.

I was helped to Walt's office. His diploma hung over the desk where the phone was located and Simon was on the phone.

"Told you he was a cinch. How are you?" Simon's tone was serious.

"Better, you just doubled my net worth," I bantered back.

"Well, believe me I have. Walt says you're going home. He is going to treat you, do what he says," Simon spoke once again as my brother.

"You are the Doctor," I laughed, a bit out of fear.

"Harry, take care of yourself. Fennimore paid your notes, now get back on your feet." He completed talking and the line went dead. He wasn't going to let me thank him. He knew I wanted to talk but his quick exit was purposeful.

The summer came and went, my routine driven by Walt. I would arrive at his home in the morning, take medication to force sickness when I drank. I would travel to his office once a week to talk. He grew irritated when I tried to drink, he could see it in my face. The days I did not show up would result in a visit at the break of dawn the next day. I wanted to give up. He told me I could recover.

The war monument I had donated years before became a constant reminder of the war raging in Europe. It had grown short on space and was expanded to accommodate additional names of courageous young men who had died. The country was bombed in December, Pearl Harbor had been destroyed, the town lost six citizens. William paid for an additional monument to honor them. Many were unknown to me, though recognized by most in the town, I simply watched funeral processions pass by while others attended.

I thought of Lou. I was struggling each day. He had been surrounded and was fighting to save others when he was unmercifully shot to death. Walt seemed to use these errant comments and life observations as a way to confuse me, place doubts, like random cards of the corruption of my soul that I could not turn over. They were puzzles of how I felt and being forced to confront.

I was forced to relive my life in small passages, with immediate memories. They had texture, I felt corrupted. The corruption of bad behavior, reconciled by others misdeeds, evoked a feeling that I was bad.

"Tell me how your father died?" he asked one day.

"Farming accident," I lied.

"How about your grandfather, he suffer the same fate, very unlucky?" he quickly asked. It threw me off guard.

"Very," I mumbled.

"The only way you are going to get better is to stop lying to yourself, to understand yourself. Your father and grandfather committed suicide," Walt reminded me.

"I don't understand," I spoke with conviction.

"It's something that comes from something, killing oneself can come from depression, illness of the mind." Somehow, he knew the truth and I was powerless to say anything.

"Depression, it's a field of study. It manifests itself into destructive behavior, for many it takes the form of drinking." Walt was speaking of my sadness, the static shocks of watching a beautiful image on any given day turn to bleakness.

Each week, each month, each year, I began to feel better. Our meetings were productive but I found times to escape, skipping medication, and drinking to muffle the sadness and the words of wisdom he had shared.

Our meetings stopped in 1945. Walt was stricken with a heart attack. He passed away in his office during the night where he had been working with a patient who had recently been brought to the hospital. The patient had suffered a seizure, just as I had in 1941. My savior was gone.

I was summoned to the college the following week. I assumed it was to help honor Walt in some way. It was not. I had been selected to help with the construction of a new football stadium. The war was ending and the college was now going to implement a gift that had been dedicated to building Charles Field.

I remember the stunned silence I felt. The president was saying that the benefactor, Winston Charles, had gifted the school the monies to build a new stadium and that the timing was right. I could barely speak. I was handed a plaque that had been prepared to be the dedication when it was completed in the fall of 1946. I had once been the Pioneer of School Spirit, the salutation in my yearbook among others. I read the words on the engraved red stone: *This stadium is dedicated by the Charles Family in honor of the college's first coach. "It is about character, doing the best you can in the face of adversity, this is a test of who you are and can become." Coach Kinnon*

My uncle had used the very words the coach had said when we played Yale, my five touchdowns still the team's record. I began to cry. I simply now felt the loss of my uncle. The president was surprised that I was unaware of the gift, unaware that my uncle was proud of my accomplishments. I attended the games in 1946, recognized by a few during the homecoming weekend that the field was dedicated. They announced my name to a smattering of applause.

I managed to stay sober for longer periods of time. I was thankful that my nephews, Winston and Henry Walter were too young to have fought, too young to not have been hurt or killed in the war. I spent more time with them and William would join me on the island to fish and camp. I did not feel safe at times. The fear of drinking forcing me to alter my plans.

I was summoned to Quinn's office in 1949, I had continued to grow the farm, built a more regional business, I easily paid the notes and managed to create wealth despite the horrific hole I had built myself.

Quinn was blunt. "Eminent domain, you are losing the narrows."

"The Canadian Company is calling your notes, however, the notes are converting to shares in a trust," Quinn continued.

I was struggling trying to understand the complexity of the conversation.

"Harry, it's a good thing." He smiled. "You would lose the land anyway, the government has the right to take land for the public good," he continued to map out.

"What shares?" I asked.

"There are 1,000 shares. Fennimore will own 50. I will own 50. You will own 650, and the principle of the barge recovery company will own 250." I still did not understand.

"Fennimore is negotiating the final valuation. It appears that each share will be worth over $1,000, making your valuation over $650,000 dollars. In other words, you are rich!" He was gleeful in his delivery.

I was about to ask when he knew the answer.

"You keep the island, free and clear," Quinn spoke with pride.

"The principle owner worked with us to create this trust. It's a very fair deal. You would lose the land anyway, and this helps increase the value and avoids tax issues, and the island stays in the family."

"Who is the principle?" I questioned.

"You don't know?" Quinn responded.

"His name is Simon Sheldon, II," he quietly responded, somewhat surprised I had no idea after all the years.

"Simon, Dear God, Simon held the notes after the crash?" I mouthed the words but nothing came out. Simon had gone to Europe and luckily avoided the carnage and had silently bailed me out.

"He is a great friend," Quinn soothed.

"He is more than that. He is my brother," I said. I wept as I left his office. Simon had saved my life, he had secretly helped me when I was in trouble, and I was now wealthy again. Walt had helped me regain my sanity. I still struggled with trying not to drink, but I worked with the doctors at the hospital that sat on the land my uncle had once owned. People I had once despised, felt contempt for were actually my friends. All of the sessions with Walter were finally making daily sense. I was under-standing what made me feel the way I felt.

I thanked Fennimore, calling him Francis when I asked him to assist in my will. I avoided Quinn's legal assistance, in part not wanting him to know, but making sure that there would be no issue in the event of my death. I was leaving the land, my island, and a majority of my holdings to my nephews. I was thinking it was a debt I owed my uncle.

In 1951, the letter I helped create mapping out the happenings of our 30th reunion arrived in my mailbox. I knew what it said, but I read it anyway. I had been on the organizing committee. There was to be a river cruise, a dance, and a dinner on the campus. Most importantly, there was a dedication to Dr. Walter Robinson. Simon had worked with the college and would be helping in the ceremony.

The dance was a blur, everyone trying to connect faces with name tags, everyone struggling with first names and not nicknames, everyone struggling with the changes that had come with age. We were all different, but the banter of days gone by helped us reconnect. The favorite story of *Sally the Sturgeon*, the *Huckster*, *Nickel Spin* fights, my five touchdowns were told a number of times.

Simon's class song was sung in unison several times. I skipped the line about drinking until I died. I owed that to Walt. I thought of the 15 who had not joined in at the Franklin. They were now part of the song, they had always been part of our class. Many toasted Francis, he had helped many in the room during the Depression and he was happily told a number of times not to fall asleep! I was sad Beth had not come despite my inviting her. She planned to come for the cruise to spend time with Simon and Rebecca. I had paid dearly for my illness. I paid for it every day.

In a moment of quiet, Fennimore pulled a sheet of stationery from his jacket.

"Simon, here is my note, my $50 and Fannie and I are going to serve you each a drink to you and your lovely wife Rebecca," Faf gleefully shared.

"After all these years. Dear God, Fennimore you kept it?" I asked.

"Those were my favorite days, days I won't forget. I kept it in a safety deposit box. Simon has helped us all," Faf gratefully shared.

"Okay, your debt is paid, well done," Simon added.

He knew the stage was Fennimore's and allowed him to share the handshakes and adulation. I was simply awestruck. He was a runner and he was a man of character. I was lucky he was my friend.

The next day, people mingled on campus, congregating at the graduation stage that had been utilized the week before, the very stage I avoided in 1921. Simon began to speak about Walter, how two words, each containing ten letters, helped define his contributions to the college, our fraternity, to his friends, patients, and family. I thought of how Walter had skipped our reunion to care for me after the Gold Cup, how he put others before himself. I thought of Lou, dying in Europe trying to save others, the times I spent discussing corruption in Walt's office, how I mentally felt saddened by my behavior that I once blamed on others.

Simon quietly finished the dedication. "That transition leads to traditions, his medical work, breathtaking in it's complexity would help millions of people. He was a pioneer, a man of compassion, taken too young but never forgotten." He began to walk down the walkway, everyone followed without being told. I stopped at the very point I had been in 1917, I thought about my fear, how the skies were filled with storms. The seven rings of the college bell flashed in my mind, the day that Simon's train had arrived.

The assembled class quietly walked to the base of the walkway, the iron gate standing guard. The last step, the very step on which I broke my collarbone, was covered in a scarlet tarp. Fennimore spoke just four words evoking a river of tears, "To our friend, Walter." It was the first time I saw Fennimore cry. He slowly pulled the tarp away as he spoke.

No one needed to know what to do, everyone began reading the engraving on the base of the marble step in unison, reciting it as a prayer, softly. People were sobbing as they spoke: "You can always recover from a bad fall. Dr. Robinson class of 1921."

The dedication step was one of many people would see on their daily visits to campus, I would spend many days reading the others as well as visiting Robinson's step many times during the coming years. I would come to call the steps my 'words on the walkway.'

What began as tears, was a resonating cheer of life. Vibrant applause rose that had cadence, it seemed to transcend the sadness. It was joy, something I now felt and that he had given me. He had given me life and I could only wipe the tears from my eyes as my hands softly came together. I lacked the emotional strength to really applaud and could only think I had not invited him to my wedding. I had been angry at him and in the end he was a better friend than I had been to him.

Simon was looking directly at me. He smiled. It wasn't an inside joke, it was a reminder to me, it was the greatest of tributes, and Walt's words were directed to all who faced the sadness I fought daily. He had cared for so many and his work would carry on after his death.

"Charles, Appleton, Barnes, Green, Faf, follow me," Simon commanded. We began to walk past the gates, onto Park Street, toward the train station that had long been closed. The trains did not bring passengers anymore, just commercial cargo that would pass at errant times. I thought of the time my father had died, each friend stopping to give their condolences. I thought of the Franklin, Vanier, and the many times we had been together. I thought deeply about Jacob. The line of friends turned toward the train station, it had a few lighted signs, it had been converted to a college hangout.

The bricks of the building were still regal as if servicing passengers, though there was no Douglas selling tickets. The door made a loud thud as we entered. I stopped. On the wall was a painting of me when I had handed the ball to the coach of Yale. Among signs of tribute to fraternities and sororities were pictures. The postcard of the *Huckster* was framed on the wall near where tickets had been sold. Brown game-worn jerseys of those who had followed me hung from the rafters, they were cherished relics of a time gone by.

The bar was a museum of memories and class pictures. Framed history was everywhere. One of Appleton's sweater letters was hanging from the rafters, it had been carefully framed and hung perfectly.

"Who owns this place?" I asked a student who was reading the paper at a table near the door, the place where passengers once waited for the trains to depart and arrive. "Danny, he is over there," he pointed as he spoke. I felt I somehow knew him. He was wearing a green vest.

"Simon, it can't be?" I could barely utter the words.

"Harry, Simon, about time you visited. I have been waiting all weekend for you dignitaries!" Daniel loudly spoke from the bar that had been built where the ticket office was located.

It was if it was only yesterday that he had built our bar and dutifully served us at the Franklin.

"Beers for all." Daniel had grown up and was now like Simon on stage as he spoke.

I thought of Simon's words: "transition leads to traditions, no matter how much time goes by, memories will fade but friendships will always remain."

Simon regaled the bar all afternoon with his class song. I cornered him when he finished one version. He had substituted "bev-rye" with barge.

"Please tell me Canadian Coal and Barge Recovery did not mean, *cocktail-cocktail-bev-rye*, that last word I created," I joked.

Simon retorted, "I wrote that word."

"You always had a plan. Thank you my friend," I spoke softly. I was humbled and felt mystified that I had not figured it out.

"You were sick. Continue to work on your recovery." His face was caring but the smirk I had known from the day I had met him spoke to my heart about how much he cared.

It was one of those magical days, a party you could not create, the perfect mix of classmates, other classes, students about to leave campus, and constant laughter. I sipped a few beers, but managed to leave my drinks half empty when a new round appeared. I owed it to Walter, my uncle, Simon, to remain sober. I laughed that Appleton wisely had not worn a sweater.

It wasn't easy not drinking as others were now the ones to be overserved. Instead of staying until the bar closed, I walked back to read Walter's dedication.

It was a quintessential day among many that I now could happily remember and would simply never forget.

Acknowledgments

My deep gratitude goes to those who were intimately involved in the publication of this work:

To Karen Mireau Rimmer, founder of Azalea Art Press, whose countless edits brought the book to life.

To my mother, Cynthia Kozlowski, who nurtured my creative nature and to my father, the late Richard Kozlowski, who taught me never to give up.

To Tom Chiarella, prominent author and retired DePauw University writing professor, whose suggestions helped guide critical improvements in the manuscript.

To artist Courtney Kuno Burds, whose amazing work is reflected in the paintings that appear throughout the book and the art that graces the back cover.

To my friend John Daly, a creative force in the world of editorial cartooning.

To my son, Charlie, for his assistance in the web design, social media and advertising for the book.

To my pledge son and friend Sargent Johnson, for his creative input, his seeing the vision of the book, and for assisting with the book's publication.

And to The Hoot Owl, the train station that was the inspiration for the book's ending.

About the Artist

Courtney Kuno Burds graduated from St. Lawrence University in 2012 and received a Masters of Fine Arts from Tufts University and the School of the Museum of Fine Arts (SMFA) in Boston in 2015.

She taught Print and Graphic Arts at SMFA after receiving their Graduate Teaching Fellowship at the University. She is currently teaching Screen Printing at Monserrat College of Art.

Courtney continues to enjoy working on unique commissioned art projects and collaborations. You can view her paintings and other work at her website at www.courtneykunoburds.com. You can contact Courtney at courtneykunoburds.fineart@gmail.com.

About the Cartoonist

John Daly studied political science at St. Lawrence University, Temple University and the University of Albany's Rockefeller College of Public Policy. His work has been appearing in major publications on a freelance basis since 1998.

Top of the Stretch was seen in the New York Racing Association Program and The Saratoga Special. He also served as the editorial cartoonist for the Albany Times Union from 2005 to 2006. John can be reached at JDtoon@hotmail.com and his work can be viewed at skewedimages.com.

About the Author

The author is a lifelong racing fan whose wit was featured in *Top of the Stretch*, a horse racing cartoon highlighting the humor in the everyday lives of the horseplayer.

His favorite day begins at a pub in Saratoga Springs and the relentless deciphering of the racing form.

Eric is a graduate of St. Lawrence University and resides in Brighton, New York with his son Charlie.

by John Daly & Eric Kozlowski

by John Daly & Eric Kozlowski

by John Daly & Eric Kozlowski

by John Daly & Eric Kozlowski

by John Daly & Eric Kozlowski

by John Daly & Eric Kozlowski

To Contact the Author
please email:
theharrowedrunner@gmail.com

Learn more at:
theharrowedrunner.com

To Contact the Publisher
please email:
Azalea.Art.Press@gmail.com

For Direct Book Orders
please visit:
www.Lulu.com